The FUTURE of Us

The FUTURE of Us

JAY ASHER & CAROLYN MACKLER

An Imprint of Penguin Group (USA) Inc.

The Future of Us

RAZORBILL

Published by the Penguin Group
Penguin Young Readers Group
345 Hudson Street, New York, New York 10014, U.S.A.
Penguin Group (USA) Inc., 375 Hudson Street,
New York, New York 10014, U.S.A.
Penguin Group (Canada), 90 Eglinton Avenue East, Suite 700, Toronto,
Ontario, Canada M4P 2Y3 (a division of Pearson Penguin Canada Inc.)
Penguin Books Ltd, 80 Strand, London WC2R 0RL, England
Penguin Ireland, 25 St Stephen's Green, Dublin 2, Ireland
(a division of Penguin Books Ltd)
Penguin Group (Australia), 250 Camberwell Road, Camberwell, Victoria 3124,
Australia (a division of Pearson Australia Group Pty Ltd)
Penguin Books India Pvt Ltd, 11 Community Centre, Panchsheel Park,
New Delhi – 110 017, India
Penguin Group (NZ), 67 Apollo Drive, Rosedale, Auckland 0632,
New Zealand (a division of Pearson New Zealand Ltd)
Penguin Books (South Africa) (Pty) Ltd, 24 Sturdee Avenue, Rosebank,
Johannesburg 2196, South Africa

Penguin Books Ltd, Registered Offices: 80 Strand,
London WC2R 0RL, England

10 9 8 7 6 5 4

First published in hardcover by Razorbill 2011
Published in this edition 2012

ISBN 978-1-59514-516-1

Library of Congress Cataloging-in-Publication Data is available

Printed in the United States of America

Carolyn Mackler
to Jonas, Miles, and Leif Rideout

Jay Asher
to JoanMarie and Isaiah Asher

Our past, present, and future

In 1996 less than half of all American high school students had ever used the Internet.

Facebook would not be invented until several years in the future.

Emma & Josh are about to log on to their futures.

sunday

1://Emma

I CAN'T BREAK UP with Graham today, even though I told my friends I'd do it the next time I saw him. So instead, I'm hiding in my bedroom, setting up my new computer while he plays Ultimate Frisbee in the park across the street.

My dad shipped me the computer as yet another guilt gift. Last summer, before he and my stepmom moved from central Pennsylvania to Florida, he handed me the keys to his old Honda and then started his new life. They just had their first baby, so I got this desktop computer with Windows 95 and a color monitor.

I'm scrolling through various screensavers when someone rings the doorbell. I let my mom answer it because I still haven't decided between a shifting brick wall maze and a web of plumber's pipes. Hopefully it's not Graham at the door.

"Emma!" my mom shouts. "Josh is here."

Now *that's* a surprise. Josh Templeton lives next door, and when we were little we constantly ran back and forth between our houses. We camped in our backyards, built forts, and on Saturday mornings he carried over his cereal bowl to watch cartoons on my couch. Even after we got to high school, we hung out all the time. But then, last November, everything changed. We still eat lunch with our small group of friends, but he hasn't been in my house once in the past six months.

I select the brick wall screensaver and head downstairs. Josh is standing on the porch, tapping at the doorframe with the scuffed toe of his sneaker. He's a grade behind me, which makes him a sophomore. He's got the same floppy reddish-blond hair and shy smile as always, but he's grown five inches this year.

I watch my mom's car backing out of the driveway. She honks and waves before turning into the street.

"Your mom said you haven't been out of your room all day," Josh says.

"I'm setting up the computer," I say, avoiding the whole Graham issue. "It's pretty nice."

"If your stepmom gets pregnant again," he says, "you should talk your dad into buying you a cell phone."

"Yeah, right."

Before last November, Josh and I wouldn't have been standing awkwardly in the doorway. My mom would've let him in, and he would've jogged straight up to my room.

"My mom wanted me to bring this over," he says, holding up a CD-ROM. "America Online gives you a hundred free hours if you sign up. It came in the mail last week."

Our friend Kellan recently got AOL. She squeals every time someone sends her an instant message. She'll spend hours hunched over her keyboard typing out a conversation with someone who may not even go to Lake Forest High.

"Doesn't your family want it?" I ask.

Josh shakes his head. "My parents don't want to get the Internet. They say it's a waste of time, and my mom thinks the chatrooms are full of perverts."

I laugh. "So she wants *me* to have it?"

Josh shrugs. "I told your mom about it, and she said it's okay for you to sign up as long as she and Martin can have email addresses, too."

I still can't hear Martin's name without rolling my eyes. My mom married him last summer, saying this time she found true love. But she also said that about Erik, and he only lasted two years.

I take the CD-ROM from Josh, and he stuffs his hands in his back pockets.

"I heard it can take a while to download," he says.

"Did my mom say how long she'd be gone?" I ask. "Maybe now would be a good time to tie up the phone line."

"She said she's picking up Martin and they're driving into Pittsburgh to look at sinks."

I never bonded with my last stepdad, but at least Erik didn't rip apart the house. Instead, he talked my mom into raising parakeets, so my junior high years were filled with chirping birds. Martin, however, convinced my mom to start a major renovation, filling the house with sawdust and paint fumes. They recently finished the kitchen and the carpets, and now they're tackling the downstairs bathroom.

"If you want," I say, mainly to fill the silence, "you can come over and try AOL sometime."

Josh pushes his hair away from his eyes. "Tyson says it's awesome. He says it'll change your life."

"Right, but he also thinks every episode of *Friends* is life-changing."

Josh smiles and then turns to leave. His head barely clears the wind chimes that Martin hung from the front porch. I can't believe Josh is nearly six-feet tall now. Sometimes, from a distance, I barely recognize him.

* * *

I SLIDE IN THE CD-ROM and listen to it spin inside the computer. I click through the introductory screens and then hit Enter to begin the download. The blue status bar on the screen says the download is going to take ninety-seven minutes. I glance longingly out the window at the perfect May afternoon. After a blustery winter, followed by months of chilly spring rain, summer is finally arriving.

I have a track meet tomorrow, but I haven't been

running in three days. I know it's stupid to worry about bumping into Graham. Wagner Park is huge. It stretches along the edge of downtown all the way to the newer subdivision of homes. Graham could be playing Frisbee anywhere. But if he sees me, he'll hitch his arm around my shoulder and steer me somewhere to make out. At prom last weekend, he was all over me. I even missed doing the Macarena with Kellan and Ruby and my other friends.

I consider interrupting the download to call Graham's house and see if he's home yet. If he answers, I'll hang up. Then again, Kellan told me about a new service where some phones display the number that's calling. No, I'll be a grown-up about it. I can't hide in my room forever. If I spot Graham in the park I'll just wave and shout that I have to keep running.

I change into shorts and a jog bra, and twist my curly hair into a scrunchie. I strap my Discman around my arm with Velcro and walk out to my front lawn, where I stop to stretch. Josh's garage door opens. A moment later, he rolls out on his skateboard.

When he sees me, he stops on his driveway. "Did you start the download?"

"Yeah, but it's taking forever. Where are you headed?"

"SkateRats," he says. "I need new wheels."

"Have fun," I say as he pushes toward the street.

There was a time when Josh and I would have talked

longer, but that's been a while. I jog over to the sidewalk and take a left. When I get to the end of my block, I cut across and meet the paved trail leading into the park. I push Play on the Discman. Kellan made this running mix for me, starting with Alanis Morissette, then Pearl Jam, and finally Dave Matthews.

I run the three-mile loop hard and fast, relieved not to see any Frisbee games. As I'm nearing my street again, the opening guitar of "Crash into Me" comes on.

Lost for you, I mouth the words. *I'm so lost for you.* The lyrics always make me think of Cody Grainger. He's on the track team with me. He's a senior and an incredible sprinter, ranked in the top twenty in the state. Last spring, on the ride home from a meet, he sat next to me and told me all about the college scouts who've been calling him. Later, when I couldn't hold back a yawn, he let me rest against his shoulder. I closed my eyes and pretended to fall asleep, but I kept thinking, *Even though I don't believe in true love, I could reconsider that for Cody.*

Kellan says I'm delusional about him, but she's one to talk. When she got together with Tyson last summer, you'd think the girl invented love. She's got a genius IQ and writes intense editorials for the school paper, but all she could talk about was Tyson this and Tyson that. When he broke up with her after winter break, she crashed so hard she missed two weeks of school.

While I may pine for Cody, I still have to live my life.

For the past two months I've been going out with Graham Wilde. We're in band together. He plays drums and I play saxophone. He's sexy, with shoulder-length blond hair, but his clinginess at prom was annoying. I'll definitely end it with him soon. Or maybe I'll just let things dissolve over the summer.

* * *

THE STATUS BAR is still chugging along.

I take a shower and then settle into my papasan chair to read over my notes for the biology final. I've been getting A's in biology this year, definitely my strongest subject. Kellan has been trying to convince me to sign up with her for a biology course at the college next fall, but I don't think that's going to happen. I want a low-key senior year.

When the download is complete, I close my textbook and then restart the computer. As I dial in to AOL, the modem crackles and beeps. Once I'm on, I check to see if *EmmaNelson@aol.com* is available, but that email address is already taken. So is *EmmaMarieNelson*. Finally I settle on *EmmaNelson4Ever*. For my password, I consider a few options before typing "Millicent." Last summer, when Kellan and Tyson were all over each other, Josh and I made fun of them by pretending we were a lovesick middle-aged couple named Millicent and Clarence who devoured Hamburger Helper and drove around town in a beat-up ice-cream truck. Kellan and Tyson never thought it was funny, but it sent Josh and me into hysterics.

I click Enter and the same AOL screen I've seen on Kellan's computer now appears on mine.

"*Welcome!*" chimes an electronic voice.

I'm about to write my first email to Kellan when a bright light flashes across the screen. A small white box with a blue border pops up, asking me to re-enter my email and password.

"EmmaNelson4Ever@aol.com," I type. "Millicent."

For about twenty seconds, my monitor freezes. Then the white box snaps into a tiny blue dot and a new web-page fades in. It has a blue banner running across the top that says "Facebook." A column down the center of the screen is labeled "News Feed" and under that are tiny photos of people I don't recognize. Each photo is followed by a brief statement.

Jason Holt
Loving NYC. I've already eaten two Magnolia cupcakes!!
3 hours ago · Like · Comment

> **Kerry Dean** And you didn't share one with me?
> I want chocolate frosting and sprinkles.
> 2 hours ago · Like

Mandy Reese
I just walked into a spiderweb and didn't freak out. Woo to the hoo!
17 hours ago · Like · Comment

I circle the mouse around the screen, confused by the

jumble of pictures and words. I have no idea what any of this means, "Status" and "Friend Request" and "Poke."

Then, just under the blue banner, something makes me shiver. Next to a small picture of a woman sitting on a beach, it says "Emma Nelson Jones." The woman is in her thirties with curly brown hair and brown eyes. My stomach tingles because this woman looks familiar.

Too familiar.

When I move the mouse over her name, the white arrow turns into a hand. I click and another page slowly loads. This time, her picture is larger and there's so much information I don't know where to begin reading. In the center column, next to a smaller version of the same picture, I see:

Emma Nelson Jones
Contemplating highlights.
4 hours ago · Like · Comment

It says Emma Nelson Jones went to Lake Forest High School. She's married to someone named Jordan Jones Jr. and was born on July 24. She doesn't list the year, but July 24 is *my* birthday.

I sink my forehead into my hands and attempt to take a deep breath. Through my open window, I hear Josh skating toward his house, his wheels bumping over the lines in the sidewalk. I run down the stairs and burst out the front door, squinting my eyes in the bright sun.

"Josh?" I call out.

He rides up his driveway and kicks the skateboard into his hand.

I clutch the railing on my front porch to steady myself. "Something happened after I downloaded AOL."

Josh stares at me, the wind chimes ringing through the silence.

"Can you come upstairs for a second?" I ask.

He looks down at the grass, but doesn't say a word.

"Please," I say.

With his skateboard in his hand, Josh follows me into the house.

2://Josh

I FOLLOW EMMA up her stairs and count on my fingers from November to May. It's been six months since I've been in her house. Before that, this was like my second home. But after we all went to the opening night of *Toy Story*, I misread things and thought she wanted to be more than friends.

She didn't.

When we get to her room, Emma waves a hand at the computer. "Here it is."

The monitor plays a screensaver that makes it look like you're moving through a maze of brick walls.

"It's nice," I say, leaning my skateboard against her dresser. "You can barely hear it run."

Her room looks the same as before, other than a vase of wilting white roses on her dresser. Several red paper lanterns dangle from the ceiling. Two corkboards near her bed are packed with photos and ticket stubs from movies and school dances.

Emma shakes her head. "I'm sorry," she says, laughing to herself. "This is stupid."

"What's stupid?" I push my sweaty hair out of my eyes. After picking up my new wheels, I met Tyson in the First Baptist parking lot to skate. Between the morning and evening services, the lot is empty, and they have some killer banks in the asphalt.

Emma stands beside her desk chair and turns it toward me. "Okay, I need you to humor me for a second."

I sit down and Emma swivels me back around until I'm facing the monitor.

"Jiggle the mouse," she says, "and tell me what you see."

I'm not sure if it's being back in her room or the strange way she's acting, but this whole situation is making me uncomfortable.

"Please," she says, and then she walks to her window.

I give her mouse a shake. The brick wall freezes and then disappears. A website appears with words and tiny pictures thrown everywhere, like a kaleidoscope. I have no idea what I'm supposed to be looking at.

"This woman looks like you," I say. "That's cool!" I glance over at Emma but she's staring outside. Her window faces the front lawn, as well as my upstairs bathroom window. "She doesn't look *exactly* like you. But if you were older she would."

"What else do you see?" Emma asks.

"She has your name, just with Jones at the end."

The website says "Facebook" at the top. It's disorganized, with graphics and writing all over the place.

"You didn't make this, did you?" I ask. I'm taking Word Processing I this year, which is all about creating, altering, and saving files on the computer. Emma's a year ahead, in Word Processing II.

She turns toward me, her eyebrows raised.

"Not that you *couldn't* do it," I say.

It looks like Emma made this website as a class assignment, creating a fantasy future for herself. She says that Emma Nelson Jones went to our high school, now lives in Florida, and married a guy named Jordan Jones Jr. Her husband's name sounds fake, but at least she didn't call herself Emma Nelson Grainger, after that track guy. Or Emma Nelson Wilde after her current boy toy. Speaking of Graham, didn't she say she was going to break up with him by now?

Emma sits on the edge of her bed, her hands pressed between her thighs. "What do you think?"

"I'm not entirely sure what you were going for," I say.

"What are you talking about?"

"When's it due?" I ask.

"When's *what* due?"

Emma walks up beside me and stares at the screen, tapping two fingers against her lips. With her hair dripping onto her shirt, tiny rainbow-colored stars on her bra begin to appear. I try not to look.

"Josh, be honest," she says. "How did you do this?"

"*Me?*"

"You're the one who told me to download that CD-ROM," Emma says. She reaches down and presses Eject on the computer's disc drive. "You said it was from AOL."

"It was!" I point at the screen. "You think *I* know how to do this?"

"You have plenty of pictures of me. Maybe you scanned one at school and—"

"And changed it to make you look older? How could I do that?"

My hands start sweating. If Emma didn't do this, then . . .

I rub my palms across my knees. One side of my brain whispers that this could be a website from the future. The other side of my brain screams at the first side for being an idiot.

On the screen, Emma Nelson Jones, with slight creases at the corners of her eyes, is smiling.

Emma flicks her hand at the monitor. "Do you think this is a virus?"

"Or a joke," I say. I take the CD-ROM out of her

computer and study it. Maybe someone at school knew Emma was getting a new computer, so they created this realistic looking disc and . . . put it in *my* mailbox?

On the screen, there is a series of short sentences running down the center of the page. They're written by Emma Nelson Jones, with other people responding.

> **Emma Nelson Jones**
> Contemplating highlights.
> 4 hours ago · Like · Comment
>> **Mark Elliot** Don't change anything, E!
>> 57 minutes ago · Like
>> **Sondra McAdams** Let's do it together!! :)
>> 43 minutes ago · Like

"If it's a joke, I don't get it," Emma says. "What's it supposed to mean?"

"Obviously it's supposed to be from the future." I laugh. "Maybe this webpage means you're famous."

Emma cracks up. "Right. How would I become famous? The saxophone? Track? Or do you think I'm a world famous rollerblader?"

I play along. "Maybe rollerblading is an Olympic sport in the future."

Emma squeals and claps her hands together. "Maybe Cody qualifies in track and we'll go to the Olympics *together*!"

I hate the way she can bring Cody Grainger into any conversation.

She points toward something at the bottom of the page. "What's that?"

Emma Nelson Jones
Anyone want to guess where my hubby was all last weekend?
20 hours ago · Like · Comment

Below that text, mostly hidden by the bottom of the screen, there's a photo. The top of the picture looks like ocean water. I roll the mouse over it.

"Should I click to see if—?"

"No!" Emma says. "What if this is a virus and the more we open, the worse it gets? I don't want to screw up my new computer."

She grabs the CD-ROM from me and drops it in her top desk drawer.

I turn in the chair to look directly at her. "Come on, even if it's a prank, don't you want to see who they say you end up marrying?"

Emma thinks about it for a second. "Fine," she says.

I click on the photo and a new screen appears. We watch the large square in the center slowly fill from top to bottom. First, choppy ocean waves. Then a man's face. He's wearing black sunglasses. Then his fingers, gripped around the sword-like nose of a fish. When the picture has fully loaded, we see that the man is standing at the bow of a fishing boat.

"That fish is huge!" I say. "I wonder where he is? I guess it's supposed to be Florida."

"He's hot!" Emma says. "For an older guy. I wonder where they got this picture."

We're startled by a rapid knock on Emma's door, followed by her mom entering the room.

"Do you like your new computer?" she asks. "Are you two surfing the World Wide Web with all those free hours?"

Emma moves slightly in front of the monitor. "We're researching swordfish."

"And future husbands," I say, which gets the back of my arm a sharp pinch.

"Can you work on it later?" her mom asks. "Marty has to call a client before dinner and he can't do it while you're on that Internet."

"But I'm not done," Emma says. "I don't know if I'll be able to get back to this website again."

She's right. What if we can't get back here? Even if it is a joke, there's so much more to check out. Emma needs to say something convincing to keep us online.

"There's *one* phone line," her mom says. "Write down the website name on a piece of paper and go back to it later. If this Internet thing is going to be a problem—"

"It won't," Emma says. She grabs the mouse, exhales slowly, and signs out of AOL.

The electronic voice offers a cheery, "*Goodbye!*"

"Thank you," Emma's mom says. Then she tilts her

head at me. "It's nice to have you over again, Josh. Would you like to stay for dinner?"

I stand up and grab my skateboard, avoiding Emma's eyes. "I can't. I've got too much homework, and my parents . . ." As I trail off, I feel my cheeks flushing.

The three of us walk downstairs. Emma's mom joins Martin in the bathroom where he's arranging plastic bags from Home Depot. Emma opens the front door for me and leans in close.

"I'll try to get back online later," she whispers.

"Okay," I say, my eyes shifting down to my skateboard. "Call me if you need anything."

3://Emma

ALL I CAN THINK ABOUT during dinner is Emma Nelson Jones.

"You can hardly tell it's low-fat cheese," my mom gushes to Martin as she nibbles her pizza. "And pears instead of pepperoni? Delicious."

"I agree," Martin says.

We're eating on TV trays while watching *Seinfeld*. They record it on the VCR every Thursday and then watch it on Sunday night. I grab another slice of pizza and transfer it onto my plate.

"Be careful with that," Martin reminds me.

"The new carpet," my mom adds.

The show breaks for commercials. Rather than fast-forwarding, Martin moves closer to my mom and strokes her arm. I can't deal with this. I balance my plate in one hand, grab my glass of milk, and head up to my room.

I sit cross-legged on my bed, eating pizza while staring at the brick wall screensaver on my computer. Maybe this isn't a prank or a virus. Maybe there really is a woman in her mid-thirties named Emma Nelson Jones. She went to Lake Forest High years ago and just happens to have my birthday. But even if all those coincidences are true, why is she showing up on my computer?

I pick up the phone and dial Josh. I know his number so well I don't have to look at the list on my corkboard. But then I set the phone back on its cradle. Josh doesn't want to be dragged into this. He sprinted out of my room as soon as he had a chance.

I try Kellan, but her line is busy, and I can't decide whether to call my dad. Back when he and Cynthia lived in Lake Forest, we saw each other all the time. We took runs together, and when he played sax with his jazz band, I'd often come up on stage and join them for a song. But now whenever I call it feels like I'm intruding on their time with the new baby. I've only been down to see him twice since he moved, for a week at Christmas and four days at spring break.

I finish my pizza and head to the bathroom. Since the downstairs bathroom is out of commission, I have to cut through my mom and Martin's room every time I need to pee. As I look in the mirror, I think about Emma Nelson Jones and her highlights.

I've always liked my hair color, especially in the summer when I spritz it with Sun-In and lay out in the backyard. But maybe someday I'll contemplate high-lights, too.

Maybe someday I am.

I hurry to my computer and jiggle the mouse. When I dial into AOL, it's just the regular homepage. But then I look in the "Favorite Places" box, where I know Kellan stores links to all the webpages she likes.

And there it is. Facebook. When I click on the word, that box appears asking for my email and password, which I quickly enter.

Joy Renault
Watching the Harmony Alley Carjackers for the first time since college. Squee!!!
17 hours ago · Like · Comment

Gordon Anderson
I feel silly ordering apple juice as an adult, like I should be pronouncing it "appa doos."
4 hours ago · Like · Comment

> **Doug Fleiss** It always reminds me of baby breath.
> 2 hours ago · Like

In the top corner, next to where it says "Emma Nelson Jones," there's a different photo than last time. When I click her name, a page appears with a larger version of the same photo. She looks glamorous in a wide-brimmed hat and sunglasses.

Below the photo, I click on a tab labeled "Info."

High School Lake Forest High School Class of 1997

1997? That's when *I'm* going to graduate. That's next year!

I force my eyes away from the graduating class that hasn't happened yet and scroll down. Emma Nelson Jones has created lists of her favorite movies, music, and books.

Movies American Beauty, Titanic, Toy Story 3

I haven't heard of the first two movies, though I'm happy to see *Toy Story* apparently has two sequels, but it's the books section that really jumps out at me.

Books Tuck Everlasting, Harry Potter, The Help

I don't know what *Harry Potter* or *The Help* are, but Josh gave me *Tuck Everlasting* for my eleventh birthday. I still remember reading the scene where Tuck rows Winnie across the lake. The boat gets stuck in a tangle of roots and Tuck explains how the water rushing by is like time flowing on without them. Reading those words made me feel deep and philosophical.

I click back to the page where Emma Nelson Jones talked about wanting to highlight her hair, but I can't find anything about that now. It still says she's married to Jordan Jones Jr. but there's no photo of him with the fish.

That's odd. How did everything I saw before change like that?

> **Emma Nelson Jones**
> Thursday, May 19 is a day that will go down in history. The question is, in a good way or a bad way? I'll think about that as I make dinner.
> 2 hours ago · Like · Comment

Today is May 19! So that means this is all happening right now. But today isn't Thursday. It's *Sunday*.

Three people have responded to Emma, asking what she's cooking. She's replied with, strangely enough, one of my favorite meals.

> **Emma Nelson Jones** Mac and cheese. Desperately need comfort food.
> about an hour ago · Like

A few more people have written, saying how much they love comfort food. And then, at the bottom, Emma wrote something just twelve minutes ago. As I read it, my arms prickle with goose bumps.

4://Josh

MY PARENTS GOT HOME LATE, so it's scrambled-eggs-with-hot-dog night in the Templeton home. Any other night I'd be loving it, but now I'm a little distracted. I tried calling Emma before we sat down to eat, but her line was busy.

"You seem quiet," Dad says. He tilts the frying pan toward my plate and slides on more hot dog wedges.

The telephone rings. As Dad goes down the hall to answer it, I push around the eggs with my fork. The website on Emma's computer doesn't make any sense. It has to be a prank, but if it is, I don't get it. If I were going to make a fake future for someone, I'd put in outrageous stuff, like they're going to win the lottery or own a castle in Scotland. Why go to all that trouble for hair coloring and fishing trips?

Dad walks back to the table. "It was Emma. I told her you'd call her back after dinner."

"How is Emma?" Mom asks me. "Did she want that America Online CD?"

"CD-ROM," I say, shoveling some hot dog into my mouth to avoid the rest of her question.

"Is Sheila going to let her use AOL?" Mom asks.

I nod and fork in more hot dog. Why did Emma call? She knows my parents hate getting phone calls during dinner. Did she find an inconsistency, proving the website is a prank? Or maybe she figured out who did it!

"Things change so fast when you're a teenager," Dad says, spooning salsa onto his eggs. "You and Emma used to be so close. Last summer Mom and I started to worry that you needed to hang around with other people, too."

"I hang out with Tyson," I say.

"Other girls," Dad says.

"At least we know Emma," Mom says. She looks at Dad and laughs. "Remember how David was always going to that girl Jessica's house after school, but they never came over here? We finally insisted they study here, and look what happened with *that*."

"The next day," Dad says, "he broke up with her."

David is my older brother. My parents assumed he'd go to school at Hemlock State, where they're both sociology professors. Instead he moved to Seattle for college, more than two thousand miles from here. I honestly wonder if he chose Washington State to keep Mom and Dad from probing into his life so much. He even stays there during the summer to do internships. I had to fly out over spring break to spend time with him.

The phone rings again. Dad looks at his watch and shakes his head, but it doesn't ring a second time.

"I think I'm done," I say. I wipe my hands in my napkin and crumple it on my plate.

"Are you sure?" Mom asks. "There's plenty more."

"My stomach kind of hurts," I say, which isn't a complete lie. I'm feeling queasy because I think Emma is trying to reach me. I carry my plate into the kitchen and set it in the sink, then walk back down the hall. The phone is on a small table by the stairs. I pick up the receiver, dial Emma's number, and then stretch the cord as far as possible from my parents' earshot.

Within the first ring, Emma answers.

"Josh?" she asks breathlessly.

"What's the matter? Was that you who called a—"

"I don't know where to begin," she says, her voice tight. "I got onto that website again, but—"

"It was there? How did you find it?" I can't help feeling excited.

"Can you come over?" she asks. It sounds like she's been crying. "My mom and Martin just left for a walk so you can use the emergency key to let yourself in."

"Will you tell me what's going on first?"

"I think the website might be real," Emma says. "And I'm not happy."

"I can tell. But why?"

"No," she says. "I'm talking about the future. I'm *never* going to be happy."

5://Emma

"HEY," JOSH SAYS, pushing open my door.

I look up from my bed. He's standing at the edge of my room, holding the spare key we hide under a rock by the garage. It has a Scooby-Doo keychain that lights up when you press the nose.

"Sorry I took so long. My parents made me load the dishwasher." Josh pushes his hands into his pockets. "So what's going on? You found something bad?"

I'm worried if I open my mouth I'll start crying again. As it is, Josh already looks uncomfortable being up here. It's kind of sad, because we always used to be there for each other. He went on so many bike rides with me when my parents were splitting up. That was back in fifth grade. When Josh broke his leg skating, I hung out in his backyard even though everyone we knew was swimming at

Crown Lake. Josh sat with me at my mom's wedding last September, pinching my arm every time I succumbed to inappropriate giggles.

And here he is again, yet things feel like they'll never be as easy between us as they once were.

"I was able to get back to that website," I say, wiping my eyes. "Only it was different."

I catch Josh glancing at the wilted roses on my dresser. Graham gave them to me before prom, when we were taking photos in my yard. I make a mental note to chuck them as soon as Josh leaves.

"It still says Emma Nelson Jones went to Lake Forest High," I say, "and it's still says 'Facebook' at the top. No matter where you click, it always says that."

"Do you think Facebook is the name of her company?" Josh asks.

"Maybe." But that's not the point. The point is what the website says about her. Thinking about it makes my chest hurt.

"Emma, you still don't know what this thing is, or whether it's even real," Josh says. "Somebody's probably just screwing with—"

"No, they're not!" I sit up and touch the necklace resting against my collarbone. "Emma Nelson *Jones* was wearing *this* necklace in her photo."

Josh looks at the gold chain I always wear, with the delicate *E* pendant dangling from it. "The woman's name is

Emma," he says. "What other letter would she put on her necklace?"

"And she said it's Thursday, May nineteenth."

Josh's forehead wrinkles in confusion.

"Today is *Sunday*, May nineteenth," I say. "That means she's writing all this from another year where May nineteenth is a Thursday."

Josh shakes his head. "If someone is trying to prank you, they would've thought of all that."

"But *everything* was different! When I checked just now, it was a brand new picture of Emma. And there were different people saying things to her. You think all that could change with one corrupted CD-ROM? Don't you get it? This thing . . . Facebook, or whatever it's called . . . it's from the future."

Josh sets the keychain on my desk and sits down. When he jiggles the mouse, the brick wall disappears and everything's right where I left it, with Emma Nelson Jones writing about macaroni and cheese.

"Why does it say she has three hundred and twenty friends?" Josh asks. "Who has that many friends?"

"Scroll down," I say, peering over his shoulder.

Emma Nelson Jones You know why I need comfort food? JJJ hasn't come home for three nights. His trip was only supposed to last one day. I feel hopeless.
12 minutes ago · Like

Josh looks up at me. "Who's JJJ?"

"My husband. Jordan Jones Junior. The guy with the fish. I never say why he hasn't come home, but obviously I'm suspicious. When I saw that, it made me sick."

Josh rubs his forehead with the tips of his fingers. "Maybe he went on another fishing trip."

"Keep reading," I say, reaching past Josh for the mouse.

> **Emma Nelson Jones**
> Hit my sixth month of unemployment. They say it's the economy, but I'm starting to believe it's me. Thirty-one is too young to have a failed career.
> Tuesday at 9:21am · Like · Comment

"Thirty-one," Josh says. "So this is supposed to be fifteen years from now."

I point to the next sentence.

> **Emma Nelson Jones**
> Can't even afford a decent therapist.
> Monday at 8:37pm · Like · Comment

Josh turns to me. "I can't believe she's writing these things."

"Not *she*," I say. "*Me*."

"Why would anyone say this stuff about themselves on the Internet? It's crazy!"

"Exactly," I say. "I'm going to be mentally ill in fifteen

years, and *that's* why my husband doesn't want to be around me."

Josh leans back in the chair and crosses his arms against his chest. When he does that, he looks like his brother. I haven't seen David since last year, but he was always a fun person to have in the neighborhood. Guys wanted him to be their older brother, and girls had a crush on him.

"Listen, Emma. I think . . ." Josh says, but then he pauses.

"Just say it."

Josh points toward the screen. "We don't know for sure who Emma Nelson Jones is or what we're looking at. But even if it's real, you're still reading a lot between the lines."

The front door closes. Josh and I jump back from the computer.

"Emma?" my mom calls. "Marty says he locked the door when we left, but—"

"It's okay," I shout. "Josh is here, that's all."

"Are you ready to help us get email addresses?" she asks.

"Can we have another minute? Josh is helping me find something . . . an assignment."

"That's fine," my mom says. I hear her footsteps climbing the stairs. "But you need to finish up soon. It's a school night."

She cannot see this. I reach over and click the X on the

top right corner of the screen. The cheerful voice chimes, "*Goodbye!*"

My mom walks by, waving as she continues on to her bedroom.

Josh picks up the Scooby-Doo keychain. He stops in the doorway and looks back at me.

"What is it?" I ask.

"I don't think you should look at this thing alone," he says. "It's either a mean prank or it's . . ."

I feel the tears coming on again.

"Let's make a deal to only look at it together," he says.

"So you'll come over again?" I ask. "You don't mind?"

Josh stares at the keychain in his hand, pressing the Scooby nose on and off. "No, it's cool."

"How about tomorrow? After track."

"That's fine," Josh says. "Maybe Tyson and I will even stop by the meet."

I smile for the first time all evening. Last year, Josh used to come to all my home meets just to wave and cheer me on. It makes me want to be honest and tell him what else I saw on the website, before he came over. But I can't bring myself to say it. I look down at my new white carpet. What I saw would make things even more awkward between us. And for one night, I want to feel like things can be normal again.

"What is it?" Josh asks.

I'll have to tell him eventually. "Tomorrow," I say, "we should see if you have one of those webpages, too."

monday

6://Josh

AS I SQUEEZE OUT a line of toothpaste, I hear Emma's car door shut and the engine start. When I woke up this morning, I considered hitching a ride so we could have a chance to talk, but it's better if I still keep some distance. Rejection always hurts, but having it come from my best friend was the worst.

Emma shuts off her car engine. I look out the window. She's heading back into her house. Her bedroom window is across from my upstairs bathroom, so I can see her pull her saxophone case from the closet. When I was younger, I used to write notes with markers and hold them to this window for Emma to read with her pink binoculars. I still keep that can of markers on my desk, but I'm sure she sold her binoculars at one of the yard sales the Nelsons are always having.

I rinse and spit, listening to Emma start her engine again. Seconds later, it stops. This time, she slams the car door. I feel bad for Emma, but I can't help laughing. She's convinced that what we saw on the computer is her life in fifteen years. As much as I'd like to believe something like that is possible, one of us needs to remain skeptical.

I turn off the faucet and look outside. Now Emma's trunk is open and she's tossing her silver sneakers on top of her saxophone case. She slams the trunk, but it pops back open as soon as she walks away.

* * *

I KNOCK ON the passenger window of Emma's car. "Can I get a ride?"

She reaches across and unlocks the door. I lower my head to climb in, something I didn't have to do when Emma first got her license. I position my skateboard between my knees and click the seatbelt into the buckle.

Emma puts the car in reverse. "Thanks for coming down."

"Rough night?"

Emma nods. "I'm not in the mood to face certain people today."

I wonder if she means Graham. His locker is near mine, so I get to see him pull Emma into a groping session every morning.

It always fills me with so much joy.

"Want to swing by Sunshine Donuts?" I ask.

Emma turns on her blinker. "Absolutely."

A mile past Wagner Park, Emma pulls up to the orange speaker-box and orders herself coffee with cream and sugar and a cinnamon donut. I ask for a glazed donut and chocolate milk.

"I don't get it," Emma says as she pulls forward. We're still two cars back from the pickup window. "How did this happen to me?"

"Not that I'm buying into the future stuff," I say, "but I have no idea why anyone would even *joke* about your future sucking. You're really smart and—"

"Thanks for bringing that up," Emma says. "But I wasn't talking about my future sucking. I was talking about the whole website in general. How is it possible to read about something that hasn't happened yet?"

The car in front of us pulls up to the window. I reach into my back pocket and offer Emma a few crumpled dollar bills, but she pushes my money away.

"At first I thought it was the CD-ROM," she says, "but maybe it's the phone jack that made something happen during the download. Remember that electrician who rewired the house?"

"You think he accidently wired you into the future?" I say, trying not to laugh. "Anyway, that was months ago."

"But I didn't have a computer yet. Maybe we should move the computer to your house to see if the website works there."

No way. We can't start running back and forth between our houses again.

"But that still wouldn't explain *how* it happened," Emma says. "Or how we can read about things that occur fifteen years from now."

I point out the window at the cars driving by. "If you want me to play along, here's a theory. You know how Vice President Gore calls the Internet the 'Information Superhighway'? Let's say everyone's going the same direction on this superhighway. Time travel would be about finding a way to jump to a different spot."

The car ahead of us pulls away. Emma drives up to the window and then passes her money to the Sunshine woman. "So you think this website jumps us ahead somehow?"

The woman hands our drinks to Emma, who passes them to me. I place her Styrofoam cup of coffee in the drink holder so she can grab the donut bag.

"Honestly, I'm just playing along," I say. "I still think it's all a prank."

We don't say much for the drive to school. When we pull into the student parking lot, I check my watch. The bell is set to ring in three minutes.

"I know I dragged you into this," she says, turning in her seat to face me, "but I'm a little hurt that you're not taking it more seriously. If you saw *your* future and it looked terrible, I don't think you'd be so quick to blow this off."

"But it's not real," I say. I crumple up the donut bag and stuff it into my empty cup. "How about after your track meet, let's try to figure it out? Maybe whoever made it misspelled your name somewhere or got a date wrong. We'll find something."

"Why do you need to prove it's a prank so badly?" Emma asks.

"So *you* can stop worrying. Your life is going to turn out fine."

Emma looks into the rearview mirror, and then turns to me. "Josh, before you came back over last night, I found something else on that website."

The way she's staring at me gives me the chills.

"If someone's pulling a prank on me," she adds, "then they're also pulling a prank on you."

7://Emma

"ME?" Josh's eyes squint in confusion.

His webpage was one of the many things that kept me awake last night. I should have told him about it the instant he came up to my room.

"Emma." Josh waves a hand in front of my eyes. "What are you talking about?"

"Last night," I say, "before you came over, I was looking at the Facebook website. Remember where it says I have three hundred and twenty friends." I pause and exhale slowly. "It showed you as one of them."

There's silence in the car.

"It said 'Josh Templeton,'" I add, "along with a picture of you. An older you."

Josh taps the Sunshine Donuts cup against his knee. He didn't want to believe any of this. He wanted to prove it was a prank.

"You have short hair like David," I say. "And you wear glasses."

"My eyes are fine," Josh says.

"Not in the future, apparently."

Josh presses his thumbnail into the Styrofoam cup, making half-moon marks up one side. "Did you see anything else? When you clicked on Emma Nelson Jones's picture, it took you to another webpage. Could you do that with mine?"

I nod. "It has your birthday as April fifth, and it says you went to the University of Washington."

"Like David," Josh says.

"And now you live back here again."

"In Lake Forest?"

I wonder how he feels about that. Personally, I'm determined to move away someday. There's no actual forest in town and Crown Lake is nine miles down the highway, surrounded by expensive houses. The downtown is only three streets long, and you can't do anything without everyone knowing about it. But Josh is more laid back than I am. He seems to think Lake Forest is perfectly fine.

"Where's my house?" Josh asks. "They don't have me living with my parents when I'm in my thirties, do they?"

I shake my head. "I think you're out by the lake. There

was a picture of you in your yard, and you could see a dock in the background with a motorboat hitched to it."

"Very cool," Josh says. "So they made me rich."

I roll my eyes. "Why do you keep saying 'they'? Who are you talking about?"

"The people who created this joke of a website. I'm going to go to the tech lab today and see if anyone's been scanning pictures of—"

"When you say 'the people who created this,' don't you get it? At some point in the future, *we* created it. I don't know exactly what it is, but it looks like interconnected websites where people show their photos and write about everything going on in their lives, like whether they found a parking spot or what they ate for breakfast."

"But why?" Josh asks.

The first bell rings for homeroom. Graham's going to wonder where I was this morning. We usually meet at his locker and walk to band together.

I grab my bag and then reach for the door.

"Hang on," Josh says as he spins a wheel on his skateboard. "That Facebook thing, did it say whether or not I'm married?"

I flip through my keys so I can unlock the trunk. "Yeah, you're married."

"What does it say about . . . her?" Josh asks, his face pale. "My . . . you know . . . *wife*?"

"I thought you didn't believe in this," I say.

"But I still want to know. It's *my* future, right?"

"Here's the thing," I say, taking in a breath. "In the future, you're married to Sydney Mills."

Josh's mouth hangs open.

I open my car door. "We're going to be late."

8://Josh

I IMAGINE Sydney Mills standing in front of me. Her long brown hair is held back by a white headband, and her eyes are the color of sweet caramel. She opens her arms and I pull her into a kiss, the fullness of her breasts pressing into my chest.

Then I open my eyes, grab my skateboard, and meet Emma at the trunk.

"Sydney Mills?" I say. "That's ridiculous!"

Emma stuffs her silver running shoes into her backpack. "But now you want this to be true, right?"

"Why would I want to believe something that's a hoax?" I say. Even so, I'm tempted to make Emma drive us home so I can see for myself. But if we're late to school, the secretary will leave a message on our home answering machines.

Sydney Mills is a year ahead of me. She's insanely hot, she's one of the best athletes in school, and she comes from a wealthy family. I have no idea why anyone would match us up even as a joke. We've been in Peer Issues together since January and we've never said a word to each other.

"Look at you," Emma teases, bumping her arm against mine. "You're in *love*."

Emma reaches up to ruffle my hair, but I pull away. I sling my backpack over one shoulder and start walking toward school.

"Wait up, Mr. Mills," Emma calls.

I stop and turn around.

Emma shifts her saxophone case to her other hand. "It's okay. I'd be walking like a maniac, too, if I discovered Cody and I were married and vacationing in Waikiki."

Waikiki?

"I wasn't walking fast because I'm excited," I say. "I just hate it when you . . . you know . . . touch my hair and stuff."

"I'm sorry," Emma says, and I know she gets it. She doesn't want to hurt our friendship either. That's why she let me put distance between us for the past six months.

Emma points at a white convertible with its top up. "There's Sydney's car. Maybe you should leave a love sonnet beneath her windshield wiper. Or a haiku! It's probably best if you don't try to rhyme."

For the junior high talent show, I bombed with my

rap act. I thought I could be the first redheaded rapper. I called myself RedSauce. A few times a year, Emma brings it up to torture me. But that's better than my brother, who mentions it almost every time we talk.

"So, Sydney and I go to Waikiki?" I ask.

As we push through the double doors of the school, Emma leans in close. "Your future self isn't as revealing as I am," she says, her breath sweet with cinnamon. "You don't give juicy details about whether you and Sydney do it on the beach, so don't get all hot and bothered."

Emma waves goodbye, and then gets swallowed by the mob of students.

"You're just jealous!" I say, but I don't think she hears me.

9://Emma

I'M COMPLETELY DISTRACTED in band. After I miss my cue for the fourth time, Mr. Markowitz points his baton at the horn section and says, "How about everyone take a five-minute break? Flutes, come see me to talk about solos."

I glance toward percussion, but Graham isn't here yet. Sometimes he gets held up meeting with the swim coach, which is fine by me. I'm still dreading seeing him. I set my instrument on my seat and head to the water fountain. As I lean over the arc of water, I think about what happened on my computer. It all seems less real today, especially the part about Josh marrying Sydney Mills. That's like matching me with Leonardo DiCaprio.

"Guess who?" Graham covers my eyes with one hand and wraps the other around my waist.

I wipe my mouth and then turn to face him. As soon as I do, my breath catches. He shaved off his hair! All that beautiful blond hair is gone, and now his scalp is prickly and pale.

"What did you do?" I ask.

He grins and rubs his hands over his head. "Greg and Matt came over after Ultimate Frisbee and we buzzed our heads. Do you like it?"

All I can do is stare.

"Admit it," Graham says, lacing his fingers into mine. "You want to run your hands over my big, smooth head."

I'm not in the mood for this. When he presses against me, I back away.

"What's wrong?" he asks.

"I don't know," I say.

Neither of us says anything more. Sometimes it feels like if it weren't for making out, we'd have nothing to do with each other.

* * *

"IT'S TIME TO END it with Graham," I say, looking into my paper lunch bag.

We're in the cafeteria so Kellan can load up on her daily special, french fries and Sprite. Kellan is an inch shorter than me, with shiny black hair and perfect skin. And she can put away fries without gaining a pound.

"Weren't you going to break up with him in the park yesterday?" she asks.

I smile at a few girls who walk by us. "I never ended up seeing him."

"Well, what's stopping you from doing it today?" Kellan pays the cashier and heads to the condiment station. "In case you haven't noticed, *I'm* not stopping you."

"Did you see his hair yet?"

Kellan shakes her head.

"It's shaved," I say. "He and Greg and the swim team guys did it yesterday. I swear, guys in groups are capable of the stupidest things."

"Like war," Kellan says, heaping napkins and ketchup packets onto her tray.

"And jumping off rooftops."

"And lighting their farts on fire," she says.

I laugh. "Do you know anyone who's done that?"

"Tyson," she says. "Next to the Dumpster behind GoodTimez, while you were visiting your dad last winter."

Tyson's father owns GoodTimez Pizza, a restaurant that specializes in birthday parties and cheesy deep-dish pies. Because of the arcade and the prime parking-lot skating, Josh and Tyson spend many hours there.

"Was Josh with him?" I ask.

Kellan considers it for a moment. "Actually, he filmed it. But he didn't light anything."

"Good. Because I would never let him forget that."

As we push through the side doors of the cafeteria,

Kellan asks, "So how does Graham look without his golden tresses?"

"Truthfully, his hair was the only thing that made him hot," I say. "Now he looks like a peach lollipop."

It's sunny outside, even warmer than yesterday. We start across the campus to our usual lunch spot, and I turn to Kellan. "Can I ask you a physics question?"

Her face brightens at the mention of physics. She's currently taking physics at Hemlock State on Tuesday and Thursday afternoons. It's part of the same enrichment program that she tried to get me to apply to, so we could take college biology next fall.

I shift my paper bag to the other hand and say, as casually as possible, "What do scientists think about time travel?"

She lifts her tray up to her chin and pinches a fry with her teeth. "Why?"

"I'm just curious," I say. "*Back to the Future* was on cable last night."

Kellan pauses in front of a muddy patch in the grass and launches into an explanation of time dilation and special relativity. I try to follow, but I get lost somewhere around wormholes.

"Nothing's proven," Kellan says. "But nothing's ruled out, either. My personal opinion is that it's possible, but I wouldn't want to do it."

"Why not?"

She shrugs. "The past is over. We can read about it in history books. And what if in the future we're at war again, or we still haven't elected a non-white or non-male president, or the Rolling Stones are still dragging their tired old butts on stage? That would depress me way too much."

"I hope the future's better than now," I say, though I'm not sure it will be.

"You know that cute guy I told you about in my physics class?" Kellan asks. "I ran into him downtown yesterday. Seriously, Emma, you've got to take biology with me there. You won't believe the guys at Hemlock. They're *men*."

"So you're saying I should take college bio for the guys?"

Kellan shakes her head. "You should take college biology because you're smart and there aren't enough women working in science. But you and I can help change that. The guys are the icing on the cake."

"Maybe," I say, but I'm more concerned with what Kellan said about time travel. If it was definitely not possible, she would have told me. But that's not what she said.

"Besides improving the gender ratio in science," Kellan says, "I want you to fall in love before we graduate. That's a personal goal of mine."

"You know how I feel about love," I say. "It was invented to sell wedding cakes. And vacations to Waikiki."

"My parents have been in love for nineteen years," Kellan says. "And look at Tyson and me. We were probably the two most—"

"He broke your heart! How can you call it love when he hurt you so badly?"

Kellan pops another fry into her mouth. "It was love because it was worth it."

10://Josh

I'M THE FIRST ONE to the oak tree, our usual lunch spot at the far end of the campus. I set my lunch bag at my feet, pull my sweatshirt over my head, and cram it into my backpack. Then I prop it behind me as a cushion against the tree.

My peanut butter and jelly sandwiches are squished after spending hours buried in my backpack. But I'm not tasting much today. All of Emma's talk about that website has me nervous about Peer Issues, my last class of the day. It'll be impossible to look at Sydney Mills without visualizing her emerging from the warm Hawaiian ocean in a skimpy bikini.

That's *not* the kind of thing you tease a guy with!

Sydney Mills and I are in completely different orbits. She's a Mercury, with the full hotness of the sun beating down on her. I'm a Pluto. Sure, my friends appreciate me, but I'm barely holding on to the far reaches of the galaxy.

"Incoming!"

A Subway sandwich shoots through the air, smacking the ground near my feet. Every day, Tyson tosses his lunch like a bomb, though I've never understood why. Kellan says it's because his dad raised him without a female around to civilize him.

"You're a dork," I say.

"Have you seen her yet?" Tyson asks, tearing through his plastic bag.

My heart races. Did Emma tell him about Sydney?

"I know she's been talking crap behind my back," he continues. "When she's around me, she acts all cool. But when I'm not around—"

He's talking about Kellan. "No, I haven't seen her."

Tyson and Kellan are such opposites that Emma and I never imagined they'd get together. The four of us have always hung out, but last July, an intense flirtation sprouted out of nowhere. They kept it up for the rest of the summer, but on the first day of school Tyson called it off. Then they got back together, but eventually Tyson dumped her again. They were like two magnets who couldn't decide whether to attract or repel. After the last break up, Kellan was so crushed she didn't come to school for two weeks. Yet somehow, bizarrely, we all remain friends.

"She's never said anything bad to me," I say, reaching in for my second sandwich.

Tyson pulls a slice of turkey out of his sub and pops it in his mouth. "That's because she knows you'll tell me."

I spot Emma and Kellan walking toward us, their heads leaning in close.

"See," Tyson says. "They're talking about me."

The girls smile as they get closer, and then sit down. Kellan squeezes ketchup over her fries while Emma peels back the lid of her Tupperware.

"Aloha," Emma says, grinning mischievously at me. She stabs a cucumber slice with her plastic fork. "Have you seen her yet?"

"Seen who?" Kellan asks.

"Apparently Josh has a crush on Sydney Mills," Emma says.

Why is she doing this?

"Who doesn't?" Tyson says, his mouth churning with turkey and cheese.

"I never said I have a crush on her," I say.

Kellan glares at Tyson. "*Everyone* has a crush on her? Really? That is so cliché. Sydney Mills is a skanky rich bitch."

"Guys, chill," Emma says. "I wasn't trying to start anything."

"I don't even know her," I say. "I know who she is, but I wouldn't—"

Tyson ignores me and looks at Kellan. "Yes, Miss

Judgmental, I absolutely have a crush on Sydney Mills. In case you haven't noticed, she's hot."

"Only if you like skank," Kellan says. She drops a straw in her Sprite and takes a long sip.

Emma catches my eye and mouths that she's very sorry.

I bite into my sandwich, pretending not to care. After all, that website is just a prank.

* * *

I WALK PAST the open door of Peer Issues and glance anxiously inside. Sydney Mills isn't here yet.

I go straight to my seat. My fingertips drum against my desktop while students pour through the doorway. Each time someone enters, my hands and my heart beat faster.

Rebecca Alvarez walks in and I give her a quick smile. Rebecca and I went out for five months our freshman year, my longest relationship ever. We still talk at school sometimes, but never on the phone or anything.

From her seat across the room, Rebecca mouths, *Why are you staring?*

I turn back to the door. And there's Sydney!

I grip the sides of my desk, unable to look away. Her chestnut brown hair flows over her shoulders and down her back. A green knit sweater hugs her chest, the top two buttons left open. She wears a gold necklace dotted with tiny diamonds. She moves up my aisle, sliding her cell phone into a pocket of her tight jeans. My palms sweat just watching her.

Sydney looks at me and it feels like she might smile, but then she lifts her eyebrows. My face must be rearranged into something goofy.

After she passes, a backdraft of coconut floats by my nose, snipping the threads holding my heart in my chest.

* * *

TYSON AND I set our skateboards on the lowest bleacher facing the track. I suck down a cherry Slurpee while Tyson freezes his brain on blue raspberry. The cardboard pizza box at our feet is now empty. Because Tyson's dad owns GoodTimez, we get all the pizza we want for free. In exchange, sometimes I help with the birthday parties, which can mean anything from monitoring the ball pit to dressing as a smiling slice of pizza and handing out goodie bags.

Last year, Tyson and I brought pizza to every home meet. We never paid much attention to the events, but it meant a lot to Emma knowing we were there. When the first meet came around this year, I told Tyson I had too much homework. At the next meet, I said I had to help my dad clean the gutters. Eventually Tyson stopped asking. But today I need to make sure Emma drives me home after the meet and shows me what she saw on that website.

The team walks out to the field. Tyson and I shout, "Go, Emma!" Once she waves, we grab our skateboards and head to the parking lot. Next to the bike racks are two parking spaces with a couple of loose concrete blocks. Tyson grabs one end of a block, and I grab the other.

"Lift!" I say.

We drag both blocks, one after the other, to the center of a parking space, and then Tyson pulls a chunk of Sex Wax from his backpack and tosses it to me. Surfers use this to keep their feet from slipping off their boards, but skaters love it, too. Especially Tyson, who laughs at the name every time we use it. I rub the sticky wax across the top of both blocks and then step back. Tyson lands his board sideways and slides the entire length, then skates to the next block and grinds across it on his trucks.

"Speaking of Sex Wax," Tyson says, grinning, "are you really thinking of asking out Sydney Mills?"

I walk my board a few feet out of the parking space and set it down. "I don't know why Emma brought that up."

I skate up to the first block and grind its length with only my rear truck. On the next I try a nosegrind, but I can't keep up the momentum.

"You have Peer Issues with her, right?" Tyson asks.

"With Sydney Mills? Why?"

Tyson pushes his board a few feet ahead, jogs after it, and then jumps on. "So when you talk about sexual issues, you've probably heard her say 'vagina.'"

I laugh. "What does that have to do with anything?"

He skates up to the block and stops. "It's cute when girls use proper words like that."

"Sorry to disappoint you," I say, kicking my board into my hand, "but I've never heard her say 'vagina.'"

Tyson raises his eyebrows suggestively. "Maybe you would if you asked her out."

On the track, someone must've crossed the finish line because the crowd on the bleachers applauds.

11://Emma

CODY SET A SCHOOL RECORD in the hundred-yard dash today, leading the Lake Forest Cheetahs to victory. I, on the other hand, placed fourth in the sixteen hundred and was the second slowest leg of my relay. I'm usually a stronger link, but I'm going on practically no sleep, and my brain is scattered. Before last night I'd never heard of Jordan Jones Jr., and suddenly I'm in a bad marriage to him.

It made me feel better to see Josh and Tyson in the stands, clapping and waving as we took the field. I know they don't actually stay to watch the meets, but I'm still glad they came. They're probably skating over those concrete blocks in the parking lot.

The meet is over and the visiting team is heading toward their buses. I'm sitting on the grass, sipping Gatorade and watching Cody chat with a girl from the other team.

She's tall and tan and they're standing close, laughing and touching each other's arms. I wonder if they've ever hooked up, or if that's coming soon. The word on the team is that Cody can be quite the stud.

I personally have never had sex. It's not like I'm waiting for love because who knows if that will ever happen, but it always felt like I would be giving too much of myself to a guy. Like Graham. I *definitely* wouldn't want him to be the one I lose my virginity to. Cody, though, is in a different category. If he and I ever got together, I can imagine myself not wanting to stop. The guy is seriously gorgeous.

"Is the meet over?" Graham asks, plopping down next to me. He has on the blue gym shorts and white T-shirt he always wears when he goes to the weight room. And he's sweaty, which makes his newly shorn head shiny and slick.

"It just ended," I say. I stretch my legs in front of me and lean forward until my forehead touches my knees. "We won."

"You're very flexible," he says. "It could give a guy some ideas."

Maybe he caught me in the wrong mood, but I sit up and snap at him. "Why do you *always* go there?"

"Where?"

"You know where."

Graham shrugs. "Hey, my buddies are hanging out on the baseball diamond. Do you want to go?"

I look around for Josh and Tyson, hoping they'll rescue

me. Josh and I didn't make specific plans, but I figured we'd meet up here and drive home to check out my computer.

I look over at Cody again. He's still with that girl, but now he's jotting something in a notebook. He tears out a page and hands it to her. She smiles and hugs him good-bye, her hand lingering on the small of his back. They are definitely going to have sex.

"Sure," I say to Graham. I grab my gym bag and hoist myself to my feet. "Let's go."

* * *

GRAHAM'S FRIENDS ARE GONE by the time we get to the baseball field, so we settle on a wooden bench in the dugout. My head is resting in his lap and he's running his fingers under my shirt, trying to reach up my jog bra. I keep swatting away his hand.

"I'm too sweaty," I say.

"I don't mind. You always look hot after your meets."

I push his hand away again. I'm wearing my orange mesh tank top with the cheetah on the front, and my black shorts. They're faded and wrinkled from years of Cheetah girls before me.

Nothing about me feels sexy right now. Maybe I'm just tired from last night. Or maybe it's because I can't stop thinking about Emma Nelson Jones, and whether I really become an unhappy person with a husband who doesn't come home.

Graham runs his hand back under my shirt. "You have an awesome stomach. Your belly button is so sexy."

Maybe this is the best it gets.

This time, when Graham's fingers touch my bra, I don't push him away. I sit up and lean into him and we start kissing. His hand slides beneath my bra, and I turn to make sure no one can see us.

That's when I notice Josh. He's standing frozen near second base. I pull back from Graham and tug down on my top, but Josh is already sprinting away.

12://Josh

IT'S ALL TYSON'S FAULT! He went on and on about Sydney Mills, which made me want to hurry up and get back to Emma's computer. So I left my board with Tyson and went to find Emma. She wasn't on the track, but Ruby Jenkins told me she saw Emma heading toward the baseball fields.

Ruby didn't say Emma was with *Graham*. If she told me that, I never would've gone up there.

Instead, I casually walked to the baseball fields, looking around. And then I saw Emma in the dugout. She was resting her head in Graham's lap. His face was slung low like he was talking to her, and I fooled myself into thinking she was finally dumping him.

But then Emma sat up and started kissing him, and Graham's hand shot up her shirt.

What the hell was that? Is that how she rejects a guy? Because it's not how she rejected me.

Before I had a chance to turn around, Emma saw me. For a brief second, we looked right at each other. I don't know what she was thinking, but I was feeling disgust and revulsion.

I'm sprinting back across the field, wanting to kick something or scream or beat the hell out of Graham.

"Did you find her?" Ruby asks as I pass the track.

"She's not there!" I shout.

Out of breath, I make it back to the parking lot. Tyson is sitting on a concrete block, admiring my latest skateboard sketch of Marvin the Martian.

"Is Emma giving us a ride home?" he asks.

"No. Let's just go," I say.

Tyson holds out a hand and I pull him up. "Can you draw something like this on my board?" he asks. "Maybe Yosemite Sam?"

I grab one of the concrete blocks and begin dragging it toward the metal rods. "Can you help me with this?"

Tyson lifts the other end of the block. We position the concrete over the rods and shimmy it down to the asphalt.

"I've got a question for you," Tyson says. "And maybe one day you'll be in a position to answer it."

"Just help me put this other one back, okay?"

We carry opposite ends of the next concrete block and stagger over to the metal rods, then lower it down.

"My question is," Tyson says as he claps the dust from his hands, "and I want you to find out the answer for me: are Sydney's tits real, or did her parents buy them for her? I'll appreciate them either way. I just want to know."

If the block hadn't already been on the ground, I would've dropped it on Tyson's foot.

13://Emma

AS I'M DRIVING HOME, I blast the new Dave Matthews album. My car doesn't have a CD player, so I bought the cassette tape when it came out last month. But even with Dave singing "Crash Into Me," I can't drown out what just happened on the baseball field. Josh saw Graham feeling me up. And Graham didn't even get it. He ran his palm over his scalp and said, "It's not like he's never seen two people kiss before."

I pushed him off me and ran to the locker room to get my backpack and clothes, then out to the parking lot to search for Josh and Tyson.

But they were gone.

When I pull into my driveway, I glance toward Josh's house. Even if he's home, there's no way I'm knocking on his door. I know we said we'd look at my computer after track, but now everything is screwed up.

I set my saxophone case in the hallway at the bottom of the stairs and head to the kitchen to splash water on my face. My mom left a Post-it note next to the sink telling me to preheat the oven and put in the casserole dish of macaroni and cheese. When I turn the dial on the oven, I spot another Post-it on the counter in my mom's handwriting. "MrsMartinNichols@aol.com." I guess that's the email address she wants. The password she picked is "EmmaMarie."

I slide the macaroni pan into the oven and head upstairs. After I sign on, I add my mom as MrsMartinNichols. Then I check to see if she can get onto the Facebook website from her account, but there's no sign of it in her Favorite Places.

Relieved, I sign out and collapse back in my chair. Our secret is safe. But I still don't know what this thing is, or how I'm going to figure it out if Josh doesn't come over.

Which he's never going to do.

I sink into my papasan chair to do homework. I can smell the food cooking downstairs. My mom and Martin arrive home. A few minutes later, she calls me down for dinner.

I've always considered mac and cheese the ultimate comfort food. It looks like I still do fifteen years from now. But today the noodles clump in my throat. Maybe it's because they're whole wheat, as my mom proudly explains to Martin. Or maybe it's because nothing could comfort me right now.

* * *

AFTER WE FINISH the dishes, my mom and Martin continue their demolition of the downstairs bathroom. They're blasting Led Zeppelin and using a hammer and chisel to remove old tiles. I pour a glass of water, head upstairs, and lie on my bed.

I'm sorry that Josh saw Graham feeling me up, but I'm allowed to kiss whoever I want. And Graham and I are going out, so it's not like Josh can call me a slut. Even so, I feel terrible about it. Especially after what happened last November.

It was the opening night of *Toy Story*. A bunch of us went to see it, taking up a whole row. I sat next to Josh, and during the scenes with Sid's creepy toys, I buried my face in his shoulder. I've always loved Josh's smell. It reminds me of tree forts and the lake. Most people went home after the movie, but Kellan, Tyson, Josh, and I went to the graveyard to visit Tyson's mom. She died when he was a baby and, as long as I've known him, he's stopped by to drop off flowers or just say hi. Kellan and Tyson took a walk while Josh and I went in search of Clarence and Millicent. They're the names we once discovered on two gravestones that belonged to a married couple. Clarence and Millicent died on the same date when they were both in their nineties. We loved the idea that they never had to live a day without the other. That's how we got the names for our Hamburger Helper couple, and also how I picked my password.

We were standing right next to Clarence and Millicent when Josh said, "I really like you, Emma."

I smiled. "I really like you, too."

"I'm glad," he said, and then he stepped close like he was about to kiss me.

I stumbled back. "No," I said, shaking my head. "You're . . . *Josh*."

As soon as the words were out of my mouth, I could see how much I hurt him.

But I meant it. For my whole life, Josh had been the one person I could always count on. If something happened between us and it didn't work out, I knew I would lose him. But in trying to protect us, I ended up losing him anyway.

I close my eyes and, for the first time all day, let exhaustion overcome me.

A short while later, my mom startles me awake.

"Emma?" she calls from downstairs. "Can you hear me?"

"Yeah," I say. I sit up and rub my eyes.

"Josh is here. I'm sending him up."

14://Josh

BEFORE ENTERING EMMA'S ROOM, I take a deep breath to calm down, but my fingers are clenched. The last time I saw Emma, she was getting felt up. While I considered not coming over tonight, I need to see what she read about me. I want to prove this is a hoax, tell Emma to get over it, and then go back to acting like I don't live next door to her.

Emma is sitting on the edge of her bed, still in her orange and black track uniform. Her hair is matted, and her cheek is creased like she just woke up. She smiles weakly, but she's having trouble making eye contact.

Emma shakes her head. "I'm sorry if—"

"I don't care," I say, looking at her computer. "Let's just forget it."

"I'm sure it hurt, so I want you to know—"

"It didn't hurt," I say. "I was just surprised because I thought you were breaking up with him."

"Not that it's any of your business," Emma says, "but I am going to break up with him soon."

"Oh, I see. You just needed your tits grabbed one more time."

Emma's eyes flash with anger, and I know I've gone too far.

"You're lucky I'm a nice person," she says, "because I'll pretend I didn't hear that. I know why you said it, but—"

"*Why* did I say it?" I ask. I want her to tell me that I'm jealous of Graham so I can laugh in her face.

"Josh, if you want me to show you that website, then you really need to shut up."

Emma stomps to her desk. It feels good to know I'm not the only one pissed off right now.

The brick wall screensaver is running. Emma jiggles the mouse. I can see her enter "EmmaNelson4ever@aol.com," then begin typing "M-i-l-l-i-c"

"Is your password seriously *Millicent*?" I ask.

Emma looks up at me. "How did you guess that?"

"I saw the first several letters and . . . do you want to hear something weird?"

Emma shrugs, but doesn't say anything.

"On the school email accounts they gave us," I say, "I chose *Clarence* for my password."

"No way!" Emma says. "Our Hamburger Helper eating—"

"Ice-cream-truck driving—"

"Middle-aged married couple."

"That's them," I say, and for the briefest moment we exchange a look as if we can both remember what it felt like to be best friends.

Emma hits Enter and the computer beeps and crackles as it dials up to AOL.

"Did you see Sydney today?" she asks, swinging her chair around.

"We have Peer Issues together."

Emma smiles. "Did you say anything to her?"

"I didn't need to. My stupid face did all the talking."

Emma points a finger at me as if looking down the barrel of a gun. "But you didn't think this was real."

"I still don't," I say. "While being able to see my future—especially *that* future—would be unbelievably awesome, it's also unbelievable."

"*Welcome!*" the electronic voice says.

Emma turns back to her computer and continues typing. "It's funny hearing you act skeptical. You used to believe in Bigfoot and UFOs. And remember the Goatman?"

"I never believed in the Goatman," I say. "I just thought he was interesting."

Emma double-clicks where it says "Facebook," and a white box opens in the middle of the screen. She retypes her email address and password, but instead of pressing Enter, she looks at me.

"I always imagined time travel would be so big and life-changing," she says. "Like *A Wrinkle in Time* or *Back to the Future*. But here, all most people care about are lame vacation photos and trivial things."

I almost say: *Or marrying the hottest chick in school.*

"So why do you think people write all this stuff about cupcakes or whatever?" I ask.

"It's not everyone," Emma says. "I talk about real issues, but only because I'm not afraid to admit when life sucks." She laughs bitterly. "And my life sucks."

At the top of the screen, it says "Emma Nelson Jones." Her picture is small, but I can tell it's different from the one that was here yesterday. Emma clicks the photo and it enlarges. Now Ms. Jones is standing in front of a white stucco wall, her hands clasped by her waist. She's wearing a yellow sweater and a gold necklace with the letter *E*.

Emma Nelson Jones
Last night's lasagna heated up great, but work is stressing me out.
2 hours ago · Like · Comment

"That's odd," Emma says. "Yesterday, it said I made macaroni and cheese. I wonder why it . . ." Emma turns to me, her eyes wide. "I bet the mac and cheese at dinner tonight turned me off to it . . . even in the future."

I try to suppress a smirk. She's taking this too far.

I look back at the monitor. "If work is stressing you out, that means you have a job. Weren't you unemployed yesterday? This is a cause for celebration!"

"You're right." Emma touches her finger to the screen and scans down. "It's *all* different. None of this was here yesterday."

"I was teasing," I say. "It's a prank, Emma."

"No, now you're wrong," she says. "If it was a prank, nothing would've changed between yesterday and today. But everything I did differently today sent little ripples of change into the future. Being in a bad mood this morning, because of *this*, changed the way I interacted with people when I got to school. And that, fifteen years down the line—"

I laugh. "Ripples of change?"

"It's something Kellan told me."

"You told *Kellan*?"

"Of course not," Emma says. "I just asked her about time travel from a physics perspective."

"So something you did today kept you from losing your job in the future. It also made you cook lasagna instead of mac and cheese. Got it." I wave my hand toward the screen. "Then maybe you're not married to what's-his-face anymore either."

Emma looks at the screen and reads:

Married to Jordan Jones, Jr.

"Unfortunately," she says, "those ripples didn't develop into a typhoon."

"Hurricane Emma. That could do some damage."

"I know you're trying to pretend there's no difference between this and the Goatman," Emma says, "but didn't you say you made a stupid face at Sydney Mills today?"

"So?" I ask.

Emma raises one eyebrow. "You wouldn't have made any face at all if I hadn't told you about your future. I wonder what damage Hurricane Joshua inflicted."

Emma points the arrow at a group of pictures labeled "Friends." "Now I'm at four hundred and six friends. Cool! I guess I've made a lot of new friends at my job."

I crouch down beside her. "Am I in there?"

Emma smiles smugly. "I thought you weren't a believer."

"I'm just having fun."

Emma moves the arrow over "Friends (406)" and clicks it. A new page appears with more tiny pictures and names. I resist the urge to ask Emma to hurry up and find me. I don't want to seem like I think it's even a possibility that I'll marry Sydney Mills. Because it's not.

The list is organized alphabetically by first name. When she gets to the Js, she slows down. And there it is.

Josh Templeton

My heart beats faster. I don't know what to say. In the very off-chance that this is real, I don't know how to feel about what I'm going to see.

Emma moves the arrow over my name. "Josh, here you are," she says dramatically, "fifteen years in the future."

A new page slowly appears. The small picture contains a cluster of colorful balloons. At the very bottom of the photo is the face of a man with reddish hair and glasses. I don't need to ask if that's supposed to be me. Beside the photo, it says his birthday is April 5. He went to the University of Washington, and works somewhere called Electra Design.

Josh Templeton
The family just returned from Acapulco. Breathtaking! I've posted photos on my blog.
May 15 at 4:36pm · Like · Comment

"What's a blog?" I ask.

"No idea," Emma says. "But I wonder why your vacation changed. It has to be more than that face you made at Sydney. Maybe it's because you knew you were going to Waikiki, but you really wanted to go to Acapulco, so when you and Sydney began planning the vacation you made sure to change it."

Josh Templeton
Helped my son put together a model of the solar
system today.
May 8 at 10:26pm · Like · Comment

> **Terry Fernandez** We did that last year. Made
> me feel nostalgic for Pluto. That was always my
> favorite planet.
> May 9 at 8:07am · Like

> **Josh Templeton** Poor Pluto! :-(
> May 9 at 9:13am · Like

I flinch. "What the hell happens to Pluto?"

Emma shrugs. "*That*, I'm guessing, wasn't our fault."

I rock back on my sneakers. "How can you tell who
my . . . you know . . . wife is?"

Emma points to the top of the screen.

Married to Sydney Templeton

"But how do you know that's supposed to be Sydney
Mills?" I ask.

Emma looks straight at me. "You need to stop saying
things like 'supposed to be.' It's annoying."

"Fine. How can you tell that person *is* Sydney Mills?"

Emma clicks on "Sydney Templeton."

The webpage is slowly replaced by another one. This
time, the photo is of a family with three kids sitting on
a lawn. The oldest son has red hair. The girls look like

identical twin sisters with the same brown hair as their ridiculously beautiful mom.

I back up to Emma's papasan chair and sink into it.

"Are you still skeptical?" Emma asks.

"I'm just . . . I want to . . ." I want to be skeptical. I *need* to be skeptical. But this rush of impossible information is almost too much.

"Jordan Jones Junior," Emma says. "I hate him just for that stupid name. Now I have a job, but it looks like Jordan spends everything I make. Listen . . . here I wrote, 'Got my paycheck on Thursday and JJJ borrowed every last dollar to buy an iPad. Men and toys!' I put quotes around 'borrowed,' so I'm guessing he's not giving the money back."

"What's an iPad?" I ask.

"That's not the point! Whatever it is, I gave my husband enough money to buy one." She clicks around on the webpage. "We live in Florida, but he's from Chico, California. Where's Chico?"

"No idea," I say. "How do you know where he's from?"

"I clicked on his name. There's not much here, but he seems like a real asshole."

"You don't even know him and you're calling him an *asshole*?"

"Some things you can just tell," Emma says.

I feel ridiculous for even entertaining the idea that this could be real, but there's no way that wasn't Sydney Mills and me in that photo. They were older versions of us, but the resemblance was unreal.

"Check this out!" Emma says.

I push myself out of her chair.

"These pictures were attached to my website," Emma says, pointing to the screen. "It looks like each one leads to more photos, kind of like albums."

Profile Pictures	12 photos
My 30th Birthday	37 photos
High School Memories	8 photos

I point at the screen. "'High School Memories.' Let's see what you find so important fifteen years from now. I bet they're all of me."

Emma laughs. "Only because I don't have any of Cody yet."

She clicks that photo album and we stare at the screen as the photos materialize.

The first is a close-up of Emma holding her driver's license. That's currently on one of her corkboards. Someone could've stolen it for a day and scanned it in the tech lab at school. The next photo shows Tyson and me using our skateboards as battle swords. That one's taped in her locker. Then there's Tyson, Kellan, Emma, and me buried up to our necks in the rainbow ball pit at GoodTimez Pizza. That's also on her corkboard. Whoever is pulling this prank could have borrowed Emma's photos and put them back without her noticing.

Emma touches her finger to the last photo, a shot of her butt in a light tan bikini. "What's this?"

She clicks on the image and a larger version begins to appear in the center of the screen.

"Is that Crown Lake in the background?" I manage to keep my voice innocent, but I know exactly where that photo was taken. I snapped it a few weeks ago when we all drove to the lake before it officially opened for the season. I thought it'd be funny to have her develop the film and wonder who took it.

The caption below the picture says, "The good ole days."

"I just bought that bikini a month ago," Emma says.

"You know," I mumble, "I think I accidentally took that picture. I was trying to move your camera out of the sand and I may have hit the button."

"Josh." Emma looks me straight in the eye. "This Facebook thing is not a joke. There's no way anyone could be pranking us."

"Someone could've stolen your pictures. I wouldn't say there's *no* way."

She reaches into her desk drawer and pulls out a yellow disposable camera. "I haven't developed the lake photos yet."

15://Emma

SO IT ALL comes down to a yellow disposable camera left over from my mom's wedding. If the lake photos are still inside, undeveloped, then Josh will have to admit that this Facebook thing is real.

We stare at the image on the screen, at the bathing suit bottom I recently bought at the Lake Forest Mall. And then, at the same moment, we shift our attention to the camera on my desk.

"Do you think we should—?" Josh begins.

"What time does Photomat close?"

"Ten," Josh says. "It's in the SkateRats plaza."

It's 8:53pm. Photomat guarantees one-hour prints.

"Let's take your car," he says.

"Too risky," I say, gesturing downstairs. If my mom heard us leave she'd tell us it's too late for a school night.

"Blade and skate?" he asks.

I nod, reaching for my orange Cheetahs fleece on the back of my chair. I'm still wearing my track uniform because I haven't had the energy to change.

"I have to grab my board from the garage," Josh says.

The screen is still open to "High School Memories." "Should we close this?"

"Definitely," Josh says.

The way he says it, so clear and direct, gives me the chills. Josh is starting to believe this is real.

*   *   *

WE MAKE IT TO PHOTOMAT at ten after nine. The guy behind the counter has thin hair and tired eyes. I fill out my name and a fake phone number, then slide the film into an envelope.

"Can you develop this before closing?" I ask, rolling my skates back and forth.

The guy glances wearily at me. "We'll see."

I clomp out to the sidewalk. "I don't think he gets the urgency of this."

"He said he'd try," Josh says.

"No, he said 'we'll see.' 'We'll see' means he's leaving it up to the universe. And it's not up to the universe. It's up to *him*!"

Josh pushes off on his board, and I blade after him across the parking lot. We settle on a raised patch of grass under the rotating time-and-temperature clock. It's dark

over here and fireflies are flickering around the lawn. I
loosen my blades and lay back on the grass, looking up
at the sky.

"Remember when we used to play T-ball over there?"
Josh asks.

I lift up onto my elbows and look at the stretch of
Wagner Park across the street from the plaza. One year,
my dad coached our Little League team. My half-sister,
Rachel, is only five weeks old, but I wonder if he'll coach
her when she gets old enough to play.

I gesture toward a trim white house in the middle of a
row of single-story homes. "That's where Cody lives," I
say.

"I know," Josh says.

"You do?"

"David used to hang out with Cody's older brother.
We went over there for pool parties. His brother, oddly
enough, isn't such a prick."

"Cody's not a prick!" I say. "You just don't know him."

"And you do?"

I decide not to tell Josh that for several months leading
up to the prom I had a fantasy that Cody would approach
me in the hall and ask me to be his date. He went with
Meredith Adams, who wore a teeny silver dress. They
came late and left early. I went with Graham, even though
I was pretty much over the relationship by that point. We
sat with his group of friends, mostly people I didn't know.

Kellan, Tamika, Ruby, and some other girls went together, sharing a limo and dancing barefoot in a big group the whole time. I joined them for a few songs, until Graham sauntered over and pulled me into a slow dance. Josh and Tyson didn't even go. They went to Tyson's house and drooled over Tony Hawk skating videos all night.

After a few minutes of watching fireflies, Josh positions a blade of grass between his thumbs and leans in to blow.

"Don't!" I shriek. "You know that freaks me out."

Josh drops the grass and turns toward me. "I'm sorry about before," he says quietly. "What I said about Graham grabbing your . . . you know. I was being a dick."

"It's okay," I say, spinning a wheel on my rollerblade.

I lean back in the grass and look up at the sky. Venus is out, and a sliver of moon. As I stare up at the stars, I wonder what becomes of Pluto. Does it get hit by a meteor?

"We should get going," Josh says, pointing at the clock. "Photomat closes in five minutes."

* * *

"NELSON?" I ASK, pushing through the door.

The guy thumbs through the Ns and fishes out my envelope. When he hands us the packet, Josh's earlobes turn pink. I give the guy a ten-dollar bill and he counts back my change.

We exit and move down a few shops until we're directly beneath a street lamp. I tear open the packet. With my blades on, I'm almost as tall as Josh. For a second, his leg brushes against mine, but he quickly pulls it away.

The first few photos are of my mom and me in the kitchen. Josh touches the stack as if to say, *faster, faster*. But now I'm not sure I want to find out. If that really is my future, and I'm not happy, maybe it would be better not to know until I get there.

Josh grabs the photos from me. He flips to the next picture, and there we all are at the lake. Tyson throwing Kellan into the ice-cold water. A close-up of Josh crossing his eyes. Kellan and me with our arms flung around each other's waists. And the bottom half of my new tan bikini with the lake stretched out in the distance.

The good ole days.

16://Josh

I'M GOING TO MARRY SYDNEY MILLS.

I'm going to *marry* Sydney Mills.

Sydney Mills is going to be my wife.

I stand in the hot shower for ten minutes. When it becomes obvious I'm not going to figure anything out by staring at the drain, I turn off the water and grab my green towel.

The porcelain sink feels cool against my palms. In the steamed bathroom mirror, I can see my scattershot red hair, thin arms, and the towel around my waist. Somehow, in fifteen years, I morph from *this* into the guy who marries Sydney Mills.

I take a step back, flex my biceps, and suck air into my chest. The hazy reflection helps me imagine stacking on some muscle. And it looks good!

I wink at myself. "Yeah, baby!"

A few more pushups and sit-ups every night and maybe I can become that guy even faster. I turn sideways and flex into the mirror, but from this angle there's no denying I'm still a skinny kid with two years of high school left to go.

I slide open the bathroom window to let out some steam. Across the lawn, the lights are off in Emma's room. She must have gone to bed early.

*   *   *

IT'S GETTING CLOSE to midnight. I glance around my bedroom, but I can't see my phone. I walk downstairs, turn on the small light in the hallway, and dial my brother. It's three hours earlier in Seattle, so I'm not worried about waking him up.

On the second ring, David answers. In the background, there's a TV audience laughing.

"Hey, it's Josh," I say. "Are you busy?"

"I'm in college," he says. "I'm eating a bowl of Lucky Charms and watching the final episode of *Fresh Prince of Bel-Air*." I guarantee, if David calls home tomorrow, he'll tell our parents he was studying in the library all night.

"Mom and Dad watched that tonight," I say. "Doesn't it scare you to know you have the same sense of humor as them?"

"A little," he says. "But it's Will Smith! Have I ever told you that every time he starts rapping the theme song, it reminds me of the time you tried rapping in the junior high—"

"I remember," I say, cutting him off. "But that's not why I called."

"Of course not," he says. "So what's going on, RedSauce?"

"There's this girl," I say.

I hear the TV shutting off. "Is she cute?"

"She's gorgeous. Any guy in school would *die* to go out with her."

"And she's interested in you?" David asks. "That's my brother!"

"No, she's not interested . . . yet." I take a breath. "It's hard to explain, but I think she *could* be interested in me . . . eventually."

"How do you know her?"

"I don't. Not really. We have Peer Issues together, but she's a year ahead of me."

"Have you ever talked to her?"

"No."

"Never?" he asks.

"No."

"So she's more like your fantasy girl," he says. "That's okay. You just need to break the ice."

"That's the part I suck at."

"Whatever you do," he says, "don't walk up and ask

her out. If you don't have any sort of a relationship yet, that can seem creepy."

"Then what do I do?"

"Hang back and play it cool," he says. "When the right moment appears, the key is not to let it pass."

That's always been my problem. I let moments pass, and then I kick myself endlessly.

I twist the phone cord around my finger. "What if it feels like the perfect moment is happening, but I'm mis-reading things?"

"You mean like what happened with Emma?" David asks. "No, definitely don't let that happen again."

tuesday

17://Emma

I ARRIVE AT SCHOOL early and head to the newspaper office. Kellan's editorials are due on Tuesdays and she always reviews last-minute changes with Tamika West, who's the editor in chief. When I enter, Kellan and Tamika are marking up papers spread out on a long table.

"Hey, Emma," Tamika says.

Kellan looks up. "What happened to you?"

"What do you mean?" This morning, I blew my hair straight and even put on makeup, which I rarely do for school. But I just needed the ego boost today.

"You look fried," Kellan says.

"I'm fine . . . just a little tired."

"Can you hang on for a second?" Kellan asks. "We're almost done."

I settle into a stained armchair at the corner of the office. It's a cluttered room, with newspaper clippings, gum wrappers, and flattened soda cans everywhere. For several weeks after Tyson broke up with her, we ate lunch at that long table.

I listen as Kellan and Tamika discuss Kellan's editorial. I read an early draft of it. It's about a school policy prohibiting girls from wearing shirts that reveal their midriffs, and whether that violates their First Amendment rights. It makes me think about Graham lusting after my belly button in the dugout yesterday. On my way here, I slipped a note through the vents in his locker, saying I wouldn't see him until band. That way he won't hunt me down for a make out session before class. Eventually we need to have the breakup talk, just not this morning.

Kellan picks up her backpack. "Ready?"

We walk into the hallway, and people are starting to arrive at their lockers. I have no idea what I'll say to Josh if I run into him. It was dark when we returned home from Photomat and said good night. But now, under the bright florescent lights of school, my emotions are too exposed.

"Did you hear about Rick's bonfire on Friday night?" Kellan asks as we walk up the stairs. "Tamika told me about it. It's at the end of Senior Skip Day, but the party isn't just for seniors. It's on the beach behind his house, and he's inviting anyone who wants to come."

Rick Rolland is a senior who plays football and throws parties and always has a beautiful girlfriend. He actually went out with Sydney Mills last year, but word is that he cheated on her with a ninth grader.

"Rick lives on the lake?" I ask, thinking about Josh and Sydney's future house.

"Yeah. Want to go?"

"I guess," I say, though it's hard planning for the end of the week when all I can think about is fifteen years in the future. As we head down the foreign language corridor, I turn to Kellan. "Do you think it's too late to sign up for that college biology course?"

Kellan claps her hands together. "You changed your mind?"

"I think so," I say.

I woke up this morning feeling sad for myself. But telling people I'm taking a college class while still in high school sounds worthy of respect. Also, I liked biology this year, especially the units on genetics and DNA.

"It'll be much harder than high school bio, but you'll do great," Kellan says. "And you've already got the grades, so you'll definitely get in."

"I hope so," I say.

Kellan links arms with me and squeals. "This is our first step on the way to med school!"

"We're going to med school now?"

"We can even live together. And do our residency at the same hospital!"

When she says this, I realize that I can try looking up Kellan on Facebook. Maybe I'll even see if she actually *does* go to med school. It's such a powerful thought that Facebook isn't limited to Josh and me. I might be able to look up *anyone* and see what their future holds.

18://Josh

TYSON AND I HAVE GYM third period. If we played a sport, we wouldn't need to take gym, but the sacrifice is worth it. With the time it takes to change and walk to the volleyball courts, class only lasts thirty minutes.

I wipe my towel beneath each arm, and then toss it back in my locker. In the next row, someone's beeper goes off.

Tyson's towel is wrapped tight around his waist. He reaches beneath it to pull off his gym shorts. "I tried getting my dad to buy me a beeper for my birthday," he says, "but he thinks only doctors and drug dealers need them."

I sniff my armpits and reach into my locker for deodorant. "Why do you want one?"

"So people can reach me if they need to," he says.

"Are you really that in demand?" I ask. "I know you're not a drug dealer, so are you secretly a doctor?"

Kyle Simpson saunters around the corner, naked as usual. He holds up his little black beeper and presses a button to make the seven digits glow. "My girlfriend's paging me," he tells us. "Anyone got a quarter for the pay phone?"

Kyle's girlfriend goes to the college, and we all know what it means when she beeps him during gym. He'll be cutting fourth period and won't return until the end of lunch.

Kyle is one of Emma's exes. They dated for a while last year, and she used to talk about how hot he was when he took off his shirt. Guys seem to love doing that if they're ripped. Needless to say, I'm a shirt-on kind of guy. I'm just thankful I didn't have gym with Kyle while they were dating. The last thing I needed was to hear him talk about Emma while parading around buck naked.

I pretend to feel around for change on my towel. "Sorry, dude."

Tyson pulls his bunched-up pants out of his locker, reaches into one of the pockets, and tosses over a quarter. Kyle slaps him on the back, then swaggers back down the aisle. When he's gone, Tyson and I look at each other and shudder.

"Why does he do that?" I whisper. "Either get dressed or wrap a towel around yourself."

"Exactly," Tyson says. "I don't need to see his schlong five days a week."

I pull my shirt over my head. "Maybe that's why you and Kellan broke up. You call it a 'schlong.'"

"If I'd had a beeper," Tyson says, "I bet we'd still be together."

"If you had a beeper, she'd be calling it nonstop. You'd spend half your life running to the nearest payphone to call her back."

The bell rings and I finish tying my sneakers. Then I yank my backpack from my locker and set it on the bench. From the front pocket, I remove a pen and a sheet of paper, which I smooth against my thigh. During first period, I began a list called "I wonder what becomes of . . .?" So far I've written the names of eighteen people I want to search for on Emma's computer. The list includes a few of the smartest people in my grade. Maybe one of them finds a cure for AIDS or designs a car that doesn't run on gas. Maybe the president of drama club makes it to Broadway. And my first girlfriend, Rebecca Alvarez. What's she doing fifteen years from now?

There are also the people too bizarre to ignore, like Kyle Simpson. Future male stripper.

19://Emma

KELLAN AND I are spending study hall in the library. Kellan, who will ace finals no problem, is taking a quiz in *YM* called "What Kind of Girlfriend Are You?" I'm trying to remember key events in the Spanish-American War for the history final, but what I'm really thinking about is my future.

I close my eyes and massage my forehead. It's hard to tell much when the future is given out a few random sentences at a time. Also, my life has changed every time we've looked, so I can't even predict what's going to make my future self miserable today.

"'You're having a girls' night in,'" Kellan reads, "'when your boyfriend calls and invites you to the movies. Do you, (A), say you can't make it but you'll be free tomorrow; (B), invite him over to join your gal pals; or (C)—'"

"None of the above," I say. "Call him on the fact that he doesn't really want to see a movie. It's just a booty call."

"You're right," Kellan says, shaking her head. "Guys are such horndogs."

I study my fingernails. "Do you ever think about who you're going to marry someday?"

"Funny you should ask." Kellan grins and folds down a corner of her magazine page. "This morning I was telling Tamika about a Husband Theory I came up with."

"You have a Husband Theory?"

"I thought of it while I was waiting at a stoplight yesterday," she says. "Okay, imagine you're about to die in a head-on collision. There you are, driving down the street, when a Ford Bronco comes hurtling toward you. You know this is it, the end. So you glance in the passenger seat and . . . who do you see?"

"That's terrible, Kel!"

"Quick, who do you see? That's your future husband."

I pick some coral polish off my thumbnail. "I'm the one driving?"

"Yes, and you're both about to die. Who is it?"

"I don't know," I say. "You, maybe."

"Impossible" she says. "We just learned in sociology that they don't allow same-sex marriage *anywhere* in the world. That's what my next editorial is about. But come on! Who's in your passenger seat?"

"No one," I say, shaking my head. "I see a tabby cat. Or

maybe one of those cockatoos like that woman downtown carries on her shoulder."

Kellan pushes out her lower lip. "You're not even playing along."

"Sorry. Okay, I'll envision Cody. What about you? Who do you see?"

"Tyson," she says, and then she opens her magazine again.

"*Tyson*?" I look over my shoulder to make sure the librarian hasn't noticed us talking. She's sitting at the front desk, reading *School Library Journal.* "He broke your heart. Twice! Why do you always forget that?"

"That's who I see," Kellan says. "I can't help it. But do you want to hear something cute? Tyson's helping some senior skaters get the wood for the bonfire on Friday night. That's so Paul Bunyan of him, isn't it?"

When Kellan goes back to her *YM* quiz, I think about my *real* future husband, Jordan Jones Jr. He didn't have much on his webpage, though he obviously enjoys fishing. But I don't know enough about him to envision him in my passenger seat.

Then it hits me. I jump out of my chair and hurry across the library. *He's* what's making my future suck. If I can get rid of him, then maybe I'll have a shot at happiness.

"Ms. Nesbit?" I say. The librarian has a pink streak in her hair and two silver hoops at the top of one ear. "Does the library have any phone books?"

She sets down her magazine, open to an article on book censorship. She's definitely one of the cooler teachers at Lake Forest High.

"Is it an emergency?" she asks, heaving out the local white pages. "I can let you use the phone in back if you need to make a call."

"Actually, I'm looking for phone books from other states."

Ms. Nesbit fidgets with one of her earrings. "Any state in particular?"

My pulse quickens. "California?"

"You should try the public library," Ms. Nesbit says. "They have phone books from all over the country. I'm sure they have some from California."

20://Josh

AFTER TAKING ATTENDANCE, Mrs. Tuttle leads our class down the hall toward the auditorium, where we'll join another Peer Issues class on the stage. Whatever we're doing, that's the only space big enough for everyone.

At the far end of the hall are the double doors to the theater. Mr. Fritz's class is already filing in. I remember David's advice about not letting moments pass me by, so I hurry to catch up with Sydney Mills. As I approach, her coconut scent washes over me and I'm reminded of suntan lotion and bikinis. And Waikiki! I mean, Acapulco.

I don't want to force a moment between us, but I need to talk to her at least once to get it over with. Otherwise, I'll keep agonizing about when she'll ever acknowledge me. Just yesterday, the two of us falling in love never would have occurred to me. But after seeing that photo of

Emma at the lake, and the one of Sydney and me with our kids, there's no way this could be a hoax.

I slide up beside Sydney and walk next to her down the hall. I need to say something clever. Something she'll always remember as the first words I ever said to her. We'll write those words on Valentine's Day cards and retell the story to our grandchildren someday.

Sydney looks over at me and smiles. Here's my moment!

"I . . . I like this auditorium we're going to."

Really? *That's* the ice-breaker that seals our fate?

"That's good," she says, her smile fading. "Because that's where we're going."

To get through the doors, our class shrinks into a compact mass of bodies. I let Sydney pull ahead while my face burns with embarrassment. "I like this auditorium we're going to" will not be appearing on any Valentine's cards.

The other class is standing near the edge of the stage with their teacher. Mr. Fritz is overweight, yet he always wears tight polyester shirts. Apparently, whenever he talks about sex he gets crescent-moon sweat marks beneath his man-breasts.

"Let's gather round," Mrs. Tuttle says. She walks close to Mr. Fritz and we form a semicircle around them.

Sydney settles at one end of the semicircle while I hang near the center.

"We are here to do a group exercise," Mr. Fritz explains.

"Hopefully it will allow you to see outside of your own lives."

Next to me, a guy from the other class whispers, "A dollar says Fritz and Tuttle do the wild thing in the teachers' lounge."

Mrs. Tuttle takes a step forward. "We thought it would be enlightening to learn how many different perspectives there can be on relationships just within our two classes." She places a hand on Mr. Fritz's shoulder.

"What'd I tell you?" the guy asks, grinning at me.

"One of the things we've been trying to get across all semester," Mr. Fritz says, "is that your well-being is affected by the relationships you have."

I glance over at Sydney. She's paying close attention as she twists back her hair. I take in her long hair and smooth skin. Everything about her is so beautiful.

Mr. Fritz points to the four corners of the stage. "Each corner will represent a different relationship philosophy. We'll give you a scenario and present you with four options, then you'll move to the corner you most agree with." He hands his clipboard to Mrs. Tuttle.

"We'll start with an easy one," she says. "Imagine that you want to go on a date with someone at our school. Would you ask them out . . . wait as long as it takes for them to ask *you* out . . . tell your friend to find out what that person thinks of you . . . or are you simply too busy to date?"

"People don't really call it *dating* anymore," Abby Law says.

A few people giggle, and Mrs. Tuttle says, "Well, whatever you call it."

The guy next to me shouts, "Hooking up!" and now the whole class is laughing.

Mr. Fritz points to the front of the stage. "Come downstage-left if you'd ask that person out. But if you'd rather—"

Abby Law cuts in again. "Actually, you're pointing upstage-right."

After the four options are sorted out, I walk to the corner where you ask a friend for help. Last fall, I should've asked Tyson to find out what Emma thought about our relationship. It would've saved me so much humiliation.

"No one's too busy to date?" Mrs. Tuttle asks, pointing toward the empty corner.

Shana Roy raises her hand. Any guy in this room would give his left nut to be asked out by her.

"I almost went over there," she says. "But if the right person asked, I'm sure I'd find the time."

"That wasn't the question," another girl says. "What would you do if *you* wanted to date someone?"

"You're right," Shana says. "I'd ask them out."

She walks across the stage, and I'm mesmerized by the strip of tan bare skin swiveling above her jeans.

At lunch, Kellan talked about the school's new midriff rule, and how she thinks it violates student rights. Tyson and I laughed, and he told her that every guy is passionately against the rule, but not because of any rights. It's the view! That pissed Kellan off and she chucked a handful of fries at him.

"This one might be tougher," Mrs. Tuttle says. She looks at her clipboard and reads, "If things are moving too fast sexually, and a girl is visibly upset, should the boy stop even if the girl hasn't said the word *no*?"

The four corners represent "yes," "no," "the boy should ask if everything's okay," and "I don't have enough information." People begin shuffling around until we're almost equally divided between "yes" and "ask if everything's okay." Surprisingly, three girls think it's fine to keep going.

Ruby Jenkins defends her point of view. "I know girls who've been in that situation. And I'm sorry, but you need to say something."

"Understood," Mrs. Tuttle says. "Now, Ruby, what if even one boy stood in your corner?"

Ruby smirks. "I'd kick his you-know-what."

The other girls in her corner laugh and give her high fives.

"That's stupid," a guy says. He's the same person who thinks Fritz and Tuttle are doing the wild thing. "That's female sexism. The girl needs to speak up."

Mr. Wild Thing is a senior who plays varsity football. Whenever I pass him in the hall, I get the urge to drop and do fifty push-ups.

"That's wasn't the question, Rick," Sydney says. "If a guy is pushing a girl too far and she's *visibly upset*, then he needs to back off."

A couple girls behind me laugh and one whispers, "I didn't know Sydney Mills had a 'too far.'"

I keep my eyes on Sydney. I don't think she could've heard that comment from the opposite end of the stage, but for a brief moment I see her bite her lip.

"I'm just saying," she says, her voice quieter, "she shouldn't have to spell everything out for him."

"So he needs to be a mind reader?" Rick asks.

"I'm just—" Sydney stops midsentence and shakes her head.

Mr. Fritz opens his mouth, but before I know it, I blurt out, "She's right. It's human decency."

Did I actually just say that? It's true, but why did I say it out loud? And "human decency"? I could've come up with something better than *that*!

"Well put," Mr. Fritz says, tapping a pencil against the clipboard. "Okay, the next question is about premarital sex, and I'm sure there will be plenty of strong opinions here, too."

"Human decency?" Abby Law whispers to me. "That sounds like something my *dad* would say."

I stare straight ahead, pretending I didn't hear her. But then, from across the stage, I notice something unusual.

Sydney Mills is looking right at me.

21://Emma

AFTER THE LAST BELL RINGS, I store my saxophone in my band locker and rush to the student parking lot. Even though a trip to the public library sounds innocent, I know I shouldn't be doing what I'm about to do. And since I'm also skipping track, it's best to leave the school grounds quickly.

"Emma! Wait up!"

Josh jogs across the parking lot, waving me down. I haven't seen him since lunch, when I let him stash his skateboard in my backseat.

"I need to get my board," he says. "Tyson and I are heading over to Chris McKellar's half-pipe."

"That sounds like a good thing to do," I say, trying to keep my nerves calm.

"Are you okay?" he asks.

"I'm fine." I open the driver's side door and get in, avoiding eye contact. I hate being dishonest with Josh, but I can't tell him what I'm about to do. My future husband didn't come home for three nights. *Three nights!* And now he's using my money to buy some gadget. Meanwhile, I can't even afford a therapist, which I most likely need in the future so I can talk about *him*!

I have to get rid of this guy.

"Where are you headed?" Josh asks. He pops the passenger seat forward and leans into the back.

"Nowhere," I say. Then, because that sounded too guilty, I add, "Just the public library to research something."

Josh glances covertly around and then whispers, "After dinner, we should go to that website again."

"Fine," I say.

"Also, I was thinking we should have a code word for it so people don't know what we're talking about."

"How about 'Facebook'?" I say, starting my engine. "No one's heard of that."

* * *

AS I'M HEADING toward the library entrance, I run into Dylan Portman. We went out at the beginning of tenth grade. We'd been counselors-in-training at the YMCA day camp that summer. By the time school started, we were a couple. We didn't have much of a connection beyond camp, though, so when he broke up with me, I didn't take it too hard. That's why it's never weird when we see each other.

"How's it going?" Dylan asks. He's carrying a huge stack of hardcover books, so I grab the door and hold it open for him. He grins at me, flashing that sexy dimple on his left cheek. Dylan knows he's hot, and he can work it.

"School lets out and you go straight to the library?" he says, walking next to me.

"Well, look at you with that massive pile of books."

"I'm returning them for my little sister." Dylan grins and adds, "I'm that kind of guy."

Generally, I wouldn't mind flirting with Dylan, but I'm on a mission and I can't let anyone get in my way, even if that person has a sexy dimple and tousled brown hair.

"I have a lot of research to do," I say. Then, to make sure Dylan doesn't come along while I look for the phone books, I add, "I might be meeting Graham later."

"Graham Wilde? Awesome how he buzzed his hair." Dylan points his chin in the direction of the returns desk and then says, "Don't work too hard."

The air conditioner is blasting in the library, and it makes me shiver. Or maybe the shiver comes from knowing that I'm about to find my future husband's phone number. I head straight to the reference desk. The guy working there is chewing on a pencil as he stares at a computer screen.

"Excuse me?" I ask. "My school librarian said you might have phone books from other states."

He taps at his keyboard and then rises from his chair, sliding the pencil behind his ear. I follow him around a corner and down a flight of stairs, finally arriving at a long shelf crammed with phone books.

The librarian crosses his arms. "Is there a particular state you're looking for?"

"California," I say. "Chico, California."

"That's in Butte County, I believe." He plucks the pencil from behind his ear, studies the bite marks, and then retrieves a medium-sized phone book. "Let me know if you need anything else."

When he disappears back into the stairwell, I sit cross-legged on the floor and hurriedly flip to the *J*s. There are hundreds of Joneses in Chico, California. I focus my eyes on the tiny print. Jones, Adam. Jones, Anthony. Jones, Anthony C. Jones, Arthur. They go on forever! But if my husband's name is Jordan Jones *Junior*, then his dad must be a Jordan, too. I flip the page, and with a stab of disappointment, I see there's no one named Jordan Jones.

If there isn't a Jordan, maybe his dad is listed by his first initial. I glance at the beginning of the Joneses where they list the single letters, but there are tons of *J*s there. Clutching the phone book against my chest, I run upstairs to find a photocopy machine.

I give the librarian a dollar and he hands me ten dimes. I spread the phone book across the smooth glass of the copy machine, close the top, and drop a coin in the slot. It lands with a tinny *plink*, and I hit the green start button.

22://Josh

I'M SITTING ON TOP of the half-pipe in Chris McKellar's backyard. My legs dangle over the lip while Tyson skates up one side and back down to the other. Chris graduated last year, but his parents still let us use the ramp. As usual, almost everyone else on the half-pipe is a senior. They're okay with us being here, though, because we always bring pizza.

Sitting beside me, a non-skater guy is full of questions. "Why do they call it a half-pipe?"

He's here with his girlfriend, who just stepped off on the deck at the opposite end.

"Really? You don't know?" I ask.

"It looks to me like a U-shaped ramp," he says.

His eyelids are half-mast and he nods slowly to himself. I wonder how much weed he's smoked today. For whatever reason, I feel compelled to answer him. "If you took another half-pipe, flipped it upside down, then placed it on top of this one, you'd have a full circle, like a pipe," I say. "Actually, I guess it'd be more of an oval."

"You know what you should call it then?" His face goes completely serious. "A half-oval."

I'm tempted to slide down the ramp, grab my backpack, and add this guy to my "I wonder what becomes of . . . ?" list, which is now up to thirty-seven names. It starts with Tyson, then my brother, my parents, and all the way down to this kid in my grade, Frank Wheeler, who once told us that if he's not a millionaire by the time he's thirty he'll jump in front of a bus.

Tyson roars up beside me, rocks the middle of his board against the lip, then rolls back down again. Across the ramp, the stoner guy's girlfriend adjusts her helmet. When she first showed up last month, no one wanted to give her a chance. But on her first drop she put most of us to shame.

"You should ask your girlfriend to teach you to skate," I say.

"No way," he says. "It requires too much balance."

Tyson skates up close, locking his rear truck against the lip. He extends his arm and I pull him onto the deck.

"Ready?" he asks. "I need to get to work and prep for a party."

Fifteen years in the future, I wonder if Tyson's running

GoodTimez Pizza. It wouldn't be a bad job. Free pizza for life sounds like a sweet deal to me. In fact, Sydney and I probably take our kids there on their birthdays.

I drop down the ramp, twisting halfway and ending in a knee-slide.

"What time's the birthday party?" I ask as Tyson and I push through the side gate.

"Five thirty," he says. "But I told Kellan I'd meet up for a few minutes before I start. She has a break in her college class and wants to talk."

I tap the tail of my board against the sidewalk. "What about?"

"Who knows," he says. "She's probably pissed at me about something. I can do no right by that woman."

"You don't have to meet her," I say. "Not if she's just going to chew you out."

We pause at an intersection and Tyson turns to me with a grin. "But she's so hot when she's mad."

We cross the street and Tyson nods toward the road leading to the cemetery. "Are you up for a quick detour?"

We lean our boards against the cemetery gate and walk along the winding gravel path. It's odd to think that only a few rows over, near Clarence and Millicent's final resting place, Emma and I began to pull apart. It was cold that night, so she snuggled against me. It's not that she hadn't done that before, but it felt different that time. She asked about the upcoming winter formal and whether I was thinking of going. I wasn't, but I said that if no one asked her, maybe we should go together. I said it with a half-smile so she could take it as a joke if she wanted. She remained quiet as we walked through the shadow of gravestones, and then finally said, "Maybe."

I liked "maybe." I pictured her in the shiny blue dress she modeled for me after a trip into Pittsburgh with her mom. I imagined slow-dancing with her. With that thought in mind, I finally told her I liked her. My heart pounded, and I did what I'd wanted to do for a long time. I leaned down to kiss her.

But Emma pulled back. "What are you doing?"

"I thought maybe—"

She shook her head. "Oh, no."

"I thought we—"

"We weren't," she said. "I couldn't. You're . . . *Josh*."

And that's when everything changed.

It's been six months since that night, and things are definitely changing again. In fact, they're changing in ways I never could've—

Oh, no.

After school, when I got my skateboard from Emma's car, something was up. Maybe it was the way she didn't make eye contact. Or how she said she was going to the library to look something up. Emma is always more specific than that. And if she's hiding something, there's only one thing it could be. It's about her future.

But if Emma's sneaking around changing *her* future, she could unintentionally mess up *mine*. And I love my future! One little ripple started today could create a typhoon fifteen years from now.

I look over at Tyson. His eyes are on the gravestone:

LINDA ELIZABETH OVERMYER
Beloved Wife of William
Beloved Mother to Tyson James
November 25, 1955 – August 15, 1982

"I need to head out," I tell him. "I forgot, but I have to check on something. I can try to swing by GoodTimez later."

"That's cool," Tyson says, nodding at me. "I'm going to be a few more minutes."

I run back up the gravel path. Once I hit the parking lot, I throw my board in front of me and jump on. When I get to the sidewalk, I dip at the knees to make the sharp turn, then push hard down the street, mentally mapping the fastest route to the library.

23://Emma

I TUCK THE PHOTOCOPIED PAGES in my backpack and hurry out to my car. Now that I have a list of numbers to try, I need to buy a phone card and get home as quickly as possible.

Dylan catches up to me in the parking lot. "You must be in some deep thought," he says. "I was calling your name since you walked out the door."

I tuck my hair behind my ear. Even though I blew it straight this morning, the warm weather's making it spring up again.

I normally wouldn't mind hanging out with Dylan for a few minutes, but I'm in a rush. I know that what I'm about to do is wrong. The ripples throughout my entire life will be huge. So I need to track down Jordan Jones Jr.

before my conscience takes over, or before I run into Josh and he tries to stop me.

"Where are you headed?" Dylan asks as we approach my car.

"I need to grab something at 7-Eleven."

"Any chance you can give me a ride?"

"That's fine," I say. "But I'm in a hurry."

"I can hop out at 7-Eleven and walk from there."

I unlock my car and we both climb in. As Dylan pulls around his seatbelt, I notice the three books on his lap. *Weetzie Bat* and two more from the Dangerous Angels series.

"You're into Francesca Lia Block now?" I ask. "Because I'm pretty sure those aren't for your little sister."

"These are for Callie. She's obsessed with this author. Have you read them?"

I drive across the parking lot. "Who's Callie?"

"My girlfriend. She lives in Pittsburgh, but she was at the prom with me."

"Oh," I say.

"We've been together since Christmas. You should see her snowboard. That's how we met."

The way he's talking about this girl sounds serious. I can't help being a little annoyed, though. The summer Dylan and I were camp counselors, I was reading all the Francesca Lia Block books whenever we had a break. The fact that he doesn't seem to remember that stings for some reason.

* * *

DYLAN HOLDS OPEN the door to 7-Eleven for me. As we say goodbye, I double-check the parking lot to make sure Josh isn't one of the skaters out there.

At the counter, I debate between a five- and a ten-dollar phone card. I choose the cheaper one, pay the guy, and then walk back to my car.

I drive home slowly, watching a father in his driveway lift up his young son so he can dunk a basket. Sprinklers quietly arch across front lawns. These neighborhoods feel so serene, almost frozen in time.

Meanwhile, Josh and I are hurtling into our futures.

I hit the power button on my radio, and turn the volume high. "Wonderwall" by Oasis is playing. That's Kellan's new favorite. She was humming it as we left study hall earlier.

And all the roads we have to walk are winding
And all the lights that lead us there are blinding

I turn off the radio. I don't need to feel any guiltier for going home, locking my bedroom door, and permanently blocking one of those winding roads.

24://Josh

I'M SWEATY when I arrive at the library, and the cold air is a shock. I don't know what Emma's looking for in here, so I have no idea where to find her. I race across the carpeted floor, looking through the aisles of fiction. No Emma. She's not at the magazines or in the children's room, either. Finally, I go to the reference desk. The man working there is staring at a computer screen.

"Excuse me?" I ask. "Was there a girl in here, probably not too long ago? She would've been looking for . . . something."

"You'll have to be more specific." The man removes a pencil from behind his ear. "What does she look like?"

"She's shorter than me," I say. "She's pretty. Her hair is curly and comes down to here." I touch behind my shoulder.

The man writes something on a yellow legal pad and then nods. "I meant to ask if she's going to college in Chico, because there's a—"

Shit!

"Why would you ask her about Chico?" I say.

His eyes notice something behind me, and then he tosses up his hands in exasperation. "I told the interns not to leave empty carts near the copy machine. People set their books there and don't return them to the shelves."

"Why Chico?" I ask again.

The man walks out from behind the desk and I follow him to the copier. "The last time I saw her," he says, lifting a phone book from the cart, "your friend was over here making copies."

He's holding a phone book from California. *Emma, what are you doing?*

I glance into the blue recycling bin next to the copier and notice a single sheet of paper in there. I pull it out. The copy is dark, but I can make out enough. Someone copied a two-page spread of phone numbers for people named Jones.

"Is your friend thinking of going to California for college?" the man asks. "Because my daughter—"

"I highly doubt it," I say, folding up the paper and stuffing it into my back pocket. "But thanks."

I hurry to the front door of the library. Once outside, I hop on my board and skate toward home as fast as I can.

25://Emma

THERE'S NO ONE AT HOME. Even so, I lock my bedroom door before pulling the two sheets of paper from my backpack. I unfold them onto my desk, pressing my fingers along the creases.

After punching in the toll-free activation number on the back of the phone card, I start by calling J.B. Jones. An answering machine picks up, saying it's the home of Janice and Bobby. I quickly hang up and cross out Jones, J.B. with a pencil.

The next number I try is an old lady who's convinced I'm her granddaughter. It takes almost five minutes before she lets me hang up. I should have gotten the ten-dollar phone card.

Next up is Jones, J.D. I follow the steps on the card and dial the number.

A woman with a singsong voice answers. "Hello?"

"Hi," I say, "is Jordan there?"

"Junior or Senior?" she asks.

I clutch the phone against my shoulder, wipe my sweaty hands on my shorts, and clear my throat. "Junior, please."

"My nephew's living with his mom now."

Think fast, Emma.

"Yeah, I know," I say. "I couldn't find his number, but I thought this might have been it."

There's silence on the other end.

"What'd you say your name was?" the woman asks.

I consider making up a name, but I feel nervous enough as is. "My name is Emma. We're friends from school."

"Jordan certainly had plenty of those. You got a pen?"

As she recites the number, I scribble it in a margin of my photocopy. We say goodbye and I hang up, staring at the phone number of my future husband.

Some people would wait. Josh, for example, would think this through carefully. He'd weigh the options, and then call David to get his brother's opinion. I, on the other hand, just flip over the phone card and start dialing.

"Hello?" It's a guy's voice.

"Jordan?"

"No, it's Mike. Hang on."

The phone gets set down. There's a television on in the background, and something that might be a blender. Mike, who I'm guessing is my future brother-in-law, shouts for Jordan and then says, "How should I know?"

The blender stops. Footsteps approach the phone, and then a guy's voice says, "What's up?"

"Is this Jordan?" I ask.

"Who's this?"

"It's Emma," I say, smiling broadly. "We met at that party . . . recently?"

I hold my breath, hoping Jordan went to a party at some point in the past month.

"Jenny Fulton's?" he asks.

I exhale. "Yeah. Jenny's."

There wasn't much to go on when I looked up Jordan on Facebook. It had his name, his picture, and his hometown. Even so, my goal is to keep him on the phone long enough to figure out how, at some point in the future, our lives intersect.

"So what's up?" he asks.

"Not much," I say. "What have you been up to?"

"Just hanging out."

Silence.

"Have you been . . . fishing recently?" I ask.

"Uh, no," he says. "I've never been fishing."

Dead silence.

"So what have you been doing?" I ask.

"Mostly looking for a summer job."

"Cool," I say.

The blender starts up again. "Listen, was there something you wanted?" he asks. "Because I should probably get back to—"

"Oh, right," I say, picking up speed. "Anyway, I was thinking about our conversation at the party."

"Are you sure you're not talking about Jordan Nicholson?" he asks. "I think he was there, too. People always get us mixed up."

It's strange, but Jordan doesn't sound like an asshole. He almost seems nice. So how is it possible that someday he becomes the kind of person who ends up staying out for three nights, most likely cheating on me? Would he believe that was possible if I told him right now?

"It was definitely you," I say. "We were talking about where we're applying to college and you—"

"Hang on," Jordan says.

I hear a screen door slam and a girl's voice say, "You ready?"

Jordan tells her it'll be a second. "Sorry," he says to me. "No, I really think you're talking about Nicholson because I'm already in college. I just got home for the summer."

"Really?" My voice catches. "Where do you go?"

I squeeze my eyes shut. Maybe this is where Jordan and I meet. I have a rough list of where I want to apply next year, all out of state, and all near an ocean.

"Tampa State," he says. "I just finished my first year."

I open my eyes and force a laugh. "You're right. It *was* Jordan Nicholson. I am so sorry."

"Do you need his number?" he asks. "I think Mike has it."

"No, that's fine. I've got it."

"Okay, well . . ." Someone shuts off the TV and I can hear the girl laugh in the background.

As I hold the phone against my ear, I actually feel sad. In the future, Jordan and I were supposed to meet at college and get married. Now, we'll probably never even know each other.

We say goodbye. When the line disconnects, I continue listening to the silence in the receiver. An automated voice eventually comes on, saying I have ninety-three cents remaining on my card. I hang up and walk over to my dresser.

In my top drawer, beneath my socks and underwear, I keep a journal. I don't write in it a lot, maybe a few times a year. I flip to an entry I wrote back in March. It's a list I made after a college counselor talked to us about the application process.

> *Emma's Top College Choices*
> *1: Tampa State*
> *2: University of North Carolina at Wilmington*
> *3: University of California at San Diego*

I grab a black marker from my desk and draw a line

through "Tampa State." If I don't go to college there, I won't meet Jordan. And if I don't meet Jordan—

There's a knock on the door. I bury my journal back in my drawer. "Who is it?"

The handle turns, but the door is locked.

"Emma," Josh says. "I need to talk to you."

When I open the door, Josh's hair is sweaty, with several strands matted to his forehead. He's holding the Scooby-Doo keychain in one hand, and a folded-up sheet of paper in the other.

"Everything okay?" I ask.

He wipes his brow. "I skated here from the public library."

I glance nervously at the paper in his hand. "I guess we just missed each other."

Josh frowns as he unfolds his paper. It's the first photocopy I made from the phone book. It came out too dark and I tossed it in the recycling bin.

"I know what you're about to do," Josh says, "but you can't unmarry your future husband."

The way he says "unmarry your future husband" makes my stomach lurch.

"You can't go around changing what's supposed to happen," he says. "I know you're upset because you're married to this jerk, but according to Facebook, *we're* still friends. I promise I'll be there for you. If you end up going through a divorce, maybe I can loan you money for a lawyer, or I can let you move into my guest room for a while."

Loan me money? Anger pulses through me. *Right, because he and Sydney are so rich!*

Josh notices my phone card on the desk, with the silver scratched off the back to reveal the activation code.

His voice is hushed. "You did it?"

I nod slowly.

"You talked to Jordan?"

"It's over," I say. "We're never going to meet."

The color drains from Josh's face.

26://Josh

JUST LIKE THAT, the future is changed forever.

Fifteen years of history—*future* history—is changed because Emma didn't like the guy she married. But she only had a few sentences from fifteen years in the future to work with. That's not nearly enough information to make such a drastic decision about her life. And *his* life! Come to think of it, any person who was impacted by their relationship, even in the slightest way, will be twisted in countless new directions.

I want to both scream *and* laugh hysterically. Instead, I crumple the photocopy in my hand and throw it across the room. The paper barely makes a sound when it hits the wall.

"You can't do that!" I shout.

"Actually," Emma says, crossing her arms, "it was easy. He goes to Tampa State, so I'm not applying there. North Carolina is now my top choice."

I collapse onto her bed and press my hands over my eyes. She doesn't get it! She knows that even the smallest change to our present will ripple into the future. On that first day, Emma was unemployed. The next day she had a job, but we have no idea what she changed to make that happen. One time we looked, Jordan had gone fishing. But later, he mysteriously hadn't come home for three days. Then macaroni and cheese became lasagna. Maybe Emma doesn't think it's important that her dinner was different, but what if next time she cooks, something causes her to make meatloaf and she gets mad cow disease and dies because one little ripple changes her dinner plans in fifteen years?

But to change her future husband? On *purpose*? Those consequences are immeasurable!

"Admit it," Emma says. "You would've done the same thing if your life looked as bad as mine."

"No." I sit up. "I wouldn't have. You have no idea what else you've changed. This is dangerous stuff, Emma."

"Look who's talking," Emma says. "You made a face at Sydney yesterday. Would you have done that if you didn't know you were going to marry her?"

"I'm talking about changing the *future*," I say.

Emma laughs. "Well, what do you think happens when you do something different in the present? It changes the future! You did the same thing as me."

"It's not the same, and you know it," I say. "Mine was a reaction, but you intentionally made a humongous change. You really wanted to go to Tampa State. I saw you and Kellan researching it in that college-ranking book, and you were saying how close it was to where your dad lives. But now you won't go there? We need to do things exactly as we would've done them before Facebook."

"Why?" Emma says, and I can see she's on the verge of crying. "So I can end up unemployed at thirty-one like the first time we checked? Or angry that my husband spends all my money when I do have a job?"

"It's more complicated than that," I say. "What if, when you were unemployed, you were just one day away from finding your perfect job? Or maybe, when your husband realized you were angry about him buying that iPad thing, he returned it the next day. Emma, all you saw were *tiny* snippets of the future."

"I don't care," she says. "I know I wasn't happy, and that needed to change."

This is making me nervous. The future seems so fragile. For instance, I already saw that I'm going to the University of Washington like my brother. And I definitely want that to happen, but what if knowing I'll get in makes me slack on the application, and then I get rejected?

"You're making that face," Emma says as she types in her email address.

"What face?"

"Like you're judging me."

Emma types her password to get into Facebook, and then turns to me with deliberate slowness. "I'm going to speak as calmly as I can," she says. "The way you're judging me means you're not even trying to understand what that life felt like for me."

"It's not that I'm not trying. I'm just—"

"You're being extremely selfish and cruel."

"How am I being cruel?"

"You know why you don't care?" Emma's getting more pissed by the second. "Because you've got your perfect wife. You've got your beautiful children. And you've got *me* living in your guest room! Do I even have a window in there?"

When Emma says that, I force myself to keep a straight face. "I get it," I say.

"You *don't* get it! You're acting superior, but what if the roles were reversed?" Emma raises an eyebrow. "That's right. What if I married Cody and got everything I wanted, and *you* didn't get shit? Actually, no, what if you *did* get shit? Because that's what I got with Junior!"

"I get it," I say, quieter this time. "I do."

"Good." Emma turns back to her computer and clicks on the tiny picture in the corner.

"Wait!" I jump off the bed and spin Emma around. "Before you look, we need to set some ground rules. This is getting way too big to figure out as we go along."

Over her shoulder, Emma's page has mostly loaded. The picture in the corner is different than yesterday. Grown-up Emma's eyes are closed. Her face is snuggled close to a baby wearing a floppy pink hat.

"What kind of rules?" she asks.

"We can't be overly picky," I say. The baby has a small spit bubble between her lips. "If your new life appears relatively happy, we leave it alone."

Emma turns her head slightly. "You see something on the screen, I can tell."

"Before you look," I say, holding tight to her chair, "you have to promise not to tweak the future unless it's absolutely terrible. Even then, we need to discuss it first."

"Fine. Now will you let me see if I got rid of him? That's all I care about."

I turn her chair around.

Emma squeals. "A baby! I have a baby!" She touches the girl's face, and then moves her finger across the screen.

Married to Kevin Storm

Emma slowly lowers her hand into her lap.

"You did it," I say. "You threw Junior to the curb." I look again at the name of her new husband. *Kevin Storm.* It sounds like the alias of a superhero.

"I just wanted to be happy," she says quietly. "But I also want Jordan Jones to be happy. Is that weird?"

"Think of it this way," I say. "Now that you've taken yourself out of the picture, you're letting him find the person he was meant to be with."

"Like that bitch he's been sleeping with the past three nights?" Emma leans in close to the monitor, and then taps the screen with her finger. "Look! I'm a marine biologist now!"

Works at Marine Biological Laboratory

"That's random," I say.

"No it's not," she says. "I love the ocean. Remember when I visited my dad in Florida over Christmas? We took a scuba diving class together."

"It takes more than loving the ocean to become a marine biologist," I say. Also, I don't want to crush her excitement, but I bet a lot of people work at that lab who aren't biologists.

Emma looks at me dismissively. "I'll have you know, I'm going to take advanced biology at the college with Kellan next year."

"Since when?"

Emma walks to her papasan chair and folds her legs in front of her. "Oh, I'm sorry. I didn't know I had to tell you everything."

I take Emma's place at the computer. "Well, now that you're happy, I'm going to make sure your bliss didn't screw things up with Sydney."

I'm about to look through Emma's list of friends to find myself when I notice my name and something I wrote right there on Emma's page.

"Listen to this," I say, and then I read it aloud.

> **Emma Nelson Storm**
> They have a farmer's market here with tons of local food. Just bought an organic peach pie. Hubby is going to be ecstatic!
> 2 hours ago · Like · Comment
>
> > **Josh Templeton** You're making me hungry.
> > 51 minutes ago · Like

"See?" Emma says. "I make my new man *ecstatic*!"

The photo yesterday had me with a bunch of balloons. Now it's just a close-up of an eyeball. I click on the eye, and while my page slowly loads I drum my fingers against the desk.

> **Married to** Sydney Templeton

"Yes!" I jump up and bat excitedly at one of her paper lanterns.

"Easy on the décor," Emma says, but she's smiling.

As she should! Our futures are looking awesome. Even with Emma changing husbands, Sydney couldn't stay away from me. This relationship is meant to be and *nothing* can stop it.

Settling back in the chair, I read my entries out loud. The first one is dull.

Josh Templeton
Good things come to those who wait.
16 hours ago · Like · Comment
> **Dennis Holloway** What are you, a fortune cookie?
> 14 hours ago · Like

The next isn't much better.

Josh Templeton
The countdown has begun.
Yesterday at 11:01pm · Like · Comment

I swivel to face Emma. "I have no idea what I'm talking about."

Emma shrugs as she bites the nail of her pinky finger.

I turn back to the computer and scroll down, scanning through more entries. "Promise me if I ever get this boring you'll—"

And then I freeze.

Emma catapults out of the chair. "What is it?"

We both stare at a photo near the bottom of the page.

It's a picture of Sydney standing sideways. She's holding her stomach, and it's huge!

> **Josh Templeton**
> My baby's having my first baby any day now.
> May 16 at 9:17am · Like · Comment

"That's cheesy," Emma says, but then she gets it. "Wait, your *first* baby?"

I stand up so fast I nearly pass out. I told her. *I told her!* This future stuff is dangerous. We can't tinker with things, plucking out details we don't like. I sit on the edge of Emma's bed and stare vacantly at the mirror hanging on her door. If changing her husband also changes my children, the future's even more fragile than I thought. The repercussions are impossible to predict.

"If what I did caused this, I'm so sorry," Emma says.

Three of my future children have been erased from existence before they had a chance to exist at all. I'll never build a model solar system with that boy, or take those twin girls to have their birthday party at GoodTimez.

Emma sits behind me on the bed. She rubs her hands together to warm them up. My mind tells me to pull away, but I can't.

"I don't understand," I say.

She presses her fingers along the muscles at the back of my neck. "I think we need to realize there's no way to control these particular types of changes."

"What do you mean, 'these particular types'?"

"Your children. My children," she says. "When you took health last semester, how much do you remember about sperm?"

I turn and glare at Emma. "What does that have to do with anything?"

Emma squeezes both of my shoulders. "No matter how small the ripple, the most vulnerable part of the future is going to be our children. If we keep looking at Facebook, we shouldn't get too attached to—"

"It altered my *sperm*?" I say. "What are you talking about?"

Emma kneads her thumbs in small circles down the sides of my spine. "All of this stuff occurs years from now. Think of how many billions of tiny details need to line up between now and then to make everything exactly the same. It's impossible. Even this massage, which wouldn't have happened yesterday, makes whatever happens next a little different."

"What does that have to do with my sperm?"

Emma slides her fingers behind my ears. "Do you remember when your teacher talked about how many sperm you guys let loose every time you—"

"On second thought, can we not talk about this?" I say, my eyes rolling back at her touch.

She rubs her fingertips down my arms. *Man, I love that so much.*

"Every time you ejaculate," she continues, "you release something like four hundred million sperm. Each one totally unique."

"I seriously don't want to talk about this."

With her fingers running back up my arms, and all this sperm talk, things are getting a little too intense down below. I lean slightly forward, conveniently placing my forearms across my lap.

"Will you just do my shoulders?" I ask.

As Emma moves her hands back up to my shoulders, there's a ping at the computer, like digital fairy dust.

"An instant message!" Emma scrambles off the bed. "I've never gotten one of these before."

I cross my legs and turn toward the computer.

"The screen name says it's from DontCallMeCindy," Emma says. "I have no idea who that is, but she's asking if I'm the Emma Nelson who goes to Lake Forest." As she taps at the keys, Emma tells me what she's writing. "'Tell me who you are first.'"

I want to watch the screen myself, but there's no way I can stand up just yet.

Another instant message appears. Emma reads it to herself, and then narrows her eyes at me. "You are in so much trouble."

"What? Why?"

She types some more words and then hits Enter. "Five

minutes ago," she says, "you were lecturing me about changing the future. But it looks like you've been tinkering with it yourself."

I laugh. "What are you talking about?"

"You are such a hypocrite! Why else would Sydney Mills be asking for your phone number?"

27://Emma

JOSH LEANS FORWARD on my bed, one leg crossed over the other. "You gave it to her, right?"

I grin and tap my chin. "Well, I had to think about whether or not—"

"Emma! Did you give my number to Sydney Mills?"

"Of course I did."

"What did she say?"

I glance at the screen. I closed the instant message box once Sydney signed out. All that's left is Josh's Facebook page with Sydney's massive belly.

Josh Templeton
My baby's having my first baby any day now.
May 16 at 9:17am · Like · Comment

That comment annoys me. It's cheesier than anything Josh would say now. I guess that's the kind of guy he becomes, all mushy and wrapped up in Sydney like he has no life of his own.

Josh looks at me with a pained sort of hope. "I need to know *exactly* what she said."

"What did you want to her to say? That she's driving over in her convertible to whisk you into the sunset?" That wasn't fair. I don't know why I'm being so bitchy. "She said she got my screen name from Graham. So I gave her your number and she said thanks."

Josh stares at me. "I thought you were happy now that you're married to Kevin Storm."

"Don't change the subject," I say. "You were so mad at me for calling Jordan, but then here comes Sydney Mills, asking for your number. You must have done more than just make a face in class yesterday."

Josh raises his shoulders. "I didn't mean to."

"But you *did*?"

"We were in Peer Issues today, talking about relationships, and this senior guy gave her a hard time. So I stood up for her. What was I supposed to do?"

"You stood up for Sydney about *relationship* issues? Who was giving her a hard time?"

"Rick something. He's in Mr. Fritz's class."

"Does he play football?"

"Do you know him?"

I can't help laughing. "You defended Sydney to *Rick Rolland*?"

Josh doesn't care about who's popular at school, or who has a history together, and that's all great. But Rick Rolland is the guy having the bonfire Kellan was excited about. He and Sydney used to date, and Josh should not be involving himself with that.

"He was being a dick," Josh says. "And besides, what I said wasn't a big deal."

But we both know it was. This ripple is going to affect Josh's future in a major way.

Josh takes in a deep breath. "So I was thinking about Facebook today. Remember last summer at the lake when Frank Wheeler said he was going to become a millionaire, and everyone laughed?"

I'm not sure where Josh is going with this, but I'm relieved to be moving on from Sydney and my husbands. "He said he'd jump in front of a bus if he doesn't make a million by the time he's thirty."

"Exactly." Josh reaches into his backpack and pulls out a folded up piece of paper. "I made a list of people we should look up on Facebook. Like my mom and dad, David, Tyson—"

"And Kellan!" I add. "I was thinking the same thing today. I want to see if she makes it into med school."

I swivel toward my computer, and jiggle the mouse.

The brick wall screensaver disappears and I get another chance to witness Sydney's pregnant belly. "First, we should refresh your page," I say. "Since you were Sydney's superhero today, and now she's going to call you, I bet everything's different. You probably weren't supposed to get together until much later, and—"

"Wait." Josh stands up.

The arrow hovers over the Refresh button, but his tone is so serious I don't click it.

Josh wriggles his feet into his sneakers and then grabs his skateboard and backpack. "I'll try to come back later. Don't look anyone up without me, okay?"

As he barrels downstairs, I shout, "I know where you're going! Don't you think babysitting your telephone is kind of—?"

Before I can finish, the latch on my front door clicks shut.

28://Josh

SYDNEY MILLS ASKED for my number!

I sprint through my front door, then up the stairs to my bedroom.

Sydney Mills asked for my number!

It still makes no sense, but I need to accept this reality. It'll start with a phone call, which will lead to marriage, children, and a house on Crown Lake. I'll have a fancy graphic-design job, and I'll probably drive a nice car, too. A BMW or, since we'll be out in the country, a Chevy Tahoe. Or both! In fifteen years, maybe I'll drive something so insane I can't even imagine it now.

My bed is unmade and T-shirts are strewn all over the floor. This does not look like the room of someone Sydney Mills would be calling. But it is! And she could be calling any second now.

Where is the phone?

I turn in a slow circle around my room. If the phone rings, I could kick piles around until I find it, but what if I answer too late? What if, because she couldn't reach me, Sydney chats with some other guy and they start going out? Maybe they'll end up getting married, and *he'll* be taking *my* tropical vacations.

I lift the gray phone cord with my index finger and follow it down the length of my mattress, picking up stray socks and shirts. Finally, I toss aside an issue of *Thrasher* magazine and unveil the glorious telephone.

Now ring, damn it!

I shake out the tension in my arms. Tonight, before bed, I'm going to add ten push-ups to my usual twenty. I want to look like the kind of guy Sydney is used to calling.

I sit on the edge of my mattress and stare at the phone. If my parents come home early I don't want them eavesdropping on this call. I'm nervous enough already. So I run to their room, grab the cordless phone from the nightstand, and then head downstairs.

I walk across my lawn toward the street. Every time Sydney comes into Peer Issues, she turns off her cell phone and slips it into her pocket. It always looks so casual and cool. I try shoving the cordless phone into my back pocket, but it's too chunky to fit.

When I reach the sidewalk, a FedEx truck speeds across the street. I carefully look both ways before crossing.

Today is definitely not the day to get hit by a truck. Today is a day to enjoy being alive! Wagner Park is full of maple trees with bright green leaves, lilac bushes, and the shouts of children playing.

I know exactly how far I can go before the phone loses contact with the cradle in my parents' room. Over spring break, while visiting my brother, I met a girl at a music festival in Seattle. We stayed in touch for a few weeks, but I never told my parents about her. Whenever I talked to her on the phone, I called from the park. As long as I didn't walk past the swings, I was okay.

I was hoping to visit her again this summer. David even offered to help pay for my flight. I think he was happy to hear me talking about someone other than Emma. But the Seattle girl didn't want a long-distance relationship. After I left a few messages that she didn't return, she mailed me a letter saying it was fun at the concert, but what was the point if it wasn't going to last?

I hear a door shut, and turn to see Emma crouched at her stoop, tying the laces on her silver running shoes. When she adjusts the Discman on her arm, I move behind a tree. If Emma walks over here and Sydney calls, she'll either roll her eyes at everything I say or coach me along in the background.

Emma crosses the street, jogs toward the running trail, and then disappears from view. I continue to the knee-high concrete barrier surrounding the swings and set the phone on the wall.

Even if I try to do everything right, the ripple effect is unavoidable. Everything changed the moment Emma discovered Facebook. If I didn't know Sydney and I would eventually get married, I may not have defended her in Peer Issues. And she wouldn't have asked for my number.

On the wall beside me, the phone remains silent.

29://Emma

MY MOM AND MARTIN are down in the den watching TV, so I go through their room to take a shower. The downstairs bathroom is usually mine, but until the construction is done I have to share with them.

My dad once asked me how I felt about Martin. We were walking on the beach over Christmas break, a few months after he moved to Florida. He was collecting shells in a mesh bag, and I was splashing my feet in the surf. I didn't want to complain about Martin to my dad because that would make my mom look bad, especially since my dad and Cynthia have been happily married since I was eleven. But I also wasn't about to sing Martin's praises.

"He's okay," I said. "They don't fight like Mom and Erik."

My mom and Erik used to have loud screaming matches with doors slamming, and ending with one of them sleeping on the couch. Come to think of it, my mom and dad fought that way, too. But so far my mom and Martin hardly argue at all.

"That's good," my dad said. "It sounds like she's happy."

I could feel a lump in my throat. "Can we not talk about this?" I asked, looking out at the bay.

I take a long shower, shave my legs, and then tie my robe around my waist. As I'm walking back through their bedroom, I pause in front of the framed baby picture my mom keeps on her dresser. It was taken in a kiddie pool when I was one. I'm wearing an embroidered hat, and I've got chubby cheeks, round eyes, and tiny heart-shaped lips.

Just like my own baby on Facebook.

When I get back to my room, I snuggle deep under my covers and think about Kevin Storm. His name is perfect. I wonder if we name our daughter Olivia. I've always loved that name, and Olivia Storm sounds like she'll grow to be a confident woman. I know I told Josh we can't get attached to our future children because there's no way every detail will line up so the same sperm will impregnate the same egg on the same day. But I can't help it.

I roll onto my side.

Tomorrow, I'm going to end things with Graham. For real this time. It was fun while it lasted, but I can't imagine letting him kiss me anymore. Not since Josh saw us together. Not when Kevin Storm is waiting in my future.

I've always said I don't believe in true love, but that I'd leave the door open for Cody Grainger to one day prove me wrong. Since I don't end up marrying Cody, maybe I should open the door a little wider so Kevin Storm can have a chance, too.

wednesday

30://Emma

MARTIN SETS A BOWL of dry oats and raisins on the counter. "It's muesli," he says, reaching for his soy milk. "The Swiss eat it for breakfast, and it's definitely growing on your mom and me."

"Good to know," I say.

I drop a frozen Eggo waffle in the toaster and look out the window at Josh's driveway. His parents' car is still there. I wish they would leave so I can yank him back here to check Facebook.

Martin slides into the breakfast nook. "Have you ever seen the statistics on life expectancy in Switzerland?"

I hover over the toaster, willing my waffle to pop up, willing Martin to shut up, and willing Josh's parents to get a move on.

My mom strolls in. "Ready to leave? I thought we could swing by the paint store on the way to work."

"I just have to finish my muesli," Martin says.

My mom sets her coffee mug in the sink. "Emma, did you call your father and thank him for the computer yet?"

I hate the way she calls him "your father." Up until last year he was "Dad." "Not yet," I say, dousing my waffle with syrup. "I started an email to him, but I haven't sent it yet."

"He left a message on Monday to see if it arrived," my mom says. "When you call, you should also ask him about their new baby. Rachel must be five weeks old already."

I'm not in the mood to call my dad and talk about the computer. The whole issue is too weird right now. Thankfully, I hear Josh's front door shut. I hurry to the window and watch his parents back their car down the driveway. Then I grab my plate and fork and slip out the door.

* * *

I PRESS JOSH'S DOORBELL for the third time and peer through the window. His backpack is on the side table, which means he hasn't left for school yet. I look behind a potted plant, relieved to see they haven't moved the emergency key. Balancing my waffle plate in one hand, I let myself in.

There's loud music coming from Josh's room.

"Josh?" I call from the bottom of the stairs.

No answer.

I haven't been in this house since December. It was a few weeks after Josh tried to kiss me, and we were barely talking. When my mom said she and Martin were going next door for dinner and television, I invited myself along in the hopes of getting a few minutes to speak with Josh. But he inhaled his food in three minutes, and then disappeared up to his room.

The entire wall next to the staircase is filled with pictures of Josh and David at every stage of development, every class picture, every bad haircut. They even have clay impressions of their handprints next to framed locks of their baby curls.

I take a bite of my waffle and then knock on Josh's door. Inside, he's blasting the song "Walking on Sunshine."

Through the door, I can hear Josh sing, *"And don't it feel GOOD!"*

I turn the knob, open the door, and—

He's doing sit-ups in his tighty-whities! His chest looks toned, but . . . *tighty-whities*?

"Emma!"

I laugh as Josh rips the sheet off his bed and wraps it around his waist.

His face is instantly red. "Haven't you heard of knocking?"

"I did knock," I say, bobbing my head to the beat. "But the bigger question is, haven't *you* heard of boxers?"

Josh reaches for a pair of pants and pulls them on under the sheet.

I take another bite of waffle and look around his room. It looks the same as before, with clothes on the floor, a Tony Hawk poster above his dresser, and Cindy Crawford above his bed. There's a can of markers for his art, and some old skateboard wheels on the floor. The only thing different are Josh's free weights. They were hand-me-downs from his brother, but ever since David left, they've been stashed in Josh's closet. Now they're in the middle of his floor.

"What are you doing here?" he asks, slipping his arms into a T-shirt.

"I need you to come over so we can go on Facebook," I say. "I can't stop thinking about Kevin Storm. And I saw a baby picture of myself last night that looks so much like—"

"Sure," Josh says. "Go ahead."

"Without you? You're not worried I'll ruin your future?"

"Just don't call Jordan Jones again, and don't try to find Kevin Storm's number. I'll come over when I finish up here."

I notice the phone on his floor, surrounded by the only patch of carpet without clothes or magazines. I wonder if Sydney's called him yet.

* * *

Married to Kevin Storm

When I click on his name, nothing happens. I try again. *Nothing!* Kevin's name isn't highlighted blue, so I'm guessing he doesn't have a Facebook page of his own.

I look down on the screen to see what I've written in this future.

> **Emma Nelson Storm**
> I can't get enough of Glee.
> 9 hours ago · Like · Comment
>> **Kathleen Podell** Netflix all the way, babe.
>> 9 hours ago · Like
>> **Emma Nelson Storm** Netflix+Glee = my life
>> 8 hours ago · Like

I have no idea what I'm talking about, but if Netflix plus Glee equals my life, I'm hoping those are good things. I keep scrolling down.

> **Emma Nelson Storm**
> Packing the boys' lunches. They're slowly settling into the new school, but I still feel guilty about moving them in the middle of the year.
> Yesterday at 7:01am · Like · Comment

Boys? I told Josh we shouldn't get too attached to our future children, but it's hard to believe I'll never see Olivia's plump cheeks again.

Emma Nelson Storm
Luke just lost his first tooth! How much does the
Tooth Fairy leave these days?
May 20 at 4:25pm · Like · Comment

Six people have commented, everything from "Congrats, Luke!" to "I dunno . . . maybe a dollar?" But it's the last comment that stands out.

Kellan Steiner Lindsay is fourteen now, so I'm
out-of-date on the Tooth Fairy. Sorry!
May 20 at 7:12pm · Like

I'm tempted to click on Kellan's name, but I promised Josh I would only look up Kevin Storm, so I force myself to stay on my own page. Mostly, I talk about my boys and Netflix, which seems to be a new way to watch movies.

Emma Nelson Storm
Kevin saved a life today. I will never browse online
while driving again. Don't worry . . . I'm writing this
at a stoplight.
May 17 at 7:18pm · Like · Comment

I have a computer in my *car*? Josh is going to freak out when he hears this. And if Kevin saved a life, maybe he's a doctor. Or a paramedic. Or a fireman! That'd be cool because firemen have great bodies.

I read through the comments of various people congratulating Kevin. The man in the eighth photo has graying hair and . . . *it's my dad!*

> **Dale Nelson** Put your phone in your purse, honey! All my love to the family.
> May 17 at 8:03pm · Like

My eyes sting with tears. Seeing my dad's name makes me miss him so much more right now.

> **Josh Templeton** Thanks for the text yesterday, Em. You BETTER not have written it while driving. Hey there, Mr. Nelson!
> May 17 at 8:18pm · Like
>
> **Dale Nelson** Nice to see you, Mr. Templeton! Emma tells me that you and the family are doing well.
> May 17 at 8:31pm · Like
>
> **Emma Nelson Storm** What is this, a reunion? Josh, say hi to Sydney and the twins for me.
> May 17 at 8:52pm · Like

I have no idea what a *text* is, but I can't help smiling. The other times we looked at Facebook, Josh's name was always in my Friends category, but we weren't talking back and forth like this.

Then my mind catches something I missed earlier. I scroll up to the comment Kellan left about the Tooth Fairy, and lean in to get a closer look at her picture. She has the same long black hair and the same devilish smile. She's wearing a black shirt and dangly silver earrings. Josh isn't here, but this is too big to ignore. I need to look at Kellan's webpage.

I click on her photo.

The most recent thing she wrote was back in February.

Kellan Steiner
Lindsay's flying to her dad's this weekend. Her first solo plane trip!
February 23 at 2:09pm · Like · Comment

> **Catrina McBride** I know you'll miss her, but enjoy your time off. Single mamas need that!
> February 27 at 6:53pm · Like

Fifteen years from now, Kellan is a single mother with a *fourteen-year-old daughter*. That means—

There's a loud knock at my door. I back-click until I return to my page.

Josh grins as he strolls in. "That was called *knocking*. And not that it's any of your business, but you'll be happy to know I'm wearing boxers now."

I smile weakly. All I can think about is whether to tell Josh about Kellan. I should, but I don't want to create any more ripples that could ruin either one of our futures.

Josh leans over my shoulder and looks at the screen. "How are things this morning?"

"Now, or in fifteen years?"

"Fifteen years," he says. "How are the Storms?"

"We're fine," I say.

Josh points to the screen. "Look! I'm talking to your dad! And now I have twins again?"

I get out of my chair. "You can click over to your page if you want. I have to finish getting ready for school."

Josh sits at my computer, and I walk into my mom's room. I close the door and sink onto the foot of her bed. If Lindsay is fourteen, and Facebook is fifteen years from now, then Kellan must become pregnant in the next few months.

Unless she already is.

31://Josh

I JUMP OUT OF EMMA'S CHAIR and slide open her window. A van drives up the street, the high-pitched drone of its engine growing louder until it eventually shifts gears. At Wagner Park, someone tosses a glass bottle into a garbage bin. It clanks, but doesn't shatter.

Perfect! If my home phone rings, I shouldn't have trouble hearing it.

I return to Emma's computer and look again at the most important bit of information.

Married to Sydney Templeton

I click where it says Photos. Emma and I need to leave for school soon, so rather than reading through dozens

of short statements that hardly make sense, I want to see
what my future *looks* like.

The first square is labeled:

Our New Casa
12 photos

When I open the album, twelve new squares slowly
load. The first one is only half filled-in, but I already
love what it shows. The house is literally on the shore of
Crown Lake. According to Mom and Dad, that's the most
expensive location in town. The rest of the photo appears,
revealing a wraparound porch leading to a long wooden
dock. Either Sydney inherited a fortune, or my graphic
design business is booming!

In the second picture, I'm laying on a hammock with
identical red-headed boys. I don't think we have twins
anywhere in my family, but for Sydney and me to have
twins in two of my futures is a bizarre coincidence.

In the next picture I'm standing in front of the house
waving at the camera. My other arm is around . . . is that
David? I click to enlarge the photo.

David is standing with one arm around me and his
other arm around a guy with short brown hair and sunglasses. We're all smiling. Beneath the picture, it says:

In this photo: Josh Templeton, Dave Templeton,
Phillip Connor

So he goes by Dave in the future. Sorry, bro, but I'm still calling you David. When I scroll the arrow over his name, it turns into a hand. I glance at the door. Emma's still not back. Anyway, she wouldn't care if I checked on David. He's family.

David's page says he now lives in Bellingham, Washington, and works as a computer engineer.

Then I notice something else.

In a relationship with Phillip Connor

Okay, that's . . . um . . . I don't . . .

Emma walks in and plops on her bed. "Anything interesting?"

"Nope!"

I click the red *X* in the corner. Facebook disappears, and AOL says, "*Goodbye!*"

"Sorry," I say quickly. I'm a little shaken by what I just saw. "Do you want me to sign back on?"

Emma tilts her head and smirks at me. "Tell me truthfully, did you change your underwear because I made fun of you?"

"No," I say. But the answer is yes. Emma walking in on me was embarrassing enough. But there's no telling when a girl I actually have a chance with might get a glimpse of my underwear. I don't want her first thought to be *Haven't you heard of boxers?*

After Emma left my house, I took a shower and swiped some boxers from my dad's drawer. They were in an unopened pack, and they're a little loose, but they work. I'm planning to buy a few pairs of my own after school.

"Remember, I can tell when you're lying," Emma says. "And if you did that for Sydney's sake, it's kind of sad. Because if you think about it, you don't even know her."

"I don't know her *yet*," I say. "But it's going to happen."

"Oh, really? Did she call you last night?"

That is the question I was hoping to avoid.

"Because if she didn't," Emma continues, "maybe she's having second thoughts."

I don't say anything. What if Emma's right? Sydney and I really *don't* know each other. Maybe she noticed me in Peer Issues sooner than she was supposed to, and now everything's rippling in ways that will push us apart.

Emma leans over my shoulder and signs back on to AOL.

"It doesn't matter," I say. "I wasn't expecting her to call me right away."

Before I came over, I carried my phone into the bathroom and plugged it into the jack near the medicine cabinet. I opened the bathroom window and set the phone on the sill. If it rings, I should be able to hear it from Emma's bedroom. Then I took the cordless phone from my parents' room and placed it by the front door. That way I can leave Emma's house, sprint across our yards, and answer the cordless before Sydney hangs up.

"You're right," Emma says. "She wouldn't call you right away. She's going to play hard to get."

"Do you think so?" I ask.

"Those are the rules," Emma says.

Emma and Kellan spend hours talking about relationships and taking quizzes in magazines. Whenever I contribute my two cents, they just laugh and call me clueless.

Emma scrolls through some comments on her Facebook page, reading each one carefully.

"It's hard to tell," she says, "but I think Kevin Storm may be a firefighter. Or a doctor."

Even if Sydney plays hard to get, she'll call me eventually. Otherwise, why would she ask for my number? I hate that Emma's trying to put doubts in my mind.

"Good for you," I say. "So he's better than Jordan Jones. Did you find anything else on there?"

Emma stares at the screen. I shouldn't have asked that question when I wouldn't answer it honestly myself. I told her I didn't find anything interesting, but my brother ends up in a relationship with someone named Phillip!

"Nothing new," Emma says. "But I have been thinking about your list, the one with people you want to look up. I'm not sure if—"

I remove the folded-up piece of paper from my backpack. Emma grabs it and turns it around, then starts reading through the names. I want to say we should crumple up the list and not check on anyone after all. If what I saw about David is true, then what else will we find that people may not want us to know?

"*Eww!*" Emma shoves the paper back at me. "Why did you put Kyle Simpson on there?"

I laugh. "What are you talking about? *You* dated the guy."

"Barely! And I have no desire to find out what's going on in his future."

"He's probably a Chippendale dancer," I say. "Or he runs a nudist colony, or—"

"Stop!" Emma tosses me a pen and says, "If you insist on looking people up, cross him off."

I cross him off, knowing we should eventually cross off every name. But if I say that to Emma, she'll know I'm hiding something from her.

"I never understood how someone can go from date-able to *eww*," I say. "I hope no one I've gone out with thinks of me that way."

"I'm sure they don't," Emma says. "But I never really *liked* Kyle before he asked me out. He was just there. Like that girl in Seattle for you."

After I got back from spring break, I talked about the Seattle girl a lot during lunch. I showed off a school picture she gave me where she wrote her phone number on the back in purple ink. I passed around the picture because she was pretty, but I also wanted to make Emma jealous.

"That was different," I say. "A long-distance relationship is one thing. But hanging out every day when you don't really like someone, isn't that hard? I'd rather already like someone at the beginning, and then fall madly in love with them over time."

"So you like Sydney?" Emma asks.

I look out toward my house. The telephone is sitting silently on my bathroom windowsill. I want to say, *Yes, of course I like Sydney*. She's beautiful, and whenever I've seen her talking to people she always seems nice. But can I see myself falling madly in love with her? That must happen, right?

"You and I are different that way," Emma says. "You're always looking for something long-term, and you'll stay with that person until you know for sure it's not right. That's why I know you weren't being honest when you said *you* broke up with the girl from Seattle. You only said positive things about her, so you never would have broken up with her."

Emma's looking at me with a gentle smile, no judgment.

"That's not what you're looking for?" I ask.

"It's what makes you great boyfriend material, but it also means you're going to get your heart broken a lot." Emma nods toward the list in my hand. "I don't think we should look up any of these people."

I tear a clean line down the middle of the paper. "I was thinking the same thing."

"Great," Emma says. "We won't look up Kellan or . . . or Tyson . . . or anyone."

"My brother, my parents, none of them," I add. "Because what if something bad happens between now and the future? If we can't find out exactly what happens, it would drive us crazy trying to figure it out."

"And some people," Emma says, "don't seem to have a page. Like Kevin Storm. So we might try to look someone up and think they died if we can't find them."

"New rule," I say. "If someone pops up on our webpage, that's cool. But no digging."

Emma smiles. "No digging."

At that moment, I hear a faint sound coming through the window. Is that . . . ?

My phone is ringing!

Emma points toward the door. "Just go, Romeo. But we should leave soon or we'll be late for school."

I bolt.

32://Emma

ON THE DRIVE TO SCHOOL, Josh and I barely speak. He's looking out his window and jiggling his knee up and down. I bet he's thinking about Sydney. He hasn't said anything, but I'm guessing it was her who called.

"Do we have time to swing by Sunshine Donuts?" Josh asks.

I glance at the clock on my dashboard. "I don't think so. We're already late."

Josh leans his head against the window and closes his eyes. Maybe it wasn't Sydney who called, after all. Or maybe Josh didn't make it to the phone in time. Either way, he's on edge.

There are so many unknowns for both of us. I want to figure out what Kevin Storm does for a living. Saving a life could mean so many things. I'm hoping it means he has a take-charge personality, which is one thing that's always attracted me to Cody. When Ruby sprained her ankle at a meet last month, Cody swooped in with an ice pack. I joked with Ruby that it made me want to get a sports injury, too.

But then I think about Kellan, and *I'm* the one on edge. Kellan—who bought my first box of tampons because I couldn't stop laughing in the aisle of the drugstore— may be pregnant *right now*. She didn't even tell me she was having sex, and that pisses me off. We tell each other everything.

Or maybe Kellan *hasn't* had sex yet. If that's the case, it'll be happening soon. But how can I sit by and watch Kellan become a teen mom? She wants to go to Penn State, and dreams of becoming a doctor or a scientist. Can she do all that with a baby screaming in the background? She might not even be able to finish high school.

The school parking lot is crowded, and the only remaining spots are way over by the field house. I pull into one and glance at Josh. He hasn't said a word since he asked about donuts.

* * *

WHEN I SLIP INTO BAND, Mr. Markowitz doesn't notice I'm late. He's busy going over the lineup for this weekend's Memorial Day parade with the girls from color guard.

I have a feeling Josh won't be so lucky with his

homeroom teacher, and that's slightly satisfying. The way he went scrambling for his phone this morning was annoying. And I don't understand why he didn't just tell me if Sydney called. When I called my first husband, at least I had the guts to tell Josh about it.

Whatever. Josh can talk to whoever he wants. I have Kevin Storm waiting for me. But the problem is, that's fifteen years from now. Today, while Josh is getting serious with Sydney Mills, I still have to deal with—

"Emma."

Graham.

He taps his drumsticks against my thigh. "How's it going?" he asks, sliding into the empty seat next to me. "I thought you'd be interested to know that my parents are going away this weekend. That means I'll have a free house."

"I assumed that's what you meant."

"So you can come over and we won't have any interruptions."

I stare at my sheet music. Last night, when I was thinking about life with Kevin Storm, I vowed to end things with Graham.

"Do you want to go to that bonfire on Friday night?" he asks. "We could stop by my place afterward."

I think about what Josh said this morning. *Hanging out every day when you don't really like someone, isn't that hard?*

"I can't do this," I say.

Graham spins a drumstick between his fingers. "Can't do what?"

"You and me. Not anymore."

"Is this because Josh saw us the other day? If you want, I can talk to him."

"No." I take a deep breath. "This has nothing to with Josh. I just need to be on my own for a while. It's nothing you did, but I—"

"Okay." Graham runs his hands over his prickly scalp. "I'm not going to try to change your mind. We always said we were going to keep things low-key."

Graham smiles sadly, and then holds out his arms like he's waiting for a hug. As I lean in toward him, I notice how similar this feels to my breakup with Dylan, and even with Kyle. Unlike other people's breakups, I never have too much drama. When Josh and Rebecca Alvarez broke up, he moped around in his room for weeks. When my mom and Erik divorced, she must have cried for a month. And when Tyson dumped Kellan—

Kellan!

I need to tell Josh about her pregnancy as soon as possible. I should have told him this morning. This isn't something I want to handle on my own.

* * *

I SPOT JOSH in a crowded hall between third and fourth periods. I call his name, but he doesn't respond. He's standing with a sophomore girl and they're both laughing. They turn and begin walking down the hall.

"Josh?" I shout again, but he still doesn't respond. Or maybe he's ignoring me? One call from Sydney and this is what happens!

I stand on my toes and watch them walk away. A few steps later, he reaches over and touches her back. That is *so* not something Josh would usually do.

"Emma?" a voice says.

I know that voice.

Slowly, I turn around. Cody Grainger is walking toward me.

33://Josh

SOMETIMES I'LL HEAR a song on the radio that launches my mood into a higher orbit. Even though I'd happily erase the moment Emma burst in on me in my underwear, "Walking on Sunshine" has been looping through my head all morning. It plays when I walk down the halls, sit in class, and say hi to people at their lockers.

When I answered the cordless phone this morning, no one responded. But then I heard Sydney's distant voice say, "He must be on his way here" before hanging up.

She called me from her cell phone! I haven't seen her yet, but that call has lit my path with sunshine all morning. I absorb it through the soles of my feet and it tingles up my legs, across my chest, shoots down my fingers . . . *and don't it feel GOOD!*

The sunshine is magnetic, too. All morning, guys

who've never said more than *What's up?* have stopped to talk to me. And the girls! Between my morning classes, three girls have walked with me, keeping my pace . . . and I have long legs.

Like Anna Bloom right now. After history, she caught up with me as I headed for the door. I ended up walking to her third-period class even though I have gym on the opposite side of school.

"If you ever want to work on history together," she says, "feel free to give me a call." She writes her number on the corner of my folder.

Anna smiles up at me and then heads into her classroom. I try not to be obvious, but I can't help checking her out as she walks away. She's cute! Then I turn and look down the hall. I swear someone had been calling my name while I was talking to Anna. It was distant, but it may have been Emma.

And there she is, at the far end of the hall, talking to . . . *Cody Grainger?*

Good for her, I guess. Cody's a conceited dick, but whatever makes her happy.

34://Emma

CODY SMILES AT ME.

He's wearing a dark blue T-shirt with DUKE written across the chest. Everyone in track knows he was accepted there with a full athletic scholarship. As usual, he looks relaxed with his spiky blond hair, pale blue eyes, and a faint shadow on his jawline.

"How's it going?" he asks.

My hands start to tremble. Kellan thinks I hold Cody up on a pedestal, but he totally deserves to be there.

"Great." I shift my books from one hip to the other. "So . . . what's your next class?"

"Photography," he says.

"That sounds fun." I fidget with the *E* on my necklace. "I've got World History."

There's a brief silence. I remind myself that one day I

will have a respected career and a life-saving husband. Even though Cody's presence turns my brain into mush, I attempt to channel the confidence I will someday have.

"Are you going to track later?" I ask. "I missed it yesterday."

He nods. "So that's why I saw you running in the park."

"You saw me?"

I went running soon after Josh left. I couldn't stand sitting in my room with the computer right there, not being able to check Facebook because I promised Josh I wouldn't. It turned out to be a kick-ass loop. I did my best time yet, and even sprinted for a half-mile.

"You looked great," Cody says, combing his hands through his spiky hair. "I was working out on the nautilus course and you ran right by me. I called your name, but you must not have heard."

"I was listening to my Discman," I say, unable to control a grin. *Cody* said I looked great!

"What were you listening to?" he asks.

"Yesterday? Mostly Dave Matthews. Hootie and the Blowfish. A little Green Day."

"Green Day?" He nods approvingly. "'Basket Case' was the first song I learned on guitar."

"You play guitar?"

Cody tells me about teaching himself to play, and I nod in all the appropriate places. I am so glad I ended things with Graham today.

"We should go running sometime," he says. "Do you live near the park?"

I happen to know that Cody lives on the east side of the park, about ten minutes from my house. To be more precise, he lives in a one-story house with purple lilac bushes and a striped mailbox.

"I live near the playground," I say.

"Great. I'm over by the baseball field," he says.

"I used to play Little League there."

"Me too," Cody says. "Hey, if you like Dave Matthews, you should come over sometime. I have a live bootleg tape from a show in Vermont."

"Okay," I say. "I'd like that."

Cody touches my shoulder and smiles. "Well, okay then."

As I watch him walk down the hall, I realize this is yet another ripple brought on by Facebook. If Josh hadn't ditched me yesterday to babysit his phone, I wouldn't have gone for a run and Cody would never have seen me, prompting him to approach me today. And not just approach me . . . *invite me to his house!* I wonder if this ripple affects my future with Kevin, a man I don't even know yet.

For Cody, I might be okay with that.

35://Josh

TYSON AND KELLAN are already at the lunch tree. I try not to read into this, but they hardly ever arrive before me. It's been even longer since they got here first *together*.

"Hey, guys," I say.

Kellan drops a ketchup-soaked french fry into her mouth.

"How's it going?" I ask, removing my first peanut butter and jelly sandwich from my bag.

Tyson smiles at me. "Groovy."

The only time Tyson says "groovy" is when he's feeling abnormally awesome, like when he nails a kickflip on his skateboard. But I still refuse to read into this. If Tyson and Kellan are getting back together, they'll tell me when they want me to know. But when Emma shows up, they'd better be more subtle or she'll flip.

"Well, that's groovy," I say, laughing as I bite into my sandwich.

According to Emma, Kellan fell way too hard for Tyson, which is why the breakup nearly wrecked her. I think that's just Kellan's personality, but Emma warned her to be more careful about love from then on.

Kellan drags another fry through the ketchup. "Anyone want to hear some gossip?"

"Sure," Tyson says. "But you need to eat more than just fries." He removes the top piece of bread from his sandwich, peels off a slice of ham, and offers it to Kellan. "Here, have some of my meat."

Still not reading into this.

"I haven't seen Emma to confirm this," Kellan says, folding the ham in half before putting it in her mouth, "but apparently, in band this morning, she dumped Graham."

What? Why didn't I hear about this?

Tyson takes a huge bite of his sandwich. "Good for her," he says while chewing. "That guy's smarmy. Did you see how he shaved his head?"

"'Smarmy'?" Kellan swats his arm. "Where are you coming up with these words?"

This morning, when Emma and I were talking about relationships, she never said she was going to dump Graham today. If she did this because of something she saw on Facebook, there's no telling what ripples she just caused. We're supposed to talk to each other about this stuff!

"I don't know if this is true," Tyson says, "but some people think Graham and those other guys shaving their heads together was some sort of gay pact. Did you hear about that, Josh?"

A lump of bread catches in my throat. Why does he think *I'd* know about a gay pact? My eyes begin to water, and Kellan shoves her Sprite at me. Have people known my brother was gay but never told me about it? While I start coughing and gagging, Tyson laughs so hard he puts his hand against the ground for support.

"Are you okay?" Kellan asks, leaning close to me. "Nod your head if you need me to give you the Heimlich."

I wipe the tears from my eyes. "I'm fine."

Kellan glares at Tyson. "That is the stupidest thing you've said all day. What on earth does shaving your head have to do with being gay? Are *you* gay because you and Greg tried to light your farts on fire?"

"You remember that?" Tyson cracks up. "Oh, man! Do you still have that tape, Josh?"

"I don't know. Somewhere." It's hard to believe David might be gay. I mean, he must be gay because I don't know any straight men in relationships with guys named Phillip. But now I have to rethink so many things I thought I knew about my brother. We never did meet that girl he spent so much time with after school. Was Jessica really a dude? He had Mom and Dad so worried about how much time they spent together. They even told him they weren't ready to become grandparents yet.

"Graham isn't gay," I say. It's still hard to say his name without seeing his hand up Emma's shirt.

Kellan throws a fry at Tyson's face. Amazingly, he catches it in his mouth.

"Anyway," she says, "I don't see why it matters to you who's gay or not."

"It doesn't matter," Tyson says, biting off more sandwich. "My dad thinks Ellen DeGeneres is gay, and we love *Ellen*!"

"Are you kidding? She's not gay," Kellan says.

"Who's not gay?" Emma asks, walking up to our group.

Kellan clasps her hands and smiles at Emma. "So is it true? You're no longer with what's-his-name?"

Emma looks right at me. "Did you—?"

"Did I what?" I ask. And then I laugh. She thinks I told them about getting rid of Jordan Jones Jr. "She's talking about Graham. We heard you broke up with him."

Emma pulls out her lunch, a clear Tupperware with steamed broccoli, carrots, and cubes of orange cheese. "It was time," she says.

Kellan offers Emma a fry. "If you want advice on finding a new romance," she says, "you should ask Mr. Templeton over there."

Emma and I look at each other, puzzled.

"Don't act so innocent," Kellan says. "I've seen you chatting up girls all over school today."

Tyson slaps me a high five. "My man!"

Emma opens a bag of pretzels and laughs. "Oh, I'm not so sure Josh has romance all figured out."

"What's that supposed to mean?" I ask. Is she talking about Sydney, and how I don't know what to do next? She'd better not be joking about rejecting me herself.

"You know what it means," Emma says.

"You guys are always teasing me, saying I'm clueless about romantic stuff," I say to Emma and Kellan, "but maybe I know more than you think."

"That's what you're hoping," Emma says. "But I don't think you have any idea what you're doing."

"Really?" I say. "Well, if you ever need advice on how to make a real relationship work, I'm right next door."

Tyson and Kellan glance at each other but don't say a word.

* * *

PEER ISSUES IS ALMOST OVER and I still haven't said a word to Sydney. Tapping my pen against the desktop, I casually look over my shoulder. She smiles when she sees me, and I smile back.

"Josh Templeton?"

I turn around and Mrs. Tuttle is looking at me. Standing beside her is Thomas Wu, a student aide from the front office. Mrs. Tuttle points me out, and then Thomas walks up my aisle.

He places a blue slip of paper on my desk. "You need to go to the front office right after class."

I look at the clock above the whiteboard. There are three minutes until the end of class. Three minutes until my first chance to speak with Sydney all day. And now I'm going to miss it!

I stuff my binder into my backpack and then zip it shut. When the bell rings, I pull my backpack over my shoulders. Behind me, I hear a sheet of paper being torn. Glancing back at Sydney, I wish I could mouth *Call me again*, but I can't do that without looking pathetic.

But then Sydney reaches forward and passes me a folded piece of paper. Our fingertips touch and I get a shock of energy through my entire body. She smiles and breezes past me, leaving me gaping at the paper in my hand.

On my way down the hall, I spot Thomas Wu at his locker.

"Do you know why they called me to the office?" I ask him.

"Your parents want you to come by their work after school," he says, turning his locker combination. "But I'm not supposed to listen in on the phone calls, so I didn't tell you that."

This must have to do with being late to school. Well,

I really don't care. Because I'm holding a note—written specifically to me—by Sydney Mills.

In the front office, I sign in and take a seat in an orange plastic chair. I unfold Sydney's note and see the words "my cell phone" and then a line of beautiful numbers scribbled across the fold.

"You're Josh, right?" a girl asks, sliding into the chair beside me. She's a foreign exchange student from Brazil. She's pretty, with long black hair and tiny freckles across her nose.

"I am," I say.

"I've seen some of your drawings on my friends' binders," she says. "You're very talented."

I smile at her. "I'm going to be a graphic designer someday."

"You'll be very good at that," she says.

Maybe it wasn't the worst thing in the world to get called to the office.

36://Emma

AFTER THE FINAL BELL RINGS, I'm walking down the stairs on my way to my locker when Kellan barrels past me. She stops on the landing below, shakes her hips, and belts out, "*Cel-e-brate good times, COME ON!*"

"What are you celebrating?" I ask.

Kellan keeps on singing, whipping her hair around her shoulders. "*We're gonna celebrate and have a good time!*"

I've been friends with Kellan long enough to know I'll be standing here until the entire song is out of her system. While she swivels and sings, I take this chance to look for a baby bump. She's wearing a black cotton skirt and a white T-shirt, and her belly looks as flat as ever. Then again, even if she's already pregnant, she probably wouldn't be showing yet.

When she's finally done singing, I ask again, "What are you celebrating?"

"You!" She follows me down the stairs. "Breaking up with Graham. I didn't have a chance to properly applaud you at lunch. So are you ready to celebrate and have a good time?"

I wish I could muster her level of enthusiasm. Yes, I'm relieved it's over with Graham. And I'm excited about Cody. But Josh's attitude at lunch bothered me. It's like the discovery of his future is changing him *now*.

"Can you skip track today?" Kellan asks.

"I probably shouldn't," I say. "I skipped yesterday, so—"

Kellan knocks her hip into me. "You just want to see Cody's gorgeous body doing sit-ups and getting sweaty and—"

I clap my hand over her mouth. Then I lean in close and say, "Cody talked to me in the hall today. *He* came up to *me*."

Kellan pulls my hand off her mouth. Even though she thinks he's self-absorbed, she understands my crush on Cody. Who wouldn't understand? He's beautiful!

"What did he say?" she whispers. "What did you say back?"

Here I am, about to spill every detail, but Kellan hasn't done the same with me. She's either having sex or is about to have sex or is possibly already *pregnant*, and she hasn't breathed a word about anything.

"He just said hi."

Kellan smirks. "Did you try out my Husband Theory again, or do you still have cats in your passenger seat?"

"Is this the theory with the car coming toward us?"

"Head-on collision."

It feels wrong to try out Kellan's theory knowing I'm supposed to marry Kevin Storm. I couldn't find any pictures of him on Facebook, so it seems unfair to imagine someone else in the car simply because I don't have a mental image of Kevin.

"Is Tyson still in your passenger seat?" I ask.

Kellan bites her lip for a moment, and then says, "Are you sure you can't go to the lake today?"

She's avoiding my question. Are she and Tyson getting back together? I felt like I was picking up signs at lunch, but I couldn't be sure. If they are getting back together, *he* could potentially be Lindsay's dad!

"Will you please come to the lake?" Kellan says. She touches my elbow. "We've barely hung out all week."

"How about tomorrow?"

"I can't," she says. "I have my college class."

The cute college guy! That's why she never wants to miss class. Could *he* be the baby's father? Has she been going back to the dorms with him after class?

"Okay," I say. "I'll come to the lake."

Kellan claps her hands together. "But you need to drive. I had a doctor's appointment before school, so my mom dropped me off."

What? "Why did you see a doctor?" This has to be about the pregnancy.

Kellan looks at me and then breaks into a laugh. "You just went completely pale! I'm not dying, Em."

I need an answer. "Then tell me why you went."

"It was just a check-up." She flips her hand dismissively. "Can we stop by your place and grab swimsuits?"

As we walk past the front office, Kellan knocks hips with me again, and this time I knock back. But then I glance through the office window and stop cold. Josh is sitting in a chair with his back to us. There's a girl leaning close to his shoulder, watching him sketch something on her notebook.

"He's drawing Pepé Le Pew," Kellan whispers. "I think our little Josh is finally learning how to hit on girls."

I grab Kellan's arm and pull her away. "If that girl wants a chauvinistic, sex-addicted skunk on her folder, that's her problem."

* * *

WE WALK UP THE STAIRS to my bedroom, and Kellan asks if she can borrow my red bathing suit. "You should definitely wear your tan bikini," she says. "Guys love it."

"How do you know?"

Kellan opens my bedroom door. "Not that we care

what Josh thinks, but when you wore it at the lake, he was checking you out."

My mind flashes to that photo on Facebook. *The good ole days.* Josh said he took the picture by accident. Well, if he *was* checking me out, he's definitely over me now. Now he's got his pick of girls at school, and it's only a matter of time before he permanently picks Sydney Mills.

I locate Green Day's *Dookie* in my stack of CDs, slide it into my stereo, and click fast-forward until I get to "When I Come Around." I've always liked this song, and Cody definitely put me in the mood for it.

"Is that your new computer?" Kellan asks, unclasping her bra beneath her shirt. "Look at that monitor!"

I wonder what would happen if I showed her Facebook. She said she wouldn't want to time travel, but how would she feel about *reading* her future . . . reading about *Lindsay*? Would her future self want her to know? And what would *my* future self want *me* to know? And Josh's?

Do they remember that, during this week in May, we've discovered a way to read Facebook? Maybe when they're writing this stuff, they're encoding what they say with subtle messages, guiding us into making different decisions. Maybe Kellan's future self knows she'll be in my bedroom today, inching closer to my computer. If that's true, then adult Kellan can tweak what she says to reflect whether or not she wants seventeen-year-old Kellan to know about the baby.

"Can I check my email?" Kellan asks, pressing the power button on my monitor.

Or maybe Josh and I are the only ones who are supposed to know about this.

Or maybe time doesn't even allow *us* to remember because it'd rip a massive hole in the universe.

"No!" I push Kellan's hand away from the computer.

She steps back, confused. "I'm not going to break it. Remember, I'm the one who showed you how to use the Internet."

"It's just that Martin's getting home soon," I say. "He and my mom have been touchy about how much time I've been spending online."

There's no way I can bring Kellan into this, too. I throw our bathing suits and flip-flops into a beach bag and send her down the hall in search of towels.

37://Josh

DAD PICKS UP his office phone and dials Mom's extension. She's only two doors down, so I can hear it ring.

"He's here," Dad says into the receiver.

Dad's office looks the same as the last time I was here. Mind-numbingly dull. Some of their best friends teach history, and their offices have powerful posters with cool quotes like "Those who cannot remember the past are condemned to repeat it" and "History is written by the victors." The only poster on Dad's wall is a black and white photo of a bald sociologist inspecting his glasses.

Mom eases the door shut, and then sits in the chair beside me.

"Why were you late for school this morning?" Dad asks.

I knew this would happen. When Emma and I finally

arrived at school, we were already ten minutes late. I was hoping if the school left a message on our answering machine, I could erase it before my parents got home. But apparently their work numbers are at the top of the contact list.

"Dad and I give you a lot of freedom," Mom says. "We don't make you take the bus, but we expect you to get yourself there on time."

"We know you didn't oversleep," Dad says. "Your music was playing when we left for work."

"I caught a ride with Emma," I say. "We lost track of time. It won't happen again."

Dad taps his finger against his desk. "Did you forget to look at the clock?"

"Why did you lose track of time?" Mom asks. "Was Emma in your bedroom?"

This is what David was talking about. Before leaving for college, he warned me that Mom and Dad get way too overprotective about the opposite sex. But apparently, it wasn't the opposite sex they had to worry about with him.

"She wasn't in my bedroom," I say, which isn't a total lie. I don't think Emma actually made it through the doorway once she began laughing at my tighty-whities.

"Were you in *her* bedroom?" Mom asks.

I shouldn't have to answer that question. I've never given them any reason not to trust me, yet they're acting like I need to report back on everything I do. "In case you haven't noticed, I'm not a little kid anymore. I can even cross the street all by myself."

"That's right," Dad says. "And when you were a kid, we let you and Emma have sleepovers. The difference is, we *know* you're not a kid anymore."

"You're a teenage boy," Mom says.

"Really?" I ask. "Wow."

Dad leans forward. "Why were the two of you late for school?"

I lean back in my chair and chuckle. "You want to know if we were having sex, right?"

Dad's voice is tight. "That's not what I said."

Mom lifts a hand to her chest. "Were you?"

I stand up and pull my backpack over my shoulder. "No, we weren't having sex. And I'm only telling you that so you don't have a heart attack. But you're assuming an awful lot just because I was a few minutes late to school."

"David was never late to school," Dad says.

"And yet," I say, my voice rising, "he chose to go to college over two thousand miles from Lake Forest!"

Mom and Dad turn to each other. There's nothing left to say, so I grab my skateboard and leave.

* * *

THE MAN IN A WHITE PAPER HAT passes me a sugar cone with two scoops of rocky road. Holding the ice cream in one hand, I drop a quarter in the tip jar and put the rest of the change in my pocket. I carry my board outside and sit on a wooden bench, working my way around the edges of the cone.

I'm dreading seeing Mom and Dad later. Even though they brought David's name into the discussion, I didn't need to imply that he moved to Seattle to get away from them. I don't even know if that's true.

Across the four-lane road, there's a small shopping center with a comic book store, a hair salon, and a record shop. I watch a white convertible pull into the parking lot.

That's Sydney's car! She looks at herself in the rearview mirror and tugs her hair into a ponytail as the top electronically closes around her.

In one of my pockets is Sydney's phone number written across a torn piece of paper. Her cell phone is probably in her car right now. In my other pocket are enough coins to make a call. And beside this bench is a pay phone.

No, this is ridiculous.

I wipe my lips with the back of my hand. If I call Sydney and tell her I can see her, she'll think I'm a stalker. Besides, if Emma's right and Sydney is playing hard to get, then she won't answer her phone. She'll wait to hear whatever message I leave, but I have no idea what I'd say.

I watch Sydney walk past the hair salon and open the door of the comic book store. She's into comics? Nice!

She gave me her cell number because she wants me to call, but what if this is too much too soon? Calling her right now could ruin everything. If we're meant to be together, it needs to happen naturally. I step onto my board and skate away, licking my ice cream to distract myself.

Or maybe I'm just being chicken.

At the first corner, I bend my knees and take a right.

If I was heading home, I would've gone straight.

38://Emma

"I DON'T UNDERSTAND why you're forcing me to eat ice cream," Kellan says, staring at the menu above the concession stand at the lake. "I'm craving a slushie."

"Because I'm the one with the money." I lift my sunglasses so I can read the flavors. "Besides, ice cream is healthier."

"Healthier *how*?"

"It's high in calcium," I say. When my stepmom was pregnant, she talked about needing a lot of calcium.

"What'll it be, girls?" asks the woman behind the counter.

"I'll have strawberry," I say, grabbing a handful of napkins, "with rainbow sprinkles."

Kellan turns to me. "Pretty please, slushie?"

I shake my head.

"Fine," she says. "Then cookie dough."

While the woman leans into the ice cream tubs, Kellan says, "I don't get why everyone's so concerned about my eating habits. First Tyson, now you."

I raise an eyebrow. "Since when are you and Tyson on good enough terms to discuss how you eat?"

Kellan waves off my question. "We've always been on good terms."

"Do I have to remind you how much he irritates you? Or about those two weeks you missed school?"

Kellan reaches for her cookie dough cone. "Did you know love and hate share the same nervous circuits in the brain?"

"So now you *love* him again?"

"I didn't say that. I was just stating a fact."

We walk across the sand, licking our ice creams.

"I feel like you're keeping things from me," I say.

"Like what?" Kellan asks.

I step around some little boys building a sand castle. I watch them fill the moat with a small bucket of lake water and I wonder if Kevin Storm and I will still have two sons tonight.

"You wouldn't tell me why you went to the doctor today."

"I know," Kellan says. "It's just that I feel weird talking about it."

"The only reason I'm asking is because I care about you."

Kellan licks a drip off her cone. "Okay, I went back to that therapist I saw after Tyson and I broke up. I hadn't seen her in a few months, so it was just a check-in."

"Well, I'm really glad you went," I say. "Thanks for telling me that."

We sit on our towels and finish our ice creams in silence. With the puzzle of her doctor visit solved, there's something else we need to discuss. My mind races to fabricate a believable story.

"I was in the school nurse's office today," I say, "and you'll never believe what I saw."

"Why did you go to the nurse?" Kellan asks.

"I cut myself on a music stand in band. It's fine. Anyway, this girl came in asking for a condom. Did you know the school nurse gives out free condoms?"

"You and I had health together," Kellan says. "I was there for the free condom talk."

"Oh, right."

"So who was it?" she asks.

"Who was what?"

"The girl asking for the condom."

"Some senior. I don't know her name."

"Not that I need a condom," Kellan says, "but I definitely wouldn't get one from school. Who wants the nurse knowing all your business?"

I see my chance and I move in quickly. "How would you get a condom if you needed one?"

She considers my question, but doesn't give an answer. I can tell by the way she's shifting on her towel that I'm on the verge of losing her.

"Want to hear a secret?" I ask. "But you can't tell anyone."

Kellan crosses her heart.

"Last summer, when Josh's brother came home to visit, Josh told me he stole a condom from David's toiletries bag. He stashed it in his wallet, in case he ever needs it."

Kellan cracks up. "Why do guys carry ratty old condoms in their wallets? When they finally get around to using them, they're either expired or worn out."

I instantly feel guilty for selling Josh out, even though he's been infuriating me today. It was for a good cause, putting the idea in Kellan's mind of always carrying a condom, but it's not the kind of thing Josh would want getting spread around.

* * *

KELLAN'S IN THE WATER, and I'm sitting on my towel, my sunglasses hiding my eyes. A half mile across Crown Lake is a huge house with a wraparound porch, a beautifully manicured lawn, and a dock with two kayaks.

I recognize that house from the night I saw Josh's Facebook page. Someday, he'll live there with Sydney. They'll go boating and have barbeques. His children will grow up rich and privileged and Josh will eventually get sucked into that world, too.

"Hey there," Kellan says. She shakes the sand off her towel and then wraps it around her waist.

I pull my legs to my chest and point across the lake. "Do you know who lives in that house?"

"The one with the big porch?" she asks, shielding her eyes with her hand. "I don't think anyone from school."

"Do you think Sydney's family could afford a house like that?"

"Sydney Mills?" Kellan sits next to me and unscrews the cap of her Sprite. "Why is everyone talking about her recently?"

I shake my head. "I think Josh might be interested in her."

"I thought you were joking about that the other day," Kellan says. "No offense to Josh, but she's a little out of his league. Has he ever even talked to her?"

"Actually, my very first instant message was from Sydney," I say, resting my chin against my knees. "She was asking for his phone number."

Kellan spits a mouthful of Sprite onto her legs. "Did she call him yet?"

"I know I'm the one who brought it up," I say, "but do you mind if we not talk about this?"

"Okay," Kellan says, "but I need to talk to *you* about something."

My heart races. Is she finally going to admit she's been having sex? If she does, that'll force me to make a huge decision. Either I admit to Kellan what I saw on Facebook, or I shake her by the shoulders and tell her she'd better be using protection.

"I've been thinking about you and Josh," she says.

I burrow my feet in the sand. This isn't the conversation I thought we were about to have.

"I know it got weird between you guys last fall," she says. "But this week, things have seemed . . . different."

"Like how?"

"You finally seemed to be getting close again, but then today at lunch you both had your claws out."

I wiggle my toes so they peek up from the sand.

"Let me put it this way," Kellan says. "Now that Graham's over with, do you ever . . . you know . . .?"

"*What?*"

"I'm serious."

"No!" I shriek. "Josh is . . . *Josh*."

"Because other girls are starting to notice that he's a really good guy. There's the girl we saw in the office. And now you're telling me Sydney Mills asked for his number." Kellan removes the cap from her Sprite again. "If there's even a small part of you that ever wondered what Josh would be like as more than a friend, maybe you should think about doing something before it's too late."

As Kellan takes a sip, I stare at Josh's future house on the other side of the lake.

After a minute, I make myself look away.

39://Josh

I SKATE PAST A YELLOW HOUSE with a tire swing out front. A Chihuahua scampers through the yard and starts yipping after me. If I slow down to take the next turn, he'll catch me. While I'm not afraid of him nipping my ankles, his bony head is the size of one of my wheels and I don't need that type of guilt.

By now, my ice cream is gone. I fling the remainder of my sugar cone toward the dog and it shatters on the sidewalk. As he stops to nibble a shard, I round the corner and coast toward the intersection. Across the street, Sydney's convertible is still parked and empty.

I roll up to a lamppost and hug my arm around it to keep from drifting. The traffic light changes and I could cross to the other side. When Sydney comes out of the comic book store, I could be waiting at her car.

Instead, I skate over to a vending machine and buy a can of root beer.

* * *

BY MY SECOND ROOT BEER, I've skated around the block four times and I have a major sugar rush going on. When I round the final corner again, I decide that if Sydney is walking to her car, I'll go over and say hi. If she's already left, then I'll bolt for the nearest restroom.

When the parking lot comes into view, I see her convertible pulling onto the street.

Decision time!

I skate hard toward the pay phone, and then kick the tail of my board to flip it upside down. I lift the receiver and, with shaking fingers, dial Sydney's cell phone number.

It's ringing!

Her car is stopped at a red light. I can see her lift her backpack onto her lap.

Answer it!

She brings her cell phone to her ear. "Hello?"

The light turns green and her car begins driving through the intersection.

"Sydney!" I've had way too much sugar. "It's Josh. I think I . . . are you . . . ?"

"Josh *Templeton*?" she asks.

"Are you driving?" I ask. "Because I was sitting here eating ice cream and I think I just saw you."

I watch her glance toward the sidewalk. "Where are you? I didn't know you had a cell phone."

"Pull over," I say. "I'll be right there."

"Okay," she says, and her turn signal begins flashing.

I hang up the phone, jump on my board, and skate across the street toward her car.

The passenger window is down, and I rest my elbows on the door. She smiles at me and undoes her ponytail, her hair falling like ribbons over her silky blue shirt.

"Do you live near here?" she asks.

I nod in the direction of the ice cream shop. "No, but I had an intense craving for rocky road."

"I *love* ice cream," she says. "So where are you headed? Can I give you a ride?"

"I'm just going home," I say. "I live over by the playground in Wagner Park."

Sydney glances at her watch. "I need to be back on this side of town in twenty minutes, but that should give us enough time."

I've never climbed into a beautiful girl's convertible before. For a moment, I think about vaulting over the door, but then sanity kicks in. I fit my skateboard into the small backseat while Sydney puts on her blinker and gradually changes lanes.

"You can toss your bag in the back," she says, adjusting her rearview mirror. "I know there's not a lot of room up front."

Before stopping by Dad's office, I bought a three-pack of my own boxers. It's not like Sydney's going to unzip my backpack and see the boxers, but until she mentioned it I hadn't realized I was hugging my bag so tight.

"Where do you have to be in twenty minutes?" I ask, hoping she doesn't throw out a boy's name.

"Home," she says.

Yes!

"A woman's coming over to show my family a slide-show, trying to get us to buy into a time-share package," she says. "My parents aren't very interested, but my sisters and I have been begging them to check it out. Plus, if you sit through the presentation, you get a gift card to the Olive Garden."

"I *love* their breadsticks," I say.

Sydney looks at me and smiles. "Me too!"

She's gorgeous. I mean *gorgeous*. From her perfect face to her soft, tan skin and glossy hair. She's wearing a skirt, which shows off her amazingly smooth legs. How am I allowed to sit in this car?

At my feet there's a red plastic bag from Comix Relief. I nudge it over with my sneaker to keep from stepping on it.

"I picked those up for my dad," she says. "It's his birth-day this weekend, so I bought a few of his favorite *Archie* comics."

"I used to be an *Archie* freak," I say.

She laughs. "Figures."

"Why? Because we both have red hair?"

"I didn't even think of that," she says. "But I'm con-vinced all guys secretly worship Archie. He's this average boy with two beautiful girls fighting over him. Don't tell me that's not every guy's fantasy."

One beautiful girl would be enough for me.

"Both of my sisters' fiancés collect comics," she continues. "Sometimes my dad tags along when they attend conventions, but they're more into the mutant and superhero comics. Personally, I think the good guys like *Archie*."

She is such a daddy's girl. It's kind of cute. I wonder if they'll still be going to comic conventions when I join the family. Even though it would be cheesy, I'd go along.

We stop at a light and Sydney turns toward me. "Thank you for what you said in class the other day, about being considerate."

"Human decency," I say, groaning.

She nods and eases onto the gas. "I know you were just speaking your mind, but in a way it felt like you were defending me. So thanks."

"Not a problem."

Sydney smiles as she pushes her hair behind her ear. "Anyway, I'm excited about these time-shares. You get to spend a few weeks a year at some of the coolest locations in the world. Have you ever been to Acapulco? We went in February and it was beautiful."

Acapulco? That's one of the places Sydney and I go in the future. Does this slideshow she's about to see lead to time-shares where we take our vacations?

"Have you ever been to Waikiki?" I ask. "I've always wanted to go there."

Sydney looks over at me, her eyes wide. "They have time-shares in Waikiki! Okay, now I really want my parents to buy in. They even have jumbo condos where it could be a family reunion every time we go."

Waikiki. Acapulco. When I read about Sydney and my vacations, I imagined we'd be alone, drinking fruity drinks and having sex in exotic locations. Now it seems like our trips involve a house overflowing with her family. Not that I wouldn't go. As long as I get time alone with Sydney, I'm there.

Up ahead, the road gradually rises where it meets the train tracks.

"Do you know what to do when you drive over train tracks?" Sydney asks.

"Of course," I say.

As the car bumps over the tracks, we both lift our feet off the floor.

"Feet-up-a-loo!" I shout.

Sydney laughs as the road descends. "Feet-up-a-*what*?"

"Feet-up-a-loo," I say, my face getting warm. "Everyone knows that."

"I don't think so," Sydney says, smiling. "Everyone knows you lift your feet and make a wish."

I'm tempted to ask her what she wished for, but maybe I don't want to know. Or maybe I do, but if she tells me it won't come true.

40://Emma

AFTER DROPPING KELLAN OFF, I drive along the east side of Wagner Park, heading home.

If Kellan says she has no use for condoms, then she's not even *anticipating* going all the way soon. When I get home, I need to tell Josh everything so we can figure out what to do. I just hope he's gotten over today's ego kick.

After the stoplight, I turn up the block toward my house. A white convertible is parked at the curb by Josh's house. It's Sydney's car! And Josh is in the passenger seat.

As I go past them and pull into my driveway, I can almost hear Sydney's voice saying, "Is that Emma Nelson?" I bet Josh won't tell her we've been friends since we were little. And that omission will be the first stone in the wall he builds around his precious life with Sydney.

I reach into my backseat for the swimsuits and towels,

and then step outside, slamming the car door much harder than I intended.

* * *

ONCE I GET TO MY ROOM, I look out the window. Sydney's convertible is still there. Josh tells her something and she laughs like he's the funniest guy in the world.

I peel off my sandy clothes, toss them into the laundry basket, and then pull on my robe. When Josh comes up here, I want to immediately check Facebook and see how everything that happened today affected our futures. I bet as soon as Sydney drives away, he'll be knocking at my door.

To get ready, I dial up to AOL. While my computer beeps and crackles, I go back to the window.

Sydney leans over and kisses Josh on the cheek, and then he climbs out of the car. As she drives off, Josh gives her a two-fingered salute. Now *that's* annoying. I pull away from the window and walk back to my computer. If he's going to move forward with Sydney, then I don't have to keep up my end of the pact.

I enter my email and password to log in to Facebook.

Emma Nelson Storm
What is a marine biologist supposed to do in Columbus, Ohio, anyway?
4 hours ago · Like · Comment

Life looks about the same as yesterday. I'm tempted to take a peek at Kellan or search for Josh before he gets here, but I'll wait. That's what friends do. They keep their word.

I spin around in my chair. *Where is he?*

Finally, I can't help myself. I locate Kellan in my Friends column, and click her name.

Kellan Steiner
Lindsay and I are eating Swedish meatballs at Ikea. She agreed to see the Rolling Stones 50th anniversary tour with me. I love my kid!
May 19 at 3:03pm · Like · Comment

Lindsay's still there! Okay, now I *have* to talk to Josh.

I look out the window. Josh is sitting on his lawn, facing the park. I click back to my webpage on Facebook, knot the belt in my robe, and hurry down the stairs.

41://Josh

THERE'S A BREEZE blowing through the trees over in the park, and the air is getting cooler. I fit a blade of grass between my thumbs and blow. Sitting still and whistling through grass has always soothed me, but it drives Emma crazy. Sometimes I do it just to irritate her.

Recently, it's been way too easy to irritate Emma.

When she pulled up to her house a few minutes ago, she ignored Sydney and me. Not that I expected her to run over, but a wave in our direction would've felt less intentionally rude. To give her the benefit of the doubt, I'll assume she didn't want to interrupt my time with Sydney.

* * *

"JOSH!"

Emma is stomping across her front lawn, her arms folded against her chest. She seems pissed, which looks silly since she's barefoot and wearing a fluffy white bathrobe.

"Hey," I say.

"*Hey?*" Emma stares down at me. "I assumed you would come up to my room the moment you got home. See, we have this thing called Face—"

"I'm sorry," I say. "I didn't know you were up there waiting." I hold the blade of grass to my lips and blow.

"Stop that!"

I bite the inside of my cheeks to keep from smiling. "Did you see who dropped me off?"

Emma stuffs her hands into the floppy pockets of her robe. "A lot has happened today . . . for both of us. I think we need to make sure everything's still okay."

That's definitely true. Emma dumped Graham and then hung out with Cody in the hallway. Anna Bloom wrote her number on my folder. Sydney Mills gave me a ride home. While I'm curious to find out how everything affected Emma's future, I'm actually nervous about my own.

I grab my backpack and kick my skateboard into my hand. "I'm willing to check out *your* future," I say, following Emma, "but I want to skip mine."

"Skip yours?" Emma glances back at me. "You don't want to know what that little road trip did to your future?"

The wind chimes hanging on her porch are clinking loudly.

"Sydney driving me home didn't change anything," I say, leaning my skateboard against the railing.

Emma tips her head and looks me in the eyes. Without a word, her message is clear: *We'll see about that.*

* * *

WHEN WE GET TO HER ROOM, Emma grabs a change of clothes and disappears down the hall. She returns a minute later wearing small white shorts and a red V-neck shirt. Loose curls spill around her face and neck, but her shoulders are stiff with tension.

I set my backpack on the floor at the foot of her bed.

"Why were you wearing a robe before?" I ask.

Emma sits at her computer with her back to me. "I was about to take a shower because Kellan and I were at the lake. She needed to talk. So, like the good friend that I am, I went with her."

Is she insinuating that I'm not a good friend?

"I'm sorry," I say. "I don't remember you saying you needed to talk."

"I was trying to talk to you all day!" Emma says. "But you were either flirting with random girls or arguing with me at lunch."

The last person who should be lecturing me about flirting is Emma. But she's right. I never asked her how she was doing today. Both of us are trying to figure out so much, yet I was only concerned with my own life.

I stand beside Emma as she clicks the word "Friends."

She scrolls past several rows of photos, and then slows down when she reaches the *C* names. She sighs heavily when Cindy Freeburg is followed by Corbin Holbrook, whoever those people are. It doesn't take a genius to figure out who she was hoping to find.

I tell Emma I'm going to the bathroom. I've got a few root beers talking to me, and I'm also not in the mood to hear her moan about a future without Cody Grainger.

Since the downstairs bathroom is getting renovated, I walk through her mom and Martin's room. The last time I was in here must have been back in elementary school. I probably got a splinter or cut myself climbing a chain-link fence. Her parents kept the Neosporin and Band-Aids in this bathroom.

Outside the bathroom door there's a large square frame displaying a dozen photos. I'm in a few of them, but it doesn't look like any pictures have been added since Emma started high school. In the bottom left corner is a picture of Tyson, Kellan, Emma, and me squished into the back of a minivan on the way to a middle school dance. Tyson and I are wearing cheap clip-on ties, and Emma and Kellan have their bangs curling up like waves. And we all look so small!

I remember how Emma and Kellan danced with a large group of girls. Tyson and I mostly hung out under the basketball hoop unless a girl yanked one of us onto the dance floor. The last song of the night was "End of the Road" by

Boyz II Men, and I decided to ask Emma to dance with me. With my hands barely touching her hips, and her hands on my shoulders, we spent the first half of the song staring down at our feet. I pulled her a little closer, sliding my hands onto her back, and soon Emma rested her chin beside my neck. As that final song began to fade, I closed my eyes and leaned my head until our cheeks touched.

That's when I first felt a crush forming on my best friend.

* * *

WHEN I RETURN to Emma's room, I'm ready to talk about our futures. Even though we haven't been able to speak without snapping at each other today, we need to. And I have a plan to make that happen.

"Let's play Truth," I say. "You can ask me anything, and I get to ask you anything."

Emma shakes her head. "There's nothing I want to know."

"Nothing?"

"I have a better game," she says. "No one's ever played it before. It's called Refresh."

I remove my backpack from the bed and sit down on Emma's comforter.

"While you were gone," Emma says, "I got to thinking about the Refresh icon on the computer. This is going to blow your mind."

It's nice to see Emma smiling, so I sit up and listen.

"Ever since we discovered Facebook," she says, "we noticed there were changes between when we logged off and when we logged on again. Those changes could've been made by a thousand different ripples throughout the day. But think of how cool it would be to see the effects of *one* tiny little ripple."

"I'm not really sure what you're suggesting," I say, "but I'm not causing any ripples just for fun."

Emma points at the monitor. "Check out what my update says."

> **Emma Nelson Storm**
> Forget it. I'm making Kev take me out to dinner. I can only stay cooped inside for so long.
> 1 hour ago · Like · Comment

"That doesn't sound bad," I say. "You're going out to dinner."

Emma slowly nods her head. "So *you* get to live in a huge house on the lake, and I have to stay cooped inside. That sounds fair."

Since when did this become a contest where we compare our lives?

Emma glances at her closet, then her dresser. "Now, we have to *do* something. It doesn't have to be huge, but something we weren't going to do before playing this game."

"Emma, I'm not messing with the future. Not as part of a game."

"Then don't call it a game!" she snaps. "Think of it as an award-winning science experiment."

Emma picks up the thin blue vase from her dresser. Earlier this week, it held the dying roses Graham gave her for prom. Emma slowly tips the vase until water begins dribbling onto her white carpet.

"What are you doing?" I ask. But I know the answer. She's making a small change in the present to see how it affects the future. If I grab the vase from her now, it wouldn't matter because *that* wouldn't have happened before either.

At first Emma lets the water spill onto one spot, but then she begins spiraling it into bigger circles until the vase is empty.

"The water had a little dirt in it," she explains, sitting at her computer again. "When Martin sees this, he'll probably have a long talk with my mom. My mom will lecture me, and then she'll make me clean it when I should've been doing my homework. How do you think that will change everything that comes after?"

I don't want to guess how the future just changed. It's impossible to know, and it shouldn't have been changed to begin with.

Emma looks over at me pleadingly. "Come on! It'll be fun." She scrolls over the Refresh icon. "Fast forward fifteen years *and* . . ."

She clicks the mouse and the page reloads.

Emma Nelson Storm

Going to Kev's favorite restaurant tonight. Hopefully
the babysitter shows up this time.

36 minutes ago · Like · Comment

I sit down on Emma's bed and lean over so my thumbs
press into my temples. This is so reckless. Emma doesn't
care what happens to her future because she doesn't want
the future she has. All she cares about is Cody. But since
there's no mention of him on Facebook, she has nothing
to lose.

Emma groans. "I sound about as happy as before. I
need to do something bigger."

"How do you know you're not happy in this future?" I
ask. "I thought you liked Kevin Storm."

"We're going to *Kevin's* favorite restaurant," Emma
says. "And my babysitter has a habit of not showing up."

"You're reading a lot into very few words," I say.

Emma glares at me. "If I totally screw things up, then
I'll change it back."

"You *can't* change it back!"

"You're not playing, remember? And if I screw things
up that badly, then I'll keep screwing them up until they
get better. I can hit Refresh all night if I need to."

"I'm out!" I say, heading toward the door. "I'm done with
Facebook. I'm not messing with the future anymore."

"That's because you're afraid," Emma says. "You have
no idea why Sydney likes you, so you're terrified that

something I do will break that rock solid relationship of yours."

"Sydney has plenty of reasons to like me," I say.

"Name three."

"This is stupid."

"You can't, can you?" she says. "You're afraid of reality."

"If anyone in this room is afraid of reality," I say, "it's not me."

"That's it." Emma moves the arrow from the Refresh icon and clicks on Friends.

"What are you doing?"

"I'm looking you up. Maybe things will never be perfect in my future, but I'm tired of you acting like you're better than me because your life turns out fantastic."

"I never even *thought* that." I run to the computer and pry her fingers away from the mouse, then I click back to Emma's page.

Emma jabs her finger at the screen. "Do you see where I live now?"

Lives in Columbus, OH

"Remember how I was a marine biologist?" she says. "I should be living near the ocean. I worked at the lab in Massachusetts, but we moved to Ohio. I'm sure that's because of Kevin. So I'm stating out loud that if Kevin even *suggests* moving there in the future, he's out of his mind. Right this second, I'm committing to *never* living in Ohio."

Emma's finger taps the Refresh button. The page reloads.

Lives in London, England

"It worked!" Emma says.

She touches the mouse, but I pry her hand away again. I'm not letting go until she promises to stop this game.

"This is scary," I say. "You're not even *doing* things anymore. You're just making up your mind and changing your life."

Emma looks up at me but doesn't say anything. The longer she stares, the more uncomfortable I feel. She smiles faintly, and then lifts onto her toes. Her lips press into mine, and neither of us pull away.

I close my eyes and lean into her.

Emma brushes her cheek against mine and whispers, "How do you think this will affect our future?"

I part my lips as she slides her hand behind my neck, pulling us even closer.

42://Emma

JOSH STEPS BACK FROM ME, and I immediately know I've gone too far.

"Why did you do that?" he asks. His voice is shaky.

My legs feel weak. I sit in my chair and try to make my brain focus. I did it because . . . *I don't know.*

I stare down at my hands. I don't know what to say. When he left for the bathroom a few minutes ago, I quickly opened his backpack. I'm not sure what I was looking for, maybe a note from Sydney, or a clue as to where they just were. Instead I found a pack of boxers, which clearly shows he's hoping for something to happen with her very soon. After everything that's gone on this week, it pushed me over the edge.

"It was nothing," I say. "Let's just let it go, okay?"

"Let it go?" Josh's eyes flash with anger. "You know how I felt about you! You can't jerk me around for some stupid game."

"I wasn't jerking you around."

"You rejected me," Josh says. "But now that I'm moving on, it pisses you off. Did you expect me to mope around forever?"

"Of course not," I say, fighting back tears.

"Maybe other guys don't mind when you act like this, but I do."

"Act like what?"

"Going out with people and not caring about them," Josh says. "Even with your future you got rid of Jordan Jones like he didn't matter. And today you dumped Graham and immediately moved on to Cody. I saw you in the hall with him. But in case that doesn't work out, now you're starting something with me. Who's next?"

"That is not how—"

"Yes it is!"

The way Josh says it feels like a slap across the face. I squeeze my hands into fists and say, "Take that back or get out of my room."

"Gone!" he says.

As soon Josh's feet hit the stairs, I fall onto my bed. My shoulders shake and my chest heaves. I stare at the corkboard above my bed, at all the pictures of us. There's

Kellan, Tyson, Josh, and me in the ball pit at GoodTimez. I've had that up there since last year. In one of my futures, I even posted it in an album on Facebook. Well, not anymore. I rip the picture off the corkboard, tear it into pieces, and toss it in my trash can.

* * *

I LOOK OUT my window toward Josh's bathroom, but the blinds are closed. Just this morning, he had a phone propped on that sill, waiting for Sydney to call. I didn't humiliate him by pointing it out because that's not how you treat friends.

You don't judge them. You don't humiliate them. I bet he's been judging me all along. Like this morning, judging me for going out with Kyle and Graham even though I didn't love them. And at lunch, saying I should come to him if I need advice on romance. He thinks I'll always suck at relationships.

Screw him.

I sit down at my computer again.

Screw his ground rules about Facebook.

There I am, posing with my husband in London. I enlarge the photo. My hair is lighter, and I'm wearing an orange scarf. Kevin is barely taller than me with dark brown eyes. Big Ben looms in the background. Kevin is holding a baby in his arms. An older child is peeking out from between my knees.

Emma Storm

Wishing for a better raincoat. And more sleep. And a
day that doesn't involve mashed bananas in my hair.

17 hours ago · Like · Comment

The other times I've been married to Kevin, and even
to Jordan, I kept Nelson as part of my name. What ripple
occurred in the past twenty minutes to make me give up
my maiden name?

I scroll down.

Emma Storm

I can't stand how people in England say "Good day"
all the time. It's like they're forcing me to have a
good day. And if I'm NOT?

May 16 at 10:47am · Like · Comment

Emma Storm

Diapers, meltdowns, teething, more meltdowns.
Kevin wanted me to stay home with the kids, but I
keep wondering why more men don't do it. I used to
have a better paying job than him!

May 14 at 12:09pm · Like · Comment

I'm not happy. *Again!*

When I said that I wouldn't live in Ohio, I should have
been more specific. I should have said "I will not give up
my dream job." Or "I will not live away from the ocean."

Earlier today, I wrote that I wondered what a marine

biologist does in Ohio. I was being vague, but I can tell what's going on. Kevin moved us there so he could be some kind of hero in his job, but he took me away from what I loved. And the boys we had in Ohio were having a tough time adjusting to school because they had to start in the middle of the year. Kevin doesn't care about us. He only cares about himself.

I can hear Josh warning me to stop this line of thought. He'd say that maybe my future self is having a bad week. But I know myself. Things are not good.

I click on Friends and scroll through the names. There's still no Cody Grainger. Before I can stop myself, I go down to the Js.

This time, there's also no Josh Templeton.

So that's how it goes. One mistake and he holds it against me forever.

There's a box at the top of the webpage where you can search for people. I lightly drum my fingers against the keyboard, and then quickly type "Josh Templeton." A new page loads, with more Josh Templetons than will fit on the screen. But the third Josh down is him.

Josh Templeton 2 mutual friends

I click his name and his page appears. He still lives in Lake Forest and works at Electra Design. In his photo, he's in a rowboat with Sydney and three kids, but the rest of the page is mostly blank.

Next to his name is a small rectangle that says "Add as Friend." I try clicking it, but nothing happens. I click it again, but the future won't let itself be changed that easily.

Fine. *Have fun with your happy life, Josh.*

I type "Cody Grainger" in the search area and hit Enter.

Cody's page is similar to Josh's. He's not a Friend, so I can't get much info on him either. It says he lives in Denver, Colorado, and is an architect, focusing on wind and solar energy. His hair looks as blond and spiky as ever, and he has that same sexy smile. Cody definitely ages well.

I scroll down.

Relationship Status Single
Looking for Women

How is Cody Grainger still single in fifteen years?

Okay, let's say I divorce Kevin in London, bring the kids back to the States, and marry Cody. It's a long shot, but nothing's impossible. With that thought in mind, I log off Facebook, disconnect from AOL, and lay down on my bed.

A few minutes later, the phone rings. I'm not answering. Whoever it is can just leave a message.

"Emma!" Martin calls.

How long has he been home? I hope he didn't hear my argument with Josh.

"Are you upstairs?" he asks. "Your dad's on the phone."

I unplug the cord from my computer and snap it into my phone. As I do this, I step on the damp stain on my carpet. I'm not in the mood to talk to anyone right now, especially my dad. I feel guilty that I haven't called to thank him yet. Plus, he gets all lovey on the phone, which will only make me feel worse.

"Hey, Dad," I say.

"Is there a problem?" he asks. He sounds stern. "I left you a message over the weekend, and again on Monday, and I still haven't heard back. It's Wednesday, Em. Mom said the computer arrived on Saturday."

I can't do this now. "I know. I started an email to you, but I've been—"

"Too busy to thank me? I'm pretty sure I raised you to be—"

"Oh! So *you're* raising me now."

He pauses. "That's not fair."

"Fair?" My voice rises. "You have a new family and you're trying to get rid of me by giving me gifts. Is *that* fair?"

"I don't know where this attitude—"

I slam down the receiver.

thursday

43://Josh

I TURN THE DIAL to Hot and water sprays into the washing machine, sending up waves of steam. After pouring a circle of blue detergent over the dirty clothes, I shut the lid. It's been a while since I've been inspired to clean my room, but last night I scooped all my clothes into a big heap and shoved two years' worth of *Thrasher* magazine into the closet. There's no way to predict when Sydney will first come up to my room, so I want to be ready.

I pass the table where my parents are eating breakfast. Dad is crunching on buttered toast while Mom sips her coffee.

I grab the Lucky Charms in the pantry and linger there for a moment, trying to figure out what I'm going to say to them. My parents got home late last night, and everyone was too tired to discuss what had happened in Dad's office.

"You're doing laundry before school?" Mom says. "That's unusual."

"I cleaned my room," I say from the pantry.

"Even more unusual," Dad says.

They used to bug me about straightening my room, but eventually they gave up. If they want to view this as my way of apologizing for yesterday, that's fine.

"I'll be vacuuming this weekend," Dad says. "I'll run it over your carpet now that there's a floor again."

I head to the table. "I'll take care of it," I say, shaking the cereal into a bowl. "It'll be a nice break from homework. They're piling it on before finals."

"We noticed you were in your room all evening," Mom says. "It's good to see that your studies haven't been forgotten."

I'm late for school *one* time, by just a few minutes, and now they're concerned about my homework. If they knew I become a successful graphic designer with a huge house on the lake, they'd stop stressing over one little tardy.

"I haven't fallen behind all year," I say, pouring milk over my cereal.

Mom leans across the table and touches my hand. "I didn't mean to imply that you had."

"We know we're lucky," Dad adds. "We don't take it

for granted that, other than this one time, you've been very responsible about getting yourself to school."

"After you left, we polled a few of our colleagues," Mom says, "and some of their children are late to school way more often than they're on time."

One reason my parents feel overbearing is their need to discuss *everything*. That was probably why David moved across the country. He wasn't comfortable with them knowing every part of his life.

I definitely can't tell Mom and Dad that Emma kissed me. She lives right next door! They'd be nervous wrecks every time I'm home alone. Tyson would listen, but it's not fair to drag him into this when he sees Emma every day.

Mom drops another sugar cube into her coffee. "We want you to know that we don't have a problem if you get rides to school with Emma."

I bring a heaping spoonful of Lucky Charms to my mouth.

"We love Emma," Dad says. "But getting yourself to school on time is nonnegotiable."

"Okay," I say, a line of milk dribbling from my lips. I wipe my chin with a napkin.

Outside, Emma's car door slams shut. I glance up at the clock. If she's leaving this early, that means she's intentionally avoiding me.

We are now officially not speaking to each other.

44://Emma

I ADJUST MY REARVIEW MIRROR when I reach the end of the block. If Josh expects me to apologize for kissing him, he can keep waiting. Maybe I screwed up, but the way he went off on me was hurtful. I stayed in my room for the rest of the evening, coming downstairs only for dinner. I tried practicing my sax, which usually relaxes me, but I couldn't hold any notes.

I turn left at the intersection. I need to call my dad tonight to tell him I'm sorry. It *was* generous of him to buy me a computer. I just don't understand why he didn't pick up the phone when I called him back last night. I tried his number twice, and both times it went to the answering machine.

"This is the Nelson household," Cynthia's voice said.

"Sorry we missed your call. Please leave a message after the beep."

We used to be the Nelson household.

I couldn't bring myself to leave a message.

* * *

I STEER INTO the drive-thru at Sunshine Donuts.

"What'll it be?" comes a woman's voice through the speaker-box.

I lean out my window. "One cinnamon donut. That's all."

There are three cars in front of me at the pickup window. To pass the time, I study the poster for Sunshine Donuts. The *O* is bright yellow with long rainbow-colored sun-rays. A beaming woman holding a tray of glazed donuts exclaims, "Have a Sunshine day!"

My day felt awful the moment I woke up, and it's all because of what Josh said. I was *not* jerking him around. Josh is my best friend. I wouldn't manipulate him like that.

By the time I get to the pickup window, my donut craving is gone.

The woman has puffy golden hair bridled beneath a net. She holds out a white paper bag. "Cinnamon?"

"I think I changed my mind. I'm not hungry anymore."

"You don't want it?" she asks, jostling the bag.

"I'm sorry," I say.

I leave the parking lot and merge back onto the road.

* * *

THERE ARE TWO WEEKS until finals, and teachers are starting to put on the pressure. During the history final, we'll have to compose three long essays. For the English final, we have to be prepared to analyze any of the books we read this year. In band, our overall grade will be heavily affected by our performance in this weekend's Memorial Day parade.

I'm not in the mood for studying, but I also can't screw anything up. I need a good grade point average to take that college biology class, which leads me into marine biology someday. If my future is bad, I can't blame it all on Kevin Storm. It's my responsibility, too.

Even so, everything is getting under my skin. The ticking clocks in every classroom, the halls that reek of fruity perfume, Anna Bloom's giggle in the library. I'd never paid much attention to Anna before, but after I saw her flirting with Josh yesterday, I've been seeing her everywhere. And everyone I pass is buzzing about tomorrow's Senior Skip Day and Rick's bonfire.

Between third and fourth periods, I spot Josh ahead of me. I dart into the bathroom and stay there until the bell rings.

* * *

"I *LOVE* FRIES," Kellan says as we push our trays through the lunch line. "They energize me."

I eye the wilted salad-bar lettuce and the puddles of

grease on the pizza. If I hadn't been in such a hurry to leave home before Josh, I wouldn't have forgotten my lunch on the kitchen counter.

"When we register for the college class," Kellan says, "remind me to take you to the student café. They make the best curly fries."

As I reach for a peach yogurt, I think about what I've seen of Kellan's future. I couldn't tell much about her career, just that she lives in Philadelphia and works for a sign language school. She doesn't become the doctor or scientist she always talks about, but unlike me, she sounds happy.

After paying for our food, we head to the ketchup pump.

"Will you grab me some napkins?" Kellan asks. "Get some for Tyson, too. That boy never wipes his hands, which is just plain nasty."

Something's definitely up with her and Tyson. Back when they were a couple, Tyson occupied all her thoughts. She doted on him, bringing him cookies and cough drops and packs of spearmint gum.

Kellan nods toward the door. "Ready?"

I don't move. "Can we eat inside today?"

She looks at the door, then back at me. "What about Tyson and Josh?"

I don't know how to answer.

"What's going on?" she asks.

"I could use a little space from Josh right now."

Kellan walks to the nearest open table. "Does this have anything to do with Skanky Mills getting him out of class today?"

My stomach tightens. "What are you talking about?"

"I'm not sure exactly," Kellan says, "but when I was dropping off an attendance sheet in the front office, Her Royal Highness was there. I overheard her asking the Student Council advisor for permission to excuse Josh for the rest of the afternoon. She said it was for Student Council business."

I stare at my pale orange yogurt. Whatever "business" Sydney has in mind, Josh is well-prepared with his studly new boxers.

Kellan grins mischievously, leans in close, and whispers, "I'm sure she'll be *so* impressed when he whips out his wallet and produces that antique condom."

45://Josh

"BOMBS AWAY!"

A sandwich drops from the sky and lands at my feet. Tyson charges toward me. I pick up the sandwich and underhand-toss it back to him. He catches it like a football, spins a full circle, and then plops down next to the lunch tree.

"You've been holding out," he says. "You didn't tell me you were driving around with Sydney Mills yesterday."

How did he find out? I can't imagine Emma said anything.

"Sydney-frickin'-Mills!" he adds.

"I would've called to tell you," I say, "but things got crazy last night."

Tyson's jaw drops. For effect, he pushes his chin back

in place, and then he holds up his hand for a high five. "Crazy with Sydney?"

"Not exactly," I say.

Tyson lowers his hand and begins to unwrap his sandwich.

If *Sydney* had kissed me, I would've high-fived him back. Instead, Emma kissed me. The moment our lips touched, I was back to where I was six months ago. It was the kiss I wanted last November. It felt like everything that happened this week had finally brought us together again. We could start over.

Then I realized the truth. She wasn't kissing me because of who I am. She had that chance last fall. Emma just needed something that would create a huge ripple, and she didn't care if it hurt my future. But more than that, she didn't care if it hurt *me*.

"All morning, people have been asking about you and Sydney," Tyson says. "Dude, how could you leave me hanging like that?" He takes a large bite of his sandwich.

"How did everyone find out?"

"Her convertible is hard to miss," he says. "No offense, but what were you doing in her passenger seat?"

This must be what it's like to live in Sydney's orbit. People notice everything you do and then gossip about what they saw. Even though it's happening to me now, it's not *about* me. I'm just a tiny satellite getting pulled in by Sydney's gravity.

I look across the length of the empty football field. If Emma was coming, she would've been here by now.

* * *

AFTER LUNCH, I have Word Processing ı with Mr. Elliott. The class has three long tables, all lined with desktop computers. I press the green power button on my computer and then lean back in my chair while it boots up.

Two scenarios play out in my mind. One is that Emma didn't come to the tree for lunch because she's still too mad or embarrassed. The other scenario is that Emma left school and went home to investigate Facebook alone. But since Kellan wasn't at lunch either, they're probably together. As angry as Emma may be, I can't imagine her pulling Kellan into this.

Mr. Elliott walks up to my computer and drops a blue slip onto my keyboard. "You need to head to the front office."

Again? But why this time? The slip has my name written just above the secretary's signature. The last few class periods of the day are all circled in dark black ink.

Paranoia hits me. What if Mr. Elliott has been monitoring Emma's computer and he knows what we've been doing? A computer geek might know how to do that. Maybe *that's* why Emma never made it to lunch. Maybe they nabbed her, but she wouldn't give up my location!

As calmly as possible, I ask, "Do you know what this is about?"

"All I know," Mr. Elliott says, scratching a flaky patch on the side of his head, "is you can take your stuff with you because you won't be coming back."

* * *

I CAN ALREADY VISUALIZE my parents—brows furrowed and arms crossed—waiting for me in the principal's office. The school psychologist will be there, and maybe a physics or history teacher to share their perspectives. Emma and her mom will be sitting in chairs, and Martin too, looking like he'd rather be anywhere else.

"Playing with your futures," the principal will say, shaking his head with disapproval. "Do you have any idea how dangerous that is?"

The teachers will lecture us about the potential repercussions, not only to us, but to the entire future of mankind.

"There you are!"

Sydney is standing outside the front office, grinning excitedly. She's wearing a light pink button-down shirt, jeans, and sandals. She rises onto her toes and offers a flippy little wave.

I can't help smiling back. "What are you doing here?"

Sydney points to the blue slip in my hand. "How do you like your get-out-of-jail-free card?"

"This was *you*?"

She winks at me. "You're welcome," she says, then takes the paper from my hand and opens the office door.

Mrs. Bender, the secretary, greets us from behind the counter. "All I need are your blue slips and you're good to go."

Sydney reaches across the counter, and her jeans pull tight around her perfectly shaped body. "Here they are, Mrs. B." Then she turns toward me, loops her arm into mine, and leads us out into the hallway.

"Got everything you need?" she asks. "We'll be gone until the end of school."

I'm having a hard time focusing with her body so close to mine. Also, the top two buttons on her shirt are undone.

"Where are we going?" I ask.

"Errands!"

My textbooks for tonight's homework are in my backpack. I'm not sure about reading assignments for my afternoon classes, but I can call people for those. I still don't know why we're being allowed to go, so I want to get out of here before anyone realizes there's been a mistake.

While leaving the main building, Sydney explains our mission. As president of Student Council, she has to pick up items for several year-end events. The vice-president was set to run the errands with her, but he sprained his ankle in gym and had to back out. To fill his spot, Sydney chose . . . *me*!

"I didn't know Student Council had this much power," I say. "Can you get out of class whenever you want?"

"You have to be careful. But if the school views it as a learning experience, they'll approve it," she says. "We have a lot of errands to run today, so I drove this bad boy." She taps the rear bumper of a black Jeep Cherokee SUV.

"Is this yours?" I ask. Yesterday's convertible seemed more her style.

"It's my sister's," she says. "But she and her fiancé swapped with me for the day. They live down the street from us, so it's no big deal. We do it all the time."

I walk to the passenger side and climb in. On the seat between us is a clipboard with a to-do list.

"Buckle up," she says, starting the engine. "For the next few hours, your muscles are mine."

* * *

I PICK UP a silver and black business card tucked into the drink holder. "Electra Design?"

"That's one of my dad's companies," Sydney says. "They do graphic design work."

Electra Design.

"He's always starting new businesses," Sydney adds. "My mom tells him he's a workaholic and that he needs to hire more people to help him."

He's going to hire *me*. Someday, I'm going to work at Electra Design . . . for her dad.

We pull into the same shopping center as GoodTimez Pizza, but drive across to the opposite end. Sydney backs into a parking spot in front of Trophy Town and then cuts the engine. We hop out and I help her raise the rear window and lower the tailgate. She leans in to smooth out a blue tarp in back, and I can't help catching a glimpse down her shirt. She's wearing a pale pink bra, almost the same color as her shirt. And Tyson would be happy to know that her breasts look mind-bogglingly real.

"Next Tuesday night is the sports banquet," Sydney says as we walk into the trophy shop. "We have to pick up a bunch of awards here. The weird part is, I already know I'm getting a trophy for tennis. But I'll just stash it in my closet with the others. It feels so egotistical to put trophies all over your room."

I don't tell her I kept my T-ball and soccer trophies up for years after I stopped playing.

In the middle of the store is a three-tiered trophy display. There are different colored columns to choose from in varying heights and configurations. Each trophy is topped with a gold sports figurine: baseball, basketball, bowling, even darts.

Sydney scrolls down her clipboard with a pencil. "Did you ever play a sport?"

"Baseball and soccer when I was younger," I say. "In middle school, I got really into skating. What about you? Other than tennis, of course."

"I play soccer in the fall."

"Are you any good?" I ask, but I know she is. Several times each season, she makes it onto the front page of the *Lake Forest Tribune*'s sports section. She's either stealing the ball, kicking a goal, or running with her hands in the air.

"I'm not bad," she says. "But I'm not a crazy jock like my sisters."

A short man with glasses and receding hair asks if we're from the high school. Sydney signs an invoice, and he helps us load three boxes of plaques and trophies into the back of the SUV. Then we're off to order flower arrangements.

"My sisters played tennis in high school," Sydney says. "For a while, they were ranked first and second in the county."

"At the same time?"

"They're ridiculously competitive with each other," she says, slowing at a light. "They're identical twins, but they argue all the time."

Identical twins?

"The crazy thing is," she continues, "they're both engaged to law school students, and they're both planning to get married next summer."

The first time I saw my future, I had a son and two identical twin daughters. The girls looked just like Sydney. Later, we had twin boys who looked like me.

"Identical twins run in my family," she says. "My mom's a twin, too."

I don't respond. What can I say? *Guess what! We used to have twin girls, but then we lost them. Why? Because Emma didn't like her husband, and apparently you can't change one thing about the future without changing everything else. But now it seems we have twin boys. Or at least we did yesterday.*

"You're being kind of quiet," Sydney says.

She's right. I should be talking. If I want things to happen between us, I can't sit here thinking about the future. I need to stay focused on the present. Even though we're going to get married one day, I know so little about her. I have no idea what her favorite movie is or where she likes to hang out. I don't even know what makes her laugh.

"Do you want kids someday?" I ask. If Tyson were sitting behind me, he'd smack the back of my head.

Sydney smiles as she flips on the turn signal. "That's a funny question to ask on a first date."

I know she's joking about these errands being a first date, but for those words to even pop into her mind means, on some level, she considers this the beginning of a relationship. And it is!

After we drive a few blocks in silence, I ask, "What are you up to this weekend?"

"I'm playing tennis with my mom and sisters on Saturday," she says. "And then the whole family, including my dad and the fiancés, are helping out with a picnic at the prison on Sunday."

There's a prison about halfway between Lake Forest and Pittsburgh, but I've never been out there. "They have picnics?"

"Every Memorial Day," Sydney says. "It's volunteer work. At last year's picnic I made the mistake of bringing Jeremy with me. Do you know Jeremy Watts?"

"I don't think so."

"He graduated last year," she says. "He's a decent guy, but he can be a little insensitive. The whole time we were there, he pretended to be an inmate and he kept whispering things to me like, 'Can you pass the macaroni salad? I'd get it myself, but I have handcuffs on.'"

I look out the window so she can't tell I'm holding back a smile.

"They weren't even wearing handcuffs," she adds.

I can imagine Emma and me in that same situation. If I made that handcuff joke, she'd punch me in the arm and tell me to behave, but her eyes would give her away. She'd be on the verge of laughing, too.

I point up the road to Sunshine Donuts. "Want to stop? I'll buy."

Sydney looks where I'm pointing and then crinkles her nose. "Maybe later."

We drive past, and I watch the brightly colored sign recede in the side-view mirror.

46://Emma

I HAVE TWENTY MINUTES until I need to be at track, so I'm studying in the library. There's hardly anyone in here, just two freshman boys on a computer and Ms. Nesbit quietly shelving books. The pink streak in her hair is pinned back with an intricate series of barrettes.

Everything in my life feels like it's going downhill. Everything except Cody. We smiled at each other twice in the halls today, and all I could think was *he's still single in fifteen years.* Single and hot and working as an architect in Denver. While that's not near the ocean, I could learn to love the mountains.

"How did it go with the phone books?" Ms. Nesbit asks, approaching my table. "Were they at the public library?"

"They were . . . thanks." I wish I could've stayed in my Denver fantasy a few more minutes.

"It's amazing, isn't it?"

"What?" I ask.

"The resources we have available today," she says. "You're a junior, right? So you've probably been researching colleges, but you can also look for summer jobs, camps, even internships at a library. You can plan your whole future right here."

I smile weakly. Yes, it feels great to plan your life when you believe everything can turn out fine. But what about when you're shown, again and again, how little control you have over anything? No matter what I do to try to fix my future, it doesn't work.

After Ms. Nesbit returns to her books, I watch the freshmen laugh at something on the computer, and it occurs to me that I've been using Facebook the wrong way. It's not about automatically *having* control. It's about taking control with the resources you have.

* * *

WHEN I GET TO TRACK, I explain to the coach that I had to miss the past two practices because of female problems. It's not a total lie. I was married to a jerk and had to get rid of him, and then I found out Kellan is about to get pregnant.

We start practice on the field with the whole team standing in a wide circle doing stretches. With my hands on my hips, I lean back and hold it for five seconds. Next to me, Ruby Jenkins is bent forward with her forehead touching her knees. She's telling me how she's going to skip school tomorrow even though she's not a senior. I'm only partially listening because, across the circle, Cody is smiling at me.

When we stop stretching and head toward the track, Cody jogs up beside me.

"You weren't at practice yesterday," he says.

He was looking for me?

"I was with a friend," I say, vaguely enough to let him wonder if that friend was a boy.

I look down at the ground, noticing how our legs are perfectly in sync.

Now, Emma Nelson, it's time to use your resources.

"We drove into Pittsburgh to check out some buildings," I say. "I'm fascinated by the architecture there."

"I'm thinking about taking an architecture class at Duke next year," he says.

Before I can stop myself, I blurt out more from his Facebook page. "I'm interested in wind and solar energy and how they can relate to architecture."

The second I say it, it feels like I've gone too far. But then Cody squints up at the sun and says, "I never thought about that."

I exhale. "You should. It's the wave of the future."

Cody stops and reaches into a pocket on his shorts. "I found something near the locker-room water fountains, and I thought it might be yours."

When he opens his fingers, he's holding my gold necklace with the tiny *E* pendant. I touch my hand to my collarbone. I've worn that necklace every day for eight years. I can't believe it fell off and I didn't notice.

Cody spills the necklace into my hand. As I watch him jog away, I remember what Josh said yesterday, about how I dumped Graham and now I'm moving on to Cody. What Josh doesn't understand is that Cody isn't just some guy I suddenly noticed. I've had a crush on him for a long time. I'd be crazy not to respond when I have his attention.

* * *

DRIVING HOME, I think about what happened yesterday on Facebook. By insisting I would never live in Ohio, my future shifted to London. Just thinking differently can change everything.

I'm obviously not happy with Kevin. But instead of tracking him down like I did with Jordan, maybe I can promise myself that one day when I meet Kevin Storm, I won't marry him.

I slow at a light and glance around to make sure no one is watching.

"One day," I say quietly, "I'm going to meet Kevin Storm, but I will not marry him."

The light turns green and I step on the gas.

I say it again, louder this time, and then add, "No matter what!"

47://Josh

WE'RE IN THE PARKING LOT of Sam's Club, a discount superstore ten miles outside of town. I lower the tailgate of Sydney's Jeep Cherokee and hoist myself in. The back is already crowded with supplies, and I have to duck forward to keep from banging my head.

"Ready?" she asks.

I hold out my hands and she lifts a bulk-size bag of Cheetos out of the shopping cart. She tosses it to me. Then she passes me two bags of pretzels, followed by Doritos. While she sets cases of soda onto the tailgate, I shift around the rest of the cargo to make room.

"What banquet's this for?" I ask.

Sydney lifts up a twelve-pack of Mountain Dew and holds it out for me. "These aren't for school."

I slide the soda to the back of the bed. She hands me another twelve-pack and I fit it tight against the first one, then pull at a corner of the blue tarp that's bunched underneath.

"Usually the Student Council errands take longer," she says, "but we plowed through them so fast I figured we had time for an extracurricular run."

All afternoon, I've been pushing carts, lifting boxes, and loading things into the Cherokee. And that's fine. I won't complain about spending time with Sydney Mills. I don't even mind assisting her on a personal errand, but it would have been nice to know when we made that switch.

I hop onto the pavement. "Is this for that prison party?"

"Prison *picnic*," she says, closing the tailgate. "But no. It's for my friend's bonfire tomorrow night."

I wipe my forehead with the back of my hand and climb into my seat. When she starts the engine, I lower my window halfway down.

"You can't just have alcohol at a party, or people get too drunk," Sydney explains. "You need something for them to snack on."

All week, people have been buzzing about this bonfire. Tyson is using his dad's pickup to help some senior skaters haul firewood out to the lake.

"Also, if the cops bust the party, you want to have soda around," Sydney says. "Hide the beer, grab a Coke!"

I haven't put much thought into going to the bonfire because my mind's been on other things. Mainly, it's been on Sydney.

"Rick left a message on my cell phone earlier," she says, "asking if I could pick up some things for him. I was going to do it tomorrow, but since we had time this afternoon, I figured why not. Plus, I have the Cherokee today."

For the past three hours, Sydney and I have been driving around town together. At first I couldn't believe she picked me. Every time our elbows bumped or fingers touched, I felt electricity in my whole body. But after a while, things calmed down. Maybe I was expecting an instant connection. Although we do end up together, right now we barely know each other. I'm just the guy who spoke up in class when her ex was acting like a dick.

"If you don't mind," Sydney says, "can we drop off the bonfire stuff before I take you home? It's on the way."

"That's fine."

"Have you ever been to Rick's?"

"Rick who?" I ask. And then I realize who she's been talking about. "*Rick Rolland?*"

"His house is beautiful," she says. "It's right by the lake."

"Are you talking about that guy from Mr. Fritz's Peer Issues class?"

"That's right! His parents already left for the long weekend, so he's throwing the . . . oh . . . right." Sydney turns toward me with an apologetic look. "Rick and I used to go out, but that's totally in the past."

"That's . . . no . . . it's fine."

"I know he can seem like a jerk," she says, "but he's actually a decent friend."

As Sydney merges onto the highway, I lower my window the rest of the way.

* * *

SYDNEY TAKES THE TURNOFF for Crown Lake, and then a quick left on a hard-packed dirt road. As we circle the lake, I watch for the house she and I one day live in, but I don't see anything that resembles the photos on Facebook. Maybe our home hasn't even been built yet.

We turn onto Rick's gravel driveway, stopping in front of a redbrick house with a dense forest of pine trees behind it. Sydney honks her horn twice and then shuts off the engine.

"We can wait out here," she says.

When Rick doesn't come out, Sydney pulls her cell phone from her purse and hits a few buttons.

I hope Rick's family moves away by the time Sydney and I buy our house.

"No answer," Sydney says. She sets her phone on the dashboard. "I'll be right back."

She runs up the brick walkway, turns the doorknob, and lets herself in. As she disappears into the house, I stare at the closed door.

I can't imagine casually walking into the house of someone I used to date. I try to picture the look on Rebecca
Alvarez's face if I walked in her front door without knocking. I guess people in Sydney's orbit operate differently.
For them, it's not weird to go out with someone, break up,
and then help them throw a party.

Sydney comes out first, leaving the door open behind
her. Rick emerges a moment later and looks directly at me.
He's wearing a gray T-shirt and shorts and even from here
I can tell his calves are three times as big as mine. When he
gives me a nod, there's no hint of jealousy or cockiness, or
even that he recognizes me from Peer Issues the other day.

I open the passenger door and step outside. Standing
on the driveway with Sydney and Rick, I feel like the
skinny little brother who tagged along for the ride.

"Syd tells me you helped her with the Sam's Club run,"
Rick says. "That's cool."

He calls her Syd.

"No problem," I say.

Rick turns away and I know exactly what he's thinking.
This guy's not a threat. Or maybe that's unfair. Maybe he
doesn't look threatened because there really is nothing left
between him and Sydney.

I grab two twelve-packs of soda and carry them into
Rick's house. I set them just inside the front door, next
to five kegs of beer. Sydney brings in the chips, and Rick
carries six cases of soda as if the cans were empty. When

we return to the Cherokee, he gives me a low five while Sydney closes up the tailgate.

"I'll be back in a minute," she tells me. "Rick needs to find his wallet."

Sydney and Rick walk away together. I climb into my seat and shut the door. For the next couple of minutes, I try not to think about Sydney being in Rick's house. I know they're not making out in there. I'm sure of it! But I'm still not used to their world and its relationship rules.

I touch Sydney's cell phone on the dashboard. I've never used a cell phone before, but I wish I could call my brother right now. *Just tell me what to do because I have no idea.*

When Sydney hops back in, she greets me with a smile.

"Rick's cool," she says, removing a pair of sunglasses from the visor. "I'm glad we're friends again."

With her sunglasses on and her hair spilling around her shoulders, Sydney looks content with whatever life tosses her way. It's the exact opposite of how I feel. I know that someday she and I will own a house out here and go on fancy vacations. But something amazing must happen between now and then because, at this moment, we don't feel right for each other. If we started dating now, I can't imagine things lasting through the summer.

48://Emma

I SHUT MY BEDROOM DOOR and dial my dad's number.

"This is the Nelson household," Cynthia's voice says. "Sorry we missed your call. Please leave a message after the beep."

There's a low tone, followed by two short beeps.

"Hey, Dad . . . it's Emma." I pause and close my eyes. *You need to do this.* "Maybe you're busy with the baby, but I wanted to tell you I'm sorry for what I said yesterday, and for not thanking you yet. I really do like the computer. I've just been . . ." I can't wimp out and leave this on his machine. I need to speak with him live. "Can you please call me back?"

I hang up and try to imagine who will hear my message first. I hope it's not Cynthia. She's always been nice, but I want to keep some things personal between my dad and me.

"Dale," I imagine her saying as she rocks the baby on her shoulder. "Your daughter left you a message."

Or maybe she'll say your *other* daughter. I hope not. I hope she just calls me Emma.

* * *

THE FIRST THING I CHECK on Facebook is the status of my relationship. I'm no longer married to Kevin Storm, and my new husband's name is Isaac Rawlings. I work for the University of South Carolina. It doesn't say what my job is, but there's a link to something called Marine and Coastal Services. My picture has me nuzzling my cheek against a golden retriever, and my hair is long and curly.

Then I read my first entry.

> **Emma Nelson**
> It's official. As of today, I've dropped Rawlings from my name. Isaac may have gotten the dining room set, but I'm taking the couch and my name back. Only now I have to find a home to put it in. (The couch, that is.)
> 4 hours ago · Like · Comment

I lower my head and rub my eyes. It's been less than a week since Josh gave me that CD-ROM, but have I done anything good with it? Maybe Josh was right and I shouldn't have gotten rid of Jordan Jones so quickly. Or maybe I should've stuck it out with Kevin. It wasn't perfect, but every couple has hard times. Now I'm married to Isaac Rawlings, and we're already getting divorced.

Even if I could reverse *everything*, I don't know which life I'd want to go back to. And I've caused so many ripples by now, there's no way to recover any of the exact same futures. If I go to Tampa State, where I was supposed to meet Jordan, I'll never feel comfortable around him knowing how things once turned out.

I don't even *want* to know where I meet Isaac Rawlings. Once I make up my mind not to marry him, I'll just wind up in another bad marriage.

I glance at my Friends category. This time, I only have one hundred and fourteen friends. I scroll down to the *J*s, but there's still no Josh.

I'm scrolling back up through my friends when I see the name Cody Grainger. My heart starts racing. Something *did* change between us today! In his photo, he's wearing a sports jacket and tie and his hair is brushed neatly to one side. I click on his name and—

> **Cody Grainger**
> Getting ready to deliver a lecture in Zurich. That was a mighty long flight from Tucson.
> 2 hours ago · Like · Comment

I read through his last several statements. Cody now

lives in Arizona. He's a professor of architecture, special-
izing in wind and solar energy. He speaks all over the
world. Two weeks ago, he visited the White House and
spoke before Congress. And best of all, he's still single.

In Cody's last future, he merely worked in this field.
Now he's a leading expert. And it's because of me! What I
told him about architecture today must have jump-started
his career. That is too bizarre to even *think* about.

Cody doesn't have any other photos, but on his information page he has a list of random things he likes.

> Spicy Mexican Food, Duke Alum Activities, Drive-In
> Movies, Guitar, Red Wine, Quoting Wayne's World

I wonder if I should add Duke to my list of college
choices. That would be cool.

I can't believe Cody likes *Wayne's World* so much. I went
to see that movie with Josh and Tyson a few years ago.
Tyson was howling the whole time, popping Junior Mints
and shouting at the screen. Josh and I couldn't believe
how stupid it was. We kept ourselves entertained mainly
by watching Tyson.

But if Cody can quote *Wayne's World* fifteen years from
now, and if I want to move things along with him, I need
to get my hands on that movie as soon as possible.

* * *

"Wayne's World?" asks the woman in the video store. "I just reshelved that ten minutes ago."

She points me toward the comedy section. I quickly locate the movie, return to the counter, and hand her my video card.

"'It will be mine,'" she says, grinning as she types in my name. "'Oh yes. It will be mine.'"

I have no idea what she's talking about. "Excuse me?"

The woman tips her head. "You haven't seen *Wayne's World* before?"

"I saw it in the theater, but I didn't—" Then I get what she's doing. "You're quoting from the movie! Was that Wayne or Garth?"

"Wayne, I think. My boyfriend says it all the time."

"He does? So people think that line's funny?"

She stares at me like I'm insane. "It's due back in two days."

I thank her and hurry out the door.

49://Josh

IN THE SMALL employee break room, Tyson's dad brings in two paper plates, each with a slice of pepperoni pizza.

"I know you said you weren't hungry," he says, setting a plate next to my history textbook, "but everyone has room for one slice."

I like Tyson's dad. Maybe it's because he raised Tyson by himself, but he's more approachable than most fathers. When I showed up an hour ago claiming to need a place to study, he didn't question me even though no one comes to GoodTimez for peace and quiet. He simply cleared the newspapers from the back table and asked if I wanted anything to eat.

"Will the TV bother you?" he asks, sitting in a folding chair across from me.

"No, that's fine." I flip a page in my textbook and take a bite of pizza.

Tyson's dad leans forward and presses the power button on the TV. Two men appear on CNN, arguing about President Clinton and sex.

"Weren't they talking about this the last time I came back here?" Tyson's dad asks.

I smile. "I'm sure they're almost done."

After Sydney dropped me off, I tried studying in my living room so I could keep an eye on Emma's driveway. I don't want to spend another day getting ignored by her. It's not fair for either of us. We need to talk about what happened yesterday.

But then, when Emma did get home from track, I sat frozen on my couch as she walked inside. A short while later, she got back in her car and sped off again. That's when I grabbed my backpack and skateboard and headed to GoodTimez.

"What are you studying?" Tyson's dad asks.

"Vietnam." I take another bite of pizza and then rub my fingers on a napkin. "There's going to be an essay question on the final about the domino theory."

"I remember the domino theory," he says. He watches a few more seconds of the men arguing on TV. "If we don't stop something bad from happening, it'll keep spreading until it's nearly impossible to do anything about it."

"I think that's it."

"Even with our ability to look back on that war," he says, "there's no way to know for certain what was lost and what was saved. But that's how it is. History's a bitch when you're in the middle of it."

Tyson walks in, setting his skateboard against the wall.

"What's up, Mr. Mills?" he says, saluting me. "Dad, did you just say 'history's a bitch'?"

"We were talking about Josh's essay," his dad says. "Speaking of homework, where the hell have you been?"

Tyson smiles mischievously. "With a friend. Since when do you track my every move?"

Tyson's dad balls up a napkin and chucks it at him. "Just finish your homework, T-bone, and then I need you out on the floor. You can help, too, Josh. Earn your keep."

* * *

GOODTIMEZ PIZZA has yellow booths and orange tables on one side of the restaurant and an arcade on the other. But in the very center is the reason every kid in Lake Forest wants to have a birthday party here. Three plastic tube-slides—red, blue, and green—spit the kids into a rainbow-colored pool of plastic balls.

Every few weeks, after the restaurant closes, the pit is emptied so the balls can be sanitized. Tonight, following orders, I stay to help. Tyson squeezes through a vertical strip in the netting around the ball pit and immediately sinks to his knees. He dips a white bucket into the balls and then pushes it back through the netting. I hold open a large black trash bag and Tyson overturns the bucket, letting the balls pour in.

"So nothing happened today when you were with Sydney?" Tyson asks, scooping up another bucketful of balls. "Maybe you should bring her to lunch tomorrow. I'll see what I can do to help push things along."

The other workers are cleaning tabletops, vacuuming, and emptying tokens from the video games. The music is pumped too high for them to overhear us, but I'm still not comfortable having this conversation.

"It's too early," I say quietly. "We barely know each other."

Tyson empties another bucket into my bag. "Dude, she pulled you out of school. I think she *wants* to know you."

"Maybe." I set the full trash bag off to the side. "But maybe I'm not ready."

Tyson opens the net just enough to ricochet a green ball off my forehead. "Then get ready! We're talking about Sydney Mills. It's my *dream* to be the guy who's friends with the guy who's hooking up with her."

I shake open a new trash bag. "Wouldn't you rather be that guy yourself?"

Tyson thinks about it. "Nope. Too many people talk about you."

I pick up the green ball from the floor and drop it into the trash bag. "Not to mention, it looks like you and Kellan are getting back together."

Tyson doesn't respond.

"Don't worry," I say. "I'll let Kellan tell Emma about it, if she hasn't already. But you should be prepared. Emma's going to want to have a long talk with you about—"

"About not hurting Kellan, I know." Tyson leans his back against the cushioned border of the ball pit. We've emptied enough so that his knees stick up like two islands in front of his chest. He looks at me through the netting. "I would *never* want Kellan to get hurt. Last time, I just wasn't ready."

"But you can understand why Emma's worried," I say. "The last time you two broke up, Kellan flipped."

Tyson picks up a red ball and sidearm pitches it into the blue slide. It rolls to the top, and then falls back into the pit.

"We like each other," he finally says. "And we've both done a lot of thinking this year. I don't know what else we're supposed to do."

There's nothing I can tell him. Tyson is struggling with whether or not to let himself fall for someone he's already fallen for. My situation is different. I'm supposed to be falling for Sydney, and everything appears to be lining up for that to happen. But when I think about my future, I'm not sure that's where I want it to go.

* * *

THE PORCH LIGHT is on when I get home. I set my skateboard against the front door and reach into my pocket for the key. I can hear my parents talking to each other inside. They probably won't say a word to me when I go in, but Dad will glance at his watch, letting me know I cut it close.

Emma's house is mostly dark. The outside lights are off, as are the lights upstairs. From within the downstairs living room there's a faint blue glow.

I walk across the lawn between our houses, listening to the chimes on Emma's front porch. When Martin first hung them up, Emma complained that even his noises were infiltrating her life.

Stepping softly, I approach their living room window. In the center of the room, Emma is asleep on the couch, her head cushioned against the armrest. She's facing the TV, but it's angled so I can't tell what she was watching.

I miss Emma. Even if we didn't say anything to each other, even if she remained asleep, I wish I could be sitting on that couch with her right now.

friday

50://Emma

"EMMA?" my mom calls from downstairs.

I glance at my alarm clock. It's not set to go off for another ten minutes.

"Emma!"

I groan and pull the covers over my head. I fell asleep on the couch last night, and finally stumbled to my room at two in the morning. When I got upstairs, I noticed the light was on in Josh's bathroom. He takes showers in the middle of the night when he can't sleep. I considered blinking my light a few times. If he blinked back, I would have held a note to my window like when we were kids. But I decided not to bother him. Josh doesn't want to hear from me. He spent the afternoon with Sydney, taking their first steps toward a future together.

My mom's sandals click on the stairs, and I scan my

tired brain for what I could've done to piss her off. I didn't
see her at all last night. She and Martin were buying cabi-
netry out in Pittsburgh. I ate dinner and stacked my plate
and glass in the dishwasher. I even wiped down the counter before watching *Wayne's World*.

My mom is wearing a yellow dress and her hair is
pulled back with a matching headband. She's frowning,
and holding up a black videocassette.

"*Wayne's World*, Emma?"

I rub the shoulder I was sleeping on. "Is that why you
woke me up?"

"No." She flashes a different video in her other hand.
"*This* is why I woke you up."

I grab a scrunchie from my nightstand and pull my hair
into a ponytail. "Can you be more specific?"

"You ejected our *blank* tape to watch *Wayne's World*,"
my mom says, pressing her lips tight.

I shrug. Maybe I ejected a tape. I can't remember.

"We were taping *Seinfeld*," she says. "We had it
programmed."

"I'm sorry."

"We tape it every Thursday, Emma. You know that."
She looks at the ocean poster tacked above my desk, and
then back at me. "Martin and I are concerned about your
lack of respect for this house."

I sit up. "Lack of respect? What are you talking about?"

She points to the floor by my dresser. "Martin noticed

that stain right there. Emma, we just put in new carpeting. How did you already spill something on it?"

I do *not* want to talk about that. Spilling the vase water was a dumb thing to do, but it wasn't the stupidest thing I did that afternoon.

"I tried cleaning it," I say.

"You should have asked us for help. We have products that lift stains—"

Wait a second! "What was Martin doing in my room?"

My mom sighs. "He was just measuring with the contractor."

I leap out of bed and tug my shirt down over my hips. I'm not in the mood to fight, especially after the arguments with Josh and my dad, but I can't leave this one unchecked.

"It's for his office," she adds. "But that's not until after you graduate."

"This is crazy!" I say, my pulse racing. I hold my hands near my eyes, almost as blinders. "This has been my room for sixteen years and it's *still* my room. Maybe Martin has designs to turn it into his office someday, but he does not have my permission to enter whenever he wants."

My mom sets both videos on top of my dresser.

"I'm sorry about *Seinfeld*," I say, opening a drawer and pulling out a green T-shirt and jean shorts. "I'll call around to see if anyone taped it. But you have to tell Martin to stop plotting his takeover."

My mom looks into the distance like she's fending off tears. "It's been an adjustment for all of us," she says quietly.

I consider telling her it was an adjustment when she and my dad divorced, and her brief marriage to Erik was another adjustment. I'm tired of adjustments.

"Just tell Martin to stay out of my room," I say.

* * *

Relationship Status It's Complicated

That's my future this morning. It doesn't say I'm married. It doesn't say I'm single. Now I'm a graduate of San Diego State and I live in Oakland, California.

The last thing I wrote was on Wednesday.

Emma Nelson
Hoping it doesn't rain this weekend.
May 18 at 6:44pm · Like · Comment

My photo is black and white, almost a silhouette. I'm playing the saxophone in front of an open window, and my hair is shoulder-length.

I click open my list of Friends and start scrolling down. Cody is there. He's wearing a different tie, but he looks basically the same as yesterday. I scroll down to the Js, but there's still no Josh.

I click back to my main page. I just wrote something twelve seconds ago!

> **Emma Nelson**
> I'm doing some emotional housekeeping and letting go of things I've held onto for too long. Starting with my password. I've used the same one for fifteen years. Just waiting for a new word to reveal itself.
> 12 seconds ago · Like · Comment

I'm getting rid of *Millicent*?

Clarence and Millicent represent everything good about my friendship with Josh. And now I want to let go of that? Did I ruin our friendship forever all because I kissed him? Or is it because I didn't have a clear answer when he asked *why* I kissed him?

Hang on! I can't change my password. That's how I've been able to log on to Facebook. And I *need* to be able to get onto Facebook. My relationship is complicated now. There's no mention of a career. Even though I'm not telling much, I imagine at some point I'll start revealing again. If I can't learn the details of my life, then I won't have a chance to repair things.

"Emma!" my mom calls, startling me. "Martin needs to make a work call. Can you sign off now?"

"No, I—"

"This is what we were talking about," she warns. "We're

getting another phone line soon, just for the Internet. But for now, you need to quit."

As I close my screen, I think about that photo of Kellan, Tyson, Josh, and me at GoodTimez that I tore up the other day. I hurry over to my trashcan, hoping Martin didn't empty it when he was in here. And there, underneath several crumpled tissues, are the jagged pieces of the photograph. I pick them out of the garbage, one by one, and cup them in my palm.

Maybe Josh and I aren't going to be friends in the future, but I can't throw away these memories. I open my top drawer, slide the pieces of the photo into my journal, and then close my dresser again.

51://Josh

IT'S SENIOR SKIP DAY. With a quarter of the students gone, the hallways feel uncomfortably wide and open. They're also quieter, making it too easy to get lost in my thoughts.

As I walk to third period, I slide my shoulder against the locker doors and think about time. If I could, I'd travel back six months to the night I tried to kiss Emma, and I wouldn't do it. She would still hug my arm for warmth as we walked through the cemetery, but when we got back to her car with Tyson and Kellan, there would be no awkwardness between us. If I couldn't go back that far, I'd return to Emma's porch the day she set up her new computer, and I wouldn't give her that CD-ROM. Then she never would've discovered Facebook. While we still wouldn't be as close as we once were, at least we'd be talking.

I continue down the hall until a voice behind me says, "There you are!"

I take a shallow breath, and turn around.

"Isn't this weird?" Sydney motions at the surrounding hallway. "It's like no one's here today."

She really is beautiful, with her light brown hair and amber eyes. She could be featured in one of the magazines Emma and Kellan flip through for the quizzes.

"Are your arms tired from yesterday?" Sydney asks. She reaches forward to squeeze my bicep. Thankfully, I did my extra push-ups today. "I worked you hard."

"Not a problem," I say, though my arms are pretty sore. "What about you?"

Sydney lets her shoulders and arms droop forward. "I was exhausted when I got home."

The two-minute warning bell rings and I'm grateful for the interruption.

"Where are you eating lunch?" Sydney asks, glancing at her phone.

I'm going to my usual spot at the oak tree, but I'm not sure I should invite her to join me. That's what Tyson suggested, but Emma may be there, which would be more awkwardness than I can handle right now.

"If you already have plans," Sydney says, "we can have lunch some other time."

She deserves an explanation. "It's not that I have plans," I say, "but there's been some tension with one of my friends, and I'm hoping to talk to her about it today."

Sydney momentarily looks away. I shouldn't have used the word *her*.

"That's good," she says. "I mean, that's sweet of you."

On Facebook, Sydney and I seem happy together. Even though we're different people now, we must become more similar over time. Maybe Emma was right and I pushed things too soon.

"This is going to sound weird," Sydney says, looking down. "Last night I was telling my sister, Haley, what we did yesterday, and about how much fun I had hanging out with you."

"Thanks," I say. "I had fun, too."

She sighs, and then looks up at me with a half-smile. "But when I told her I took you out to Rick's house, she called me an idiot. If that put you in an uncomfortable position, I just want to say I'm sorry."

I give a slight shrug but don't say anything. I was definitely not expecting an apology.

Sydney smiles bashfully. "Haley would probably say I'm being an idiot again for asking this, but do you want to come with me to that bonfire tonight?"

"The one at Rick's house?"

"It's not actually *at* his house," she says. "It's down by the lake."

Shana Roy bursts over. "Hey, Syd!" After a brief glance

at me, she holds her palm out to Sydney. "I need some gum or mints. Do you have any?"

As Sydney digs through her bag, I try to figure out what I'm going to say about the bonfire. If we aren't supposed to get together this early and I go with her, am I forcing things beyond the breaking point? But if I try to slow things down, will they ever pick back up again?

Thankfully, there's a way to find out. Whatever answer I give, I can go onto Facebook after school and see the repercussions. I can use Emma's emergency key and check while she's still at track. I know her email address and password, so I'll just take one quick peek and decide if—

No! If I really wish we'd never discovered Facebook, then that's how it has to be from now on. As far as I'm concerned, Facebook never existed. And if that's true, and Sydney Mills was asking me to a bonfire, I'd be stupid to say no.

Shana folds a stick of gum into her mouth and then waves goodbye. Once she's gone, Sydney smiles at me. "So do you want to go?"

"Let's do it," I say.

* * *

I UNWRAP my second sandwich. Emma lays a slice of yellow cheese on an apple wedge. She and Kellan arrived at lunch together, but Emma hasn't said more than a few words since she sat down.

Kellan throws a french fry straight at Tyson, smacking him in the chin.

He picks the fry out of his lap and pops it in his mouth. "Don't stop till you make it."

Kellan aims another one carefully and Tyson opens his mouth. The fry rockets at his face and—

"Bull's-eye!" Kellan throws her hands in the air.

Tyson coughs twice and gives her a thumbs-up.

Emma peels off another slice of cheese, and offers it to me. "If you want it."

I'm not a fan of plain cheese, but I take it anyway.

"Wow!" Tyson looks between Emma and me. "Did you two actually acknowledge each other and exchange cheese? This is a big moment. Does anyone have a camera?"

Kellan bounces a fry off his forehead. "Leave them alone."

"But this is how it all begins," Tyson says, dipping the fry in Kellan's ketchup. "The next thing you know he's offering her a bite of his sandwich. And if they're not careful—"

"Tyson!" Kellan says. "Shut up."

Tyson holds out his arms. "What? They haven't said a single word—"

This time, when the fry connects with Tyson's forehead, it's slathered in ketchup. It sticks for a moment, then drops to the ground.

Kellan slaps a hand over her mouth. "I did *not* mean to do that."

Tyson laughs. "You didn't mean to throw it, or you didn't mean to rub it in ketchup first?"

Kellan heaves her backpack onto her lap. "I've got a napkin in here somewhere."

"Forget the napkin, woman," Tyson says, standing up. "I'm wiping this off on your shirt."

Kellan screams, and then sprints toward the football field. Tyson follows right behind.

"Emma," I say as soon as they're gone, "I'm so sorry about what I said the other day. I know you would never jerk me around on purpose."

Emma runs her hand over a patch of grass. "Maybe we should accept that it's been a crazy week and leave it at that."

Kellan squeals on the field as Tyson catches her. He aims his ketchupy forehead at her chest but she tears herself away and keeps running.

Yes, it's been a crazy week, but we need to talk about it. "I just didn't know what to do after—"

"I know." Emma waves off this conversation and then whispers, "Josh, listen. You're probably going to be mad at me again, but I've been looking at Facebook a little, and this morning it said—"

"Just tell me we can stop avoiding each other," I say. "That's all I care about."

Emma pulls in a deep breath like she's close to tears. I pick a blade of grass, press it between my thumbs, and whistle. Emma covers her ears, but at least she's smiling.

"Do you find me charming and lovable?" I ask when she lowers her hands. "Or are you still mad?"

Emma cracks up. "I was never mad. I was only moderately pissed."

"And now?"

She leans over and pinches my cheek. "Charming and lovable."

Tyson and Kellan walk casually back to the tree. The ketchup is now wiped across the sleeve of his T-shirt.

"Did everyone kiss and make up?" Tyson asks.

My face instantly warms.

Kellan claps her hands together. "Next question. Who's going to this bonfire? Tyson is bringing the wood, and I know I want to go."

Emma looks at me with cautious optimism.

"Here's the thing," I say, wanting to take back the next few words even before I say them. "I already agreed to go with Sydney."

"Oh," Kellan says.

Emma closes the lid on her Tupperware. "I wish I could go," she says, "but this morning my mom and I got in a fight and I should probably stay home."

"Are you sure?" Kellan asks. "I think it would be fun."

"I've got an idea," Tyson says. "We can invite Sydney

to come with us. Kellan's car can fit everyone. When I'm done with the firewood, I'll return my dad's truck and we can all go together."

Emma picks up Kellan's Sprite and takes a sip. "No, Josh needs to go with Sydney. And I'm staying home."

As Emma puts her container back in her bag, I notice that Kellan is staring hard at me.

52://Emma

I'VE HAD A LUMP in my throat since lunch, when Josh told us he's going to the bonfire with Sydney. He looked embarrassed saying that in front of me, but he doesn't even know the latest about my miserable future. The last time he saw it, I was living in London with Kevin Storm. Since then, I've divorced Isaac Rawlings, and now I have a complicated relationship in California.

Worst of all, Josh has no idea that our friendship will never heal.

I'm walking to track, but I'd rather be sitting in front of my computer, seeing if I've changed my password yet. If I haven't, then I could read as much as possible before I lose Facebook forever.

"Hey, Emma," Cody says. He's jogging across the parking lot, a gym bag slung over his shoulder. His hair is spiky with sweat and his T-shirt is stretched tight over his chest. "Looks like we're both late."

"I was walking my friend to the chem lab," I say.

Cody falls into stride beside me. "I got stuck in traffic coming back from Senior Skip Day."

"How was it?"

He shrugs. "It was boring. I'm over all of this. Now it's just a countdown until Duke. That's where I'm going in the fall."

"Oh," I say, as if the information is new to me. I actually know more about Cody's future than he does. Someday he'll live in Denver and visit the White House. And in fifteen years, he'll still be single. But right now, he loves a movie that I just watched.

"What you said reminded me of a funny quote." I wipe my palms across my shorts as I slip into an impression of Wayne. "'I thought I had mono for a year. It turns out I was just bored.'"

"Close," Cody says, a grin sliding across his face. "'I *once* thought I had mono for a year.' I didn't know you liked *Wayne's World*."

The truth is, I hated it even more the second time.

"You've seen it?" I ask.

"A few times," he says. "So, Emma Nelson's into Green Day and *Wayne's World*. I'm impressed."

Cody slings his arm loosely over my shoulders as we walk toward the field. The sides of our bodies touch the entire time. I can feel his muscular frame against mine, and he smells like aftershave.

I can't believe it, but this actually might be working.

* * *

THE COACH CALLS OUT our times as we loop around the track. Every quarter mile, I beat my personal best.

Coach McLeod blows his whistle for encouragement. "Whatever's gotten into you, Emma, it's good stuff. Keep it up!"

I keep running even though my legs are burning. I'm doing it to impress Cody, but it's also clearing my head. I'm currently fighting with Josh, my dad, and now my mom. The only person I have left is Kellan, and I have a feeling I'm losing her to Tyson again.

"Walk it off, Emma," the coach says after my final four hundred.

I'm rounding the track, my hand pressed into my side, when Cody jogs up next to me.

"Do you feel like you're going to hurl?" he asks.

I stare at him. "I don't think so."

"It's from *Wayne's World*."

I force a laugh. "Right. Of course."

"Hey, do you want a ride home? I need to drive out and pick up my class ring, but I put that bootleg tape in the car. . . ."

"Which bootleg?" I ask, stalling to give myself time to figure out what to do. My car is in the student parking lot, and I'm supposed to pick up Kellan from the chem lab and drive her home.

"Dave Matthews," he says. "But I have to talk to McLeod about tomorrow's timed trials first. So if you want, meet me in the parking lot in ten minutes. I'm the silver Toyota."

As if I didn't know.

*   *   *

"WHY ARE YOU OUT OF BREATH?" Kellan asks, setting a beaker into a metal stand. She's wearing plastic goggles and has an assortment of chemicals in front of her. Kellan completed AP Chemistry last year, but still drops into the lab to assist the teacher.

Ms. Monroe is up front with a few students. I step closer to Kellan to make sure no one hears. "I ran here from track," I say. "Cody asked me to come with him to pick up his class ring, and then he's giving me a ride home."

"Why?" Kellan asks. She spoons yellow powder into one of the beakers, and it instantly emits a putrid-smelling gas.

I step back, waving a hand in front of my nose. "Is this safe?"

Kellan pushes her goggles up to her forehead. "I'm not going to drink it. And don't change the subject. Why does Cody want you to go with him?"

I can't hold back my smile. "We've been talking recently. It turns out we have a lot in common."

As Kellan writes something on the lab chart, I study her face. I've only seen one picture of her daughter, but it was obvious that Lindsay looks so much like her.

"Let me guess," Kellan finally says. "You're asking me to drive your car home."

I reach into my backpack and dig out my keys, setting them beside the Bunsen burner. "I don't think we'll be very long. You can hang out at my house, and then I'll drive you home. Or you can take my bike from the garage if you don't want to wait."

Kellan doesn't respond.

"Please," I say. "I'll owe you big-time."

"*Huge*-time," she says, dropping my keys into her purse. "It's like riding the Tour de France from your house to mine. And I don't need to tell you to be careful with Cody. We both know he expects a lot from girls."

"We're getting his class ring," I say. "That's all. And I'll drive you home the second I get back."

"Or maybe I'll ask Tyson to come pick me up."

"Okay, what's going on with you guys?" I ask.

Kellan turns her attention to another beaker.

"Kellan Steiner!" I say. "You barely got over Tyson from the last time. You don't need any more drama."

"I know I've had my ups and downs with him," Kellan says, looking me in the eye. "I actually called that therapist yesterday to set up another appointment. I want to be serious about keeping my emotions in check."

"So it's official? You and Tyson are getting back together?"

"I didn't say that." Kellan picks up some metal tongs, but then immediately sets them back down. "But speaking of drama, and I want the truth, what's going on with you and Josh?"

I flinch. "Nothing."

"Yesterday, you didn't even want to go to lunch because he was there. And then today you were almost in tears when he brought up Sydney."

I pull my backpack over my shoulders. "People grow apart," I say, "and sometimes there's nothing anyone can do about it."

I turn and walk out the door.

53://Josh

"BEND YOUR KNEES!" I yell through cupped hands.

Up on the half-pipe, the stoner guy is about to make his first drop. I tried talking him out of it, but he's determined to impress his girlfriend. She's standing at the other end of the ramp with her arms crossed, shaking her head. With one foot on the tail of his board, and the rear wheels locked against the lip of the ramp, he slowly lifts his other leg and sets it near the front of the board.

Tyson and I are next to the ramp, sitting on our boards.

Tyson rocks from side to side. "I've never seen anyone die on a half-pipe before."

"Keep watching," I say, and then I cup my hands again. "Bend your knees!"

The stoner guy nods like he heard me. As his board begins tipping forward, he lets out a primal scream. He flies down the ramp, but he's not bending his knees. The board jets out from under him, his legs rocket into the air, and he lands hard on his back.

His girlfriend drops in from the other end, then jumps off her board and runs over to him. She helps him stagger away.

Tyson applauds. "He didn't die. I guess that's a success."

I slide my backpack over my shoulder and stand up. "I'm heading home."

Tyson laughs. "But what if he tries it again?"

I shake my head. I'm too stressed about tonight's bonfire to enjoy anything going on here. Maybe I'm worrying over nothing. Maybe this is the night Sydney and I finally click. Or maybe this is the night we part for good.

I slap Tyson's hand. "I'll see you at the lake."

* * *

I SLIDE OPEN my closet door. On the long shelf above my shirts, I keep everything I can't throw away. Skater magazines. A cast I once wore on my leg, signed by everyone I know. A shoebox of bootleg punk tapes that David gave me. I jiggle out a box of well-worn charcoal sticks and a large sketchpad I haven't touched since last year.

It feels good to hold this sketchpad again. Years ago, I wrote "TEMPLETON" in bold letters across the front. That's what I wanted to go by when I became a famous artist.

I flip open the cover and laugh at my first masterpiece: *Twenty-one Tweety Birds*. It's twenty-one pencil sketches of Tweety, but I only colored three of them yellow. I don't remember the significance of those three, but it meant something at the time.

The next page is *Toons & Tins*. The Tasmanian Devil and Porky Pig shout into tin-can telephones, frustrated that they can't understand each other, with spittle flying everywhere. Seriously, what the hell was I on?

A few pages later, I turn the sketchpad on its side.

At the beginning of my freshman year, Emma and I were studying on her bed when I asked if I could sketch her. She set aside her book and sat patiently while I drew, but it frustrated me that I couldn't get her just right. It may have looked like her, but it *felt* like anyone.

Emma loved it, though, and she made me show it to all our friends. But I never attempted to draw anything real again. If there was one thing I should've been able to capture, it was Emma.

I flip past the next several Looney Tunes drawings and tear out the first blank sheet. I set it on top of my sketchpad, which I pull against my hip. With a broken piece of charcoal, I run a broad squiggle down the center of the page and shade a ragged patch to the right. I study it for a moment, and then add an arched horizon at the bottom. This feels like the beginning of something. I'm just not sure what.

54://Emma

THE INSIDE OF CODY'S CAR is different than I imagined. It's worn out, the seat upholstery is thinning, and the vinyl along the door is cracked in several places.

"My brother gave it to me when he left for college," he says as we pull out of the student parking lot. "I know, it's a clunker."

The fact that Cody seems embarrassed about his car is really cute. He's showing me his vulnerable side. It makes me want to burst out and tell him that one day he'll be able to buy any car he wants.

"Where does your brother go to school?" I ask.

"University of Vermont. He's into environmental causes."

Just like you someday!

Cody turns left onto Finch Road, heading in the direction

of the highway. He reaches down near my knees to open the glove compartment, which is neatly lined with cassette tapes. "Can you grab the tape labeled 'Dave Matthews'?" he asks. "That's the bootleg I was telling you about. They played near my brother's school, and he recorded it."

I pull out the cassette and push it into the tape player. A light static emits from the speakers. While I wait for the music to start, I glance over at Cody. He's such a confident driver, the way he reclines in his seat with one hand loosely on the wheel.

He merges onto the highway, and the tape begins. There are so many concertgoers talking in the background I can barely hear the music. I think they're playing "What Would You Say."

"That audience is annoying," Cody says, gesturing at the stereo. "If you're only there to get drunk and talk through the performance, you may as well go to a bar."

"My dad plays music professionally," I say. "He's always complaining about that."

Cody turns up the volume. "As a guitarist, Dave Matthews is so underappreciated. Can you hear what he's doing right there?"

I try to listen, but the quality is really poor. "It's amazing."

Cody hits the gas hard and passes two cars. We're headed in the direction of the Lake Forest Mall. Kellan and I go there a few times a year, but mostly we save our money to shop in Pittsburgh.

"Why did you have to drop off your class ring?" I ask. I can picture Cody's ring perfectly. It's silver and chunky with an orange stone in the center, the official Cheetah color.

"I'm getting it engraved with the date I'm competing in states," he says. "I know it's strange to engrave a date that hasn't happened yet, but I'm doing it for good luck."

Cody placed first in the hundred-yard dash at regionals two weeks ago. In another week he's going on to states, where he has a chance to be the top male sprinter in all of Pennsylvania.

"Maybe I'll have them look at my necklace," I say, rummaging through the small pocket of my backpack. "I wonder if they can fix the clasp."

"I'm sorry . . . the sound on this is terrible." Cody pushes the power button on the stereo. As he does, a cyclist from the bike lane swerves in front of us.

I scream. "Watch out!"

Cody jerks the car to the left. Another car honks and slams on its brakes, and I cover my eyes.

"What the hell?" Cody shouts, glancing into his rearview mirror.

In the side mirror, I watch the bicyclist plant his foot onto the side of the road. He takes off his helmet and gives Cody the middle finger.

"Look at him!" Cody says. "He almost caused an accident, and he's flipping *me* off?"

My heart is racing and my hands are trembling.

"And you should chill on the screaming," Cody says. "It didn't exactly help."

Cody pulls into the Lake Forest Mall parking lot and shuts off the engine. He steps out of the car and I get out too, leaving my backpack inside. Cody doesn't say anything about my necklace when we're in the store, and I don't mention it, either.

* * *

ONCE WE GET BACK in the car, the vibe feels better. The engraving on Cody's class ring looked perfect, and the jeweler asked him to sign a newspaper clipping that had his picture and an article about him going to states. I acted surprised when he showed it to me, but I have the same clipping in my desk drawer at home.

As Cody pulls back onto the highway, he reaches into his glove compartment for a new tape. This time, his fingers brush my knees.

"You know," he says, "my aunt and uncle's house is right up the road, and they have a killer sound system. Want to see if we can hear the bootleg better at their place?"

My stomach flutters with excitement.

"Don't worry," he adds. "They're dental surgeons and they work crazy hours. They won't be home."

"Are you sure they won't mind?"

"No, it's fine. My uncle gave me a spare key."

Cody takes a left and steers onto a road lined with McMansions and newly planted trees. He parks in front of a huge white house with a fountain in the front lawn and Roman-style columns holding up the porch.

"Nice, right?" Cody grabs the bootleg tape and steps out of the car.

If I were here with Josh, we'd both dig through our pockets for pennies to toss into the fountain. But there's no way I'd do that with Cody in his aunt and uncle's front yard.

I glance around at the houses, all gigantic and quiet. Even though no one is around, I feel the need to whisper.

"Are you sure they're not going to come home?" I ask.

Cody shakes his head. "I come here a lot."

He punches in a security code and then fits the key into the lock. As he pushes open the door, he turns and smiles at me. My stomach flips over.

55://Josh

I ARRANGE MY CHARCOAL sketches in a semicircle around me, then stand up and take a step back. Some have angular lines, some are mostly wavy, and some are very sparse. Each has a unique feel, yet they all belong together.

Through my bedroom window, I hear Emma's car pull into her driveway. I run downstairs and out the front door.

The driver's side door opens and Kellan steps out. "Were you expecting someone else?" she asks.

"Where's Emma? Is she still at track?"

Kellan's expression is a mix of concern and pity. "Probably not. I'm dropping off her car, but I'm not waiting around for her to get back."

"Did you two have a fight?" I ask.

Kellan walks toward Emma's garage, but then swivels

to face me. "Did you just ask if Emma and *I* had a fight? You guys are the ones who don't seem to be talking."

"We talked at lunch," I say.

"Barely!" Kellan continues to the side of the garage and jiggles the doorknob, but it's locked. "Josh, do you have any idea whose car she's in right now?"

I knock my shoe against a fake rock and pick up the Scooby-Doo keychain. My hands fumble as I try to fit the key in the lock. Kellan snatches it from my hand and lets herself in.

"She's with Cody," Kellan says. "That guy's an egotistical asshole, and I hold *you* responsible for this."

"*Me?*" As far as I know, Emma and Cody had one conversation in the hallway. He wasn't even her friend on Facebook.

Kellan removes a helmet from the handlebars of Emma's bike. "There's some weird competition going on between the two of you, and I don't like it," she says. She flips up the kickstand and rolls the bike toward the door.

"What are you talking about?"

"Do you really think Emma would be driving around with Cody Grainger if you were coming to the bonfire with the rest of us? But no, you're going with Sydney Mills."

I don't want to picture Emma in Cody's car.

As I follow Kellan to the sidewalk, I look down the street. I don't know what Cody drives, but as a beat-up minivan rounds the corner, I secretly hope that's him.

When I turn back, Kellan's eyes have softened. "I get that Sydney is gorgeous," she says. "But I watched you at lunch today. When you told us she was taking you to the bonfire, you didn't look like most guys would have."

"How was I supposed to look?"

Kellan lets out a shallow sigh and adjusts the strap beneath her neck. "Happy."

I don't know how to respond.

"Are you only going to the bonfire with Sydney because it feels like you should? Because she's *Sydney Mills*?" Kellan asks. "And if you say yes, I will be so disappointed in you."

"That's not what I was going to say."

"No girl, no matter how perfect she is, deserves to get hurt like that," Kellan says. "So if you're not into Sydney, you need to tell her tonight."

Kellan swings her leg over the bike and pushes forward.

I walk slowly back to my house. When I reach the front door, I hear the soft squeal of brakes. Kellan doesn't know I'm watching, but I see her stop next to Emma's car and reach for a windshield wiper. She leaves a folded-up piece of paper against the glass, and then circles back around and rides off.

* * *

I GRAB THE CORDLESS PHONE from my parents' room and head outside. When I reach the short wall surrounding the swings, I dial David's number. His machine picks up after two rings.

"This is David. I'm probably screening my calls right now, so leave your name after the beep, and we'll see if I answer."

"Hey, this is Josh," I say, weaving slowly between the swings. "You're probably in class, but if you get this—"

There's a click on David's end. "Are you still there?"

"I'm here."

"I slept through my afternoon class," he says. "But that's not something you should tell Mom and Dad."

Before I saw David's future, I would've laughed at his comment. Now I wonder how much of his life isn't for Mom and Dad—or me—to know about. Eventually, he must tell everyone he's gay because he brings Phillip to my house at the lake. In fact, one day he'll write on the Internet that he's in a relationship with a man.

With my free hand, I hold onto the chains of one of the swings. "Do you have a second to talk?"

I hear David plopping into his beanbag. "Sure. What's up?"

I can't remember why I thought calling my brother would help. There's nothing he can say if I don't reveal everything about Sydney and me and our future together. Without telling him about Facebook, it's going to sound pathetic. Who complains about going to a bonfire with Sydney Mills?

"Josh," David says, "do you understand how phones work? When you call someone, you're supposed to talk."

"I'm sorry. I'm just really confused about a girl right now."

"Emma?" David asks.

"No," I say. "Her name is Sydney Mills. She's the one I was talking about the other night."

"Wait, is she the little sister of the Mills twins?" he asks. "Dude, they were hot."

I sit down on the swing and twist to the left. Why is he saying that? Did *he* think they were hot, or is he saying *other* guys thought they were hot? If he's trying to fool me, I shouldn't have called him in the first place. I need to talk honestly with him.

"If Sydney Mills is *anything* like her sisters . . ." David lets out a low whistle. "So I'm guessing you took my advice. You saw your moment and you didn't let it pass."

"She asked me to a bonfire tonight," I say.

"Look at you go! So what's the problem?"

"It's hard to explain," I say. "She's gorgeous. And any guy in school would *love* to be with her . . . except me. And yet, I know I should."

"Is she nice?" he asks.

"She's a little self-absorbed. But yeah, she's nice."

David is quiet for a moment. "Are you worried she's more experienced than you? Because if you want, I can explain—"

"No," I say. "That's not it." I didn't call him because I'm nervous about hooking up. I'm nervous about my entire life.

"I know what your problem is," David says.

"I have a problem?"

"You're a go-with-the-flow guy," he says. "You've always been that way. And that can feel great because it means you don't have to make any hard decisions. But sometimes you need to figure out what *you* want, Josh. If that means you need to swim against the tide to get it, at least you're aiming for something that could make you very happy."

I twist the swing in the other direction.

"Where do you want to go to college?" David asks. "I know you won't have to deal with that until next year, but where are you considering now?"

I laugh into the phone. He thinks I'm going to say Hemlock State, where Mom and Dad work. But I've seen Facebook. I know where I'm going, and he's wrong. "The University of Washington," I say.

"So you'll go where your brother went," David says. "Those are some strong currents you're swimming against."

"But it's a good school."

"I know it is," he says. "But you need to pick the school *you* want to go to."

There's a beep on his end of the line, which means he has another call.

"Listen," David says. "Tonight, you need to go to the bonfire with Sydney because you said you would. But when it's over, I want you to think about something."

His phone beeps again.

"If things aren't clicking with her," he says, "maybe it's because there's someone else you'd rather be with. And if that's true, why not swim against the tide and ask her?"

Because I can't put myself through that again.

56://Emma

"THAT FEELS AMAZING," Cody groans, rolling his head from side to side.

I've been massaging his shoulders for a while now. A tank full of turquoise tropical fish is burbling, and the coffee table in front of us displays a fan of modern art books. I'm sitting on a black leather couch, while Cody's sitting on the floor, leaning back between my knees. When we first got here, he pulled two bottles of chilled water from the fridge. We listened to a few songs on the Dave Matthews bootleg, and then he slid in one of his uncle's Paul Simon CDs.

This house is amazing.

Cody is amazing.

I look at my reflection in the horizontal mirror hanging above the marble fireplace. The mirror is framed in thick bronze and probably weighs more than my dresser. If I had known this was going to happen when I woke up today, I would have worn something better than my olive-green T-shirt and jean shorts. But I suppose I could've done worse. I watch my reflection as I rub my fingers along Cody's collarbone, inside the neck of his shirt. He groans with pleasure and closes his eyes.

It feels like my future is just beginning.

"This is definitely what I needed," Cody says, turning and smiling at me. "The weight-training yesterday killed my shoulders."

I smile back at him and flex my fingers, which are starting to ache. That massage lasted a long time.

"Mine too," I say, hunching my shoulders. I unscrew the cap from my bottled water and take a sip.

"If you're done," Cody offers, "I can give you a massage back."

"Sure. Thanks."

I think about the first time Cody and I talked, and how I rested my head on his shoulder during the bus ride home from a track meet. I'd always admired him from a distance, but suddenly this perfect guy was paying attention to me. It took another year, and some knowledge of his future, but now here we are.

"Are you ready?" Cody asks. He pushes himself up from the floor and sits next to me on the couch. I turn toward the fish tank, and he starts massaging my shoulders.

It's a very different massage than the one I gave him. His hands gently touch my skin, moving slowly up my arms. He glides his fingers down my sides and then rests them on my hips. I close my eyes, feeling a light shudder in my body as his lips kiss my neck.

"You're cute, Emma Nelson," he whispers, planting a row of kisses from my collarbone up to my ear. "This is a lot more fun than when you screamed in my car on the way over."

He wraps his arm around my waist, and I tell myself to relax. I tell myself to be fun, and not that girl who screamed in the car.

This is the moment I'm supposed to turn around and kiss him back. Instead, I glance over at the mirror and realize that I don't know who I'm seeing in the reflection.

"You said you come here a lot?" I ask.

"Sometimes," Cody says, kissing down my other shoulder.

I picture that tall girl he gave his number to at the track meet. "With other girls?"

"That's sort of a personal question."

"This is sort of a personal moment," I say.

"We're just having fun."

Cody continues rubbing my shoulders. As he does, I think about the past few days. I've listened to him tell me about Duke and about teaching himself to play guitar, and I've even recited *Wayne's World* to him. But he's never asked about me. That's because he doesn't care about me for who I am. He cares about me because I've been worshipping him.

I stand up.

Cody looks at me. "What's going on?"

"I want to go home," I say.

"We just got here," he says, leaning back. His fingers are laced behind his head and his elbows are splaying out. "You should chill for a little longer."

There he goes, telling me to chill again. Just like back in the car.

Kellan's theory is wrong. When Cody jerked into traffic, then snapped at me for screaming, I didn't see my future husband. Sitting next to me in that car was a guy so different than what I'd hoped.

"I'm going home," I say.

Cody clenches his jaw, and I can tell he's pissed. I don't think many girls say no to him. "I guess I can drive you."

And get in a car with him again? "I'd rather walk," I say.

"We're three miles from your house."

I start toward the door. "I know how far away I am."

Cody follows after me and reaches for my hand. "I said I'll drive you."

"No!" I say, pulling away.

I open the front door and he grabs my shoulder, turning me around.

"Do you realize you're being a freak?" he asks.

I push his hand off me. "And yet you have no idea that you're a dick."

* * *

I WALK ALONG THE HIGHWAY facing traffic. The shoulder stays wide for half a mile before gradually narrowing. When it's no longer an option to walk on the side of the road, I cut through a section of tall grass. In the distance, beyond the railroad tracks, I see the overgrown lot where a traveling carnival used to operate during the summers.

I lift my feet high to avoid the itchy weeds brushing against my ankles. As I reach the railroad tracks, I bend down to pick thistles from my socks. When Josh and I were younger, we once biked over here with coins to set on the tracks for the train to flatten. The train never came, so we ended up searching the carnival grounds for lost treasures.

I walk across a wide area where the Ferris wheel used to stand near a rickety red Tilt-a-Whirl. Next came the taffy vendor and a game where toy guns shoot streams of water into the open mouths of plastic clown heads.

I stroll through the grounds, thinking about how ever since we discovered Facebook, I've been changing specific things in an attempt to improve my future. Jordan Jones was probably cheating on me, so I ditched him. Kevin Storm ruined my career, so I made sure we never moved to Ohio. But every time I got a new future, I still turned out unhappy.

For the past five days, I've been trying to understand why this happens to me and how I can tweak things so it won't happen again. But I'm starting to wonder if it actually has nothing to do with the future. Maybe it has everything to do with what happens now.

I step around a long plank, swollen with moisture.

Aside from Cody, most of the guys I go for are nice. Graham may have been horny, but he was never mean. And Dylan is one of the friendliest guys I know. The other day, he was checking out library books for his new girl-friend because—

Oh my god.

Dylan was getting those books because he *loves* his girl-friend. He never did those things for me because I never gave him the chance. I never told him what I was reading or what movies made me cry. I kept enough distance so I would never get hurt.

I've always protected myself when it comes to love. And maybe that's the problem. By not letting myself get hurt now, it ripples into much bigger pain later. In the future, maybe I never let my husbands see the real me either, so I never give them the chance to learn what makes me happy. Either that or I marry a conceited jerk like Cody, and then there's definitely not going to be much love.

Once I'm across the carnival lot, I step onto the broken

sidewalk. Blades of grass push through the cracks, fighting for a taste of sunlight. I've still got a long way until I'm home, but I will get there eventually.

* * *

THE FIRST THING I NOTICE when I walk into the kitchen is a note on the counter.

> *Emma,*
> *Your mom and I are having a late dinner with friends, but I'd like to take you out for ice cream tomorrow. I'm sorry I upset you by going into your room. I'll try harder to respect your space from now on.*
> *—Martin*
>
> *P.S. Your dad left a message on the machine.*

I fold the note in half and go into the bathroom to wash my face. It looks like a war zone in here with tiles torn out and pipes protruding from the walls. Along the floor, someone placed a row of delicate blue tiles, no doubt what my mom and Martin are planning to use for the remodel.

I'll have to let them know that I like what they chose.

In the kitchen, I pour myself a glass of ice water, and then push play on the answering machine.

"Hi, Emma," my dad's voice says. "I'm sorry it's taken me a while to get back to you. Things have been stressful here. We've actually been going back and forth to the hospital with Rachel. The doctors are doing tests and . . ."

My dad pauses for a breath, and I feel myself tearing up. I sent a stuffed puppy when Rachel was born, but I haven't allowed myself to think about my baby sister very much. Now I want to hold her and tell her I love her and that she has to be okay.

"Please call me back," my dad continues. "Cynthia and I would love to have you visit us for the summer. We both miss you. I miss you."

* * *

FACEBOOK IS STILL HERE in my Favorite Places.

Please keep the same password, I tell myself. *Even if it's just for right now, and then never again.*

I type in "EmmaNelson4Ever@aol.com" and "Millicent," and then press Enter.

I exhale. The password still works.

> **Emma Nelson**
> Difficult decision, but I'm considering canceling my Facebook account. I should spend more time living in the here and now. Anyone who needs to reach me knows how.
> 2 hours ago · Like · Comment

I don't check my relationship status or where I'm living. Instead, I open up my list of friends and scroll down to the *R*s, and there she is.

Rachel Nelson

In the tiny photo, my sister looks about fifteen years old, with dark brown eyes and curly brown hair just like mine. I stare at Rachel's face, then lean back in my chair, and let myself cry.

After a couple minutes, I wipe my eyes and scroll to the Js. Josh and I are friends again. He's standing in front of a jagged mountain range, a blue backpack strapped over his shoulders. His hair is shaggier than usual and he's looking straight at the camera with a huge grin. I place the arrow next to Josh's photo, but I decide not to click it. I don't want to read into things anymore. If Josh looks happy, then I should be happy for him.

Before I close Facebook, I check one final thing. I click into my Photos. At the bottom, just like before, I have an album called High School Memories. It loads slowly, but after a few minutes I see the photo of me on the day I got my driver's license. And there's the photo of Tyson and Josh using their skateboards as swords. There's the picture of my bikini butt: "The good ole days." And there, at the very bottom, is the photo of Kellan, Tyson, Josh, and me in the ball pit at GoodTimez. I lean closer to the screen. The quality isn't perfect, but I can see a spiderweb of lines where I tore the picture, and then light shadows where one day I must have taped it back together.

* * *

I UNPLUG THE CORD from the back of my computer and click it into my phone. My dad's line rings twice, and then Cynthia answers.

"Hi, it's Emma," I say.

"Hello, sweetie." Her voice sounds tired. "Your dad will be so happy you called. He's giving the baby a bottle right now. Can he call you back?"

"Of course," I say. "But he said something in his message about Rachel. Is she okay?"

Cynthia sighs heavily. "The doctors don't know why she's not gaining enough weight. It's been difficult."

I wish I could tell Cynthia what I saw on Facebook, that Rachel is going to grow up to be a beautiful girl. But all I can say is, "She's going to be fine. I know it."

"Thank you," Cynthia says, and I hear her voice catch. "I needed to hear that."

Cynthia and I talk for a few more minutes, and then she invites me down for the summer, just like my dad did. I tell her that I'm seriously considering it.

When I hang up, I slide on my flip-flops and walk outside, breathing in the cool air. A light breeze picks up, which flutters a small piece of paper tucked against the windshield of my car.

I lift up the windshield wiper and unfold the note, instantly recognizing Kellan's handwriting.

Emma,

Remember how you owe me, your amazing friend who's about to bike all the way home? Well, I'm collecting! You and I <u>need</u> to go to this bonfire. Pick me up at 8.

Love,

Kellan

I refold the paper and head back inside.

57://Josh

"IT'S NOT A DATE," I say, dipping my spoon into the turkey soup.

"Did she ask you to the bonfire?" Dad says. "Did she offer to pick you up?"

"It's still not a date," I say.

"What I don't understand," Mom says, "is why you never asked this girl out before."

Because she's Sydney Mills! I want to scream. *She's a year ahead of me and light-years beyond me.*

Instead I say, "It's complicated."

"If you're going to be dating this girl," Mom says, "we should discuss some ground rules."

I keep my eyes focused on my soup bowl. "I never said this was turning into a relationship."

"You got home a few minutes late last night," Dad says.

"I know you were helping Tyson at the pizza shop, but do you want to borrow my watch for tonight?"

He starts removing the hulking gold and silver band from his wrist, but I raise my hand.

"It's okay," I say. "Sydney's cell phone has a clock on it."

"A cell phone?" Dad says. "Well then, I don't expect you to roll in with some story about a flat tire without calling us."

"That was David," I say. He used that excuse twice for coming home late after dates with Jessica . . . or whoever it was.

Mom blows gently on her soup. "This is a three-day weekend," she says, "so your dad and I have agreed to extend your curfew by one hour."

I'm sure this is because of my comment about David moving to Seattle to get away from them. "I don't think I'll need it. I'm actually pretty tired."

"Well, if you change your mind," Mom says, "you can always call us on her cell phone."

I push back my chair. "I have to get ready."

* * *

SYDNEY CALLED from her cellphone to tell me she was running a few minutes late. One of the fiancés, I don't know which sister he belonged to, had to drop off something for her parents and borrowed her car. He just brought it back a little while ago.

One day maybe I'll meet these fiancés, and I wonder how similar we'll be. David would probably call them go-with-the-flow guys. Maybe he was right when he called me that, but I'm not so sure I want to be that kind of guy anymore. Maybe I *do* want to go to college somewhere else, like a school that specializes in visual arts. And while Waikiki and Acapulco are probably great, my dream vacation might be hiking in the mountains, or taking a train through Europe.

The doorbell rings while I'm brushing my teeth. Just like I asked them not to, I hear my parents opening the door.

I bolt down the stairs, zipping up my black sweatshirt. When I reach the front door, Sydney is standing in a sky-blue strapless dress that falls above her knees. Her hair spills down her back in waves. She's smiling and chatting with my parents while Dad examines her cell phone.

"Hello, honey," Mom says. She raises her eyebrows at me. "When you told us Sydney was pretty, you were being a little modest."

Sydney tilts her head. "Thank you, Mrs. Templeton. That's very sweet."

I take the phone out of Dad's hands and give it back to Sydney. "Ready to go?"

"It was wonderful to meet both of you," Sydney says.

I walk across the threshold and Sydney loops her arm

in mine. We start down the path, but then Dad clears his throat.

"Josh?" he calls out. "What time do you think the bonfire will be over?"

I turn back around. Haven't we already discussed this? "It's a three-day weekend. Didn't you say—?"

"You were out late last night," Mom says. "Let's stick with the regular curfew tonight. That should give you plenty of time to hang out with your friends."

58://Emma

THE ROAD TO RICK'S HOUSE takes forever. I drive slower when I reach the unpaved section, partially to avoid potholes and partially because I'm not thrilled about being dragged to this bonfire. I know Kellan is up to something. She told me she ran into Josh while dropping off my car, but she wouldn't say what they talked about.

I should have begged Kellan to cash in her favor another time. She could have driven out here with Tyson in the pickup, or taken the car she shares with her mom. But she wanted me to come with her. And knowing there's a pregnancy in her near future, I decided that a bonfire at the lake is an important place to keep an eye on her.

"It must be the endorphins from the bike ride," Kellan says, jiggling her feet in the passenger seat. "I got home, took a shower, and now I'm feeling totally refreshed."

We approach a gravel lot full of parked cars.

"Only an hour, right?" I ask.

"One hour," Kellan says. "We say hi, sit by a few fires, and if you're still hating it, we can go back to your place and watch a movie."

I almost laugh and tell Kellan I rented *Wayne's World*. But the last thing I want to admit is that I watched it to win over Cody.

I ease behind a bunch of cars. A few kids are hanging around drinking beer, but most people are heading toward a dirt path through the pine trees.

Kellan points to an open space on the right. "Park there."

At the same time, we realize that would put us two spaces from Sydney's convertible. When a truck's tires roll onto the gravel behind us, Kellan and I both glance into her side mirror.

"Tyson's pickup!" she says. "Let's park next to him instead."

I steer over and pull in beside Tyson. There's a senior guy in the passenger seat and another in the bed steadying a heap of firewood.

"Kel!" Tyson says, hopping out of the cab. "Hey, Em!"

Kellan opens her door and gets out. "We have names," she says. "Two syllables each."

The seniors slap Tyson on the back, and then they each grab an armload of logs and head toward the pine trees.

Tyson walks to the back of the truck and gathers together a stack of logs.

"Want to help?" he asks. "It's a short walk to the bon-fire pits."

Kellan crosses her arms over her chest. "Do I look like I'm built for heavy labor?"

I grab a couple logs.

"Thanks, Emma," Tyson says, shaking his head in Kellan's direction. "At least someone knows how to be useful."

Kellan lifts the tailgate of the truck, clicking it into place. "Look at me, being useful."

She skips off down the path with Tyson following. I reposition the wood in my arms, take a deep breath, and start after them.

*   *   *

THE SKY IS DEEP PURPLE with a thin streak of amber above the treetops. Most of the light down here comes from six flickering bonfires dotting the shore. On the other side of Crown Lake is the public beach. I can barely make out the shadowy outlines of the concession stand and pavilion.

"Anyone want a beer?" a guy asks. He's a senior. Scott, maybe? He pulls himself a can from a six-pack and dan-gles the rest in front of us.

"No, thanks," I say.

Kellan holds up her Sprite. If Scott gave her a beer, I

might be tempted to whack it out of her hand to keep her from drinking tonight and making any bad decisions.

Tyson eyes the cans of beer, but Kellan lowers her palm on his scalp and makes him shake his head no.

"Don't even think about it," she says. "You're driving."

"You're right," Tyson says. "My dad would murder me."

"And I'd hide the body in wet concrete," Kellan adds.

Scott shrugs and continues down the beach.

The three of us move closer to the fire. Tyson reaches for a log from a nearby pile and tosses it on. It smokes for a minute before flames start licking around the wood.

I run my fingers through the cool sand. Dozens of people are gathered around each bonfire, but I haven't seen Josh or Sydney yet. The entire time we've been here, I've watched couples peel away and head into the trees. Imagining Josh in there with Sydney makes my stomach twist up tight.

I look across the water at the quiet shore of the public beach. When Kellan and I were there the other day, I spotted Josh and Sydney's future house somewhere on this side of the lake. It's probably just a short walk down the beach. In a way, it feels sadly appropriate that the bonfire is here. Tonight, Josh will begin disappearing into a future where the only place he and I remain friends is on the Internet.

I notice Graham sitting at the next fire over, roasting two marshmallows on a long stick. As Graham pulls his stick from the fire, he catches me watching. He waves at me, and I nod back.

"There he is!" Tyson points down the beach.

I follow Tyson's outstretched arm. Two bonfires over, I see Josh. He's sitting with Sydney and her friends on a thick log. Josh is staring into the fire, his hands stuffed into the pockets of his sweatshirt.

"Josh!" Tyson shouts.

I pull my knees up to my chest and whisper, "Let's not."

"Not bother him?" Tyson says. "Seriously, if that boy's getting too A-list for us, I might have to kick his ass."

Kellan puts her hand on my back and rubs in slow circles.

"Josh!" Tyson yells again.

Josh lifts his head, but only to look out across the lake. Sydney is talking to a friend. I think it's Shana Roy, but I can only see the back of her head.

"He's kind of far away," Kellan says. "Maybe he doesn't hear you."

I grab onto Tyson's sleeve. "Just let him be, okay?"

"This'll get his attention," Tyson says. He cups his hands over his mouth and shouts, "*Yo, dumbass!*"

In a delayed reaction, Josh turns our way.

59://Josh

I WAIT FOR SHANA to start laughing again. That'll be my chance to cut into her conversation with Sydney. The drunk college guy sitting next to Shana leans in, makes some remark and . . . there she goes!

"Sydney?" I say.

She turns toward me, her lips pressed softly together.

"I'm going to say hi to my friends for a minute."

She looks down the shore to where Tyson, Kellan, and Emma are sitting in the sand around a medium-size fire. "Was that your friend who just shouted 'yo, dumbass'?"

"Tyson," I say. "I'm sure he meant it with love."

"I'll go with you," she says. She stands up and shimmies the top of her dress higher on her chest. There's no denying that she looks amazing tonight.

As we start walking, Sydney steps closer to me. "I haven't really talked to Kellan or Emma since fifth grade."

"I'll be fine," I say, both to Sydney and to myself. I know Emma will behave, but there's no telling with Kellan. Earlier this week, she was calling Sydney a skank.

We pass the largest bonfire, where twenty or thirty kids from school have gathered. Most are drinking beer, and a few are smoking. Several girls wave at Sydney as we pass, and then quickly lean into each other and whisper.

When we approach the next bonfire, Emma is resting her head against her knees. I wonder what made her decide to come here after all. She acknowledges me with a faint nod, and then gazes into the flames. Kellan is sitting beside her, rubbing Emma's back. Tyson glances at Sydney's chest, and then jumps his attention to me.

"Hey there," he says. "I didn't realize you two were here already."

"You mean the 'yo, dumbass' was for someone else?" I ask.

Tyson grins and slaps me five.

"Thanks for letting me borrow Josh for the night," Sydney says. "I know you guys are really close. Did you all drive out here together?"

Emma and Kellan don't respond, but Tyson shrugs and says, "I drove my truck. Some seniors needed help bringing out the firewood."

"Then thanks for keeping us warm," Sydney says, leaning against my arm. As she does, I catch Emma's eyes flicker in our direction.

"It's your *dad's* truck," Kellan says to Tyson. She stands

up and wipes the sand off her jeans. "So, Josh, who are you two hanging out with?"

It feels like she's challenging me, even though I'm not doing anything wrong. "We're with Sydney's friends."

"Shana's my friend," Sydney says, "but I've never met those other people before. They go to Hemlock State."

Tyson throws another log onto the fire. As Kellan looks between Sydney and me, there's an awkward silence. I shouldn't have come over here.

Finally, Sydney smiles at Kellan. "The last time we hung out was at your fifth-grade birthday party, wasn't it?"

Kellan pulls her head back. "You remember that?"

Sydney nods. "We were on the same team for the water balloon toss."

Tyson pokes at the fire with a stick.

Emma remains facing the fire, slowly rocking her chin between her knees.

"We didn't win," Sydney says, "but I take full responsibility for that. It was a bad throw."

Kellan smiles. "You're forgiven."

Tyson slides over, patting the sand next to him. "Why don't you guys sit down?"

Emma pushes herself up. "I'm getting something to drink. Does anyone want anything?"

Without waiting for an answer, she walks down the beach.

60://Emma

KELLAN APPROACHES ME at the coolers. "Are you okay?"

"I just want to leave," I say. "Has it been an hour yet?"

Kellan dips her hand into the cooler, fishing out some ice. "I'm so sorry. It was stupid to make you come out here," she says. "I was hoping things would be different."

"They're not," I say. But in truth, they'll never be the same.

Kellan throws an ice cube into the lake.

I glance over to our bonfire. Josh and Sydney aren't there anymore. Tyson is laughing at some guys who are spitting beer on the flames.

"It was a dumb idea," Kellan says, "but I was hoping you and Josh might—"

"Josh is with Sydney now," I say firmly. "Didn't you

see them? If I had a chance with him, I missed it. No, I didn't miss it. I threw it away."

Kellan stares at me, but there's nothing for her to say.

"Please," I say. "I just want to go home."

"Who's going home?" Tyson strolls over and slings one arm around each of us. "No one's going home yet. We just got here."

Kellan looks from Tyson to me.

"You should stay," I tell her. "I'm fine driving home by myself."

"No way," Kellan says, touching my hand with her cold fingers. She turns to Tyson. "We're going to head out, maybe go over to Emma's to watch a movie."

"Why?" Tyson asks. "Aren't you having a good time?"

"I'm just not feeling—" I catch a glance between Kellan and Tyson. She's not ready to leave, but she's too loyal of a friend to tell me. "I'm too tired for a movie. When I get home, I'm going straight to bed."

Kellan studies my face. "I can leave right now if you want."

"You should stay," I say. "I'd feel bad if you left."

Tyson grins at Kellan. "I can drive you home."

When I was grabbing wood from the back of Tyson's truck, I noticed a couple of rolled up sleeping bags. On their way home, what if Tyson and Kellan pull onto a side road in the middle of nowhere? What if they hop in back and unroll the bags beneath the night sky?

Ta-da. Lindsay is conceived.

"Are you okay?" Kellan asks me. "You made this weird face for a second."

I point a finger at Kellan and then Tyson. "Don't move. Seriously. Don't go *anywhere.*"

I turn and sprint up the beach.

* * *

I STOP RUNNING as I near Sydney's group.

Behind the log Josh and Sydney are sitting on, the pine trees cast huge shadows. I walk through the darkness and tap Josh's shoulder. He shifts his body around. When he realizes it's me, he smiles.

Sydney turns around, too. "How's it going, Emma?"

"Hey, Sydney," I say. "Sorry to bother you guys, but I . . ."

Everyone around the bonfire is staring at me now.

Josh scoots over to make room on the log. "Want to sit?"

"I can't," I say. "I was just wondering . . . would you mind . . . can I borrow your sweatshirt?"

As he unzips it, I lean close to his ear and whisper, "And your wallet, too. I'll bring it back in a second, I swear."

Josh must realize everyone's watching because he sets his sweatshirt on the log before slipping his wallet into it, and then he passes them both to me.

"I'll be right back," I say.

I disappear into the shadows. Draping Josh's sweat-shirt over one arm, I slowly open his wallet. I slide my finger into the fold behind his student I.D. and . . . there it is!

I pull out the condom, its wrapper creased and worn, and stuff it into the pocket of Josh's sweatshirt. Then I sneak up behind him again. I press the wallet against his side and he casually takes it.

* * *

"I'M STILL HERE," Kellan says when I get back. "But Tyson went down to spit Mountain Dew into the fire. That boy is hard to control."

Kellan tries sounding annoyed by Tyson's antics, but I know she loves it.

"So why did you want me to wait?" she asks.

I look down at Josh's sweatshirt in my hands. I feel stupid for what I'm about to say, but I don't know what else to do. "It's getting cold," I tell her, lifting the sweatshirt between us.

Kellan stares at the sweatshirt, and then at me.

"I just thought . . . you're going to need this," I say.

She raises one eyebrow like I've gone insane. When I don't move, she takes the sweatshirt and slides her arms into the sleeves. If Kellan and Tyson are going to have sex tonight, she needs to at least have the option of using protection. Of course, she may not discover the condom in time. Or she may find the condom but decide not to use it because it's too ratty. But if I can't warn her about the pregnancy, this is the best I can do.

"Is this Josh's sweatshirt?" she asks. She holds the cuff to her nose. "Have you ever noticed how Josh smells like a pine forest?"

My throat squeezes up tight. I give her a hug and say, "It's a great sweatshirt. You should put your hands in the pockets. They're *so* warm."

Then I say goodbye and walk to the path between the trees.

61://Josh

I SIT WITH MY FEET buried in the sand, my sneakers beside me. With my knees facing the fire and a thick blanket around my shoulders, I'm able to stay warm. I'm not sure whose blanket this is, but Shana was wrapped in it before. When she left with one of the college guys, I claimed it.

Sydney went up to the parking area a few minutes ago. Someone called her cell phone saying there were hot drinks available. A few of her friends are still sitting on the log on the other side of the bonfire. They're juniors like her, but I don't know their names.

The fire where Emma, Tyson, and Kellan were sitting has almost burned out. All that remains are glimmering orange embers. A few times, I saw Tyson and Kellan walking along the shore, but it's been a while since I've seen them. And I haven't seen Emma since she brought back my wallet.

I turn and look out at the water. The dark sky and the trees blend seamlessly. The lake is nearly black, with small moonlit ripples lapping toward the shore.

"Do you have room for me?" Sydney asks. She's standing above me, her fingers wrapped around a Styrofoam cup.

I take the warm cup and she sits in the sand next to me. The steam rising from the opening in the plastic lid smells like hot chocolate.

"I'll share it with you," she says, "if you'll share the blanket."

I lift a corner of the blanket and she scoots her body close to mine, wrapping us together. The voices around the bonfire settle into a hush.

Sydney holds out her hand and I give her the cup. She takes a small sip. "That was sweet of you to give Emma your sweatshirt. I always knew you were one of the nice guys."

I turn to her. "How do you mean?"

She smiles and offers me the cup. "Trust me, not every guy would give up his sweatshirt just because a girl asks."

I take a sip of hot chocolate. "Emma and I have been close for a long time."

Sydney exhales slowly, tilts her head back, and looks up at the stars.

"If you told me you were cold," I say, "I would've given my sweatshirt to you, too."

She hugs her knees against her chest.

"And to be fair," I add, "I think you're one of the nice girls."

"Unfortunately," she says, "being nice doesn't mean you get everything you want."

It feels like she's talking about us. Even though a relationship with Sydney isn't what I want, hearing her say those words makes me sad.

I pull the blanket tighter around us. If Sydney wanted to rest her head against my shoulder, I would let her. But she doesn't. So we just sit here, side by side, sharing the warm drink until it's gone.

62://Emma

I DON'T TURN ON my bedroom light or even my desk lamp as I sit in front of my computer and sign onto AOL.

"Welcome!"

I click on Facebook in my Favorite Places. The white box opens and I type in my email address and password. The moment my finger presses Enter, the monitor crackles and flashes. As the light fades, the AOL screen reappears.

"Welcome!"

When I look in Favorite Place again, it no longer lists Facebook. I turn away from the computer and stare into my dark room.

Fifteen years from now, I did exactly as I said I would. It's over.

* * *

I'M RELIEVED that my mom and Martin are still out. I head into their bathroom, where I brush my teeth and pull my hair into a scrunchie. It's strange to see myself without my *E* pendant on.

When I get back to my room, I take the broken necklace out of my backpack and set it next to the blue vase on my dresser. At some point I'll get around to having it fixed.

I change into a long T-shirt and climb into bed.

Maybe my future self really did need to focus more on the life around her. Maybe it'll help make things better. Or maybe my future self feels a connection to my current self, and she knew that *I* needed to focus on *my* here and now.

I reach over to my stereo and slide in *Kind of Blue*. My dad used to play Miles Davis for me when I couldn't fall asleep.

Outside, I hear a car drive up the street. For a moment, I think it's my mom and Martin returning from their night out, but it idles in front of Josh's house, the headlights reflecting onto my window.

I don't have to look outside to know it's Sydney's car. She's probably leaning over to kiss Josh's cheek right now. If she leans in again, he'll turn, pressing his lips against hers.

I didn't feel it coming, but suddenly tears are pouring down my face.

I'm crying because Josh is going to marry Sydney and

they're going to have a beautiful life together. And maybe I'll have an okay life, too, but I'll never meet someone like Josh again. Josh is loving and kind, and he knows me better than anyone. He knows the real me, and he likes me for who I am. Josh is . . . Josh. And now he's gone.

I press my wet face into my pillow. This is what heartbreak feels like.

63://Josh

"DON'T TURN OFF the engine until you get home," I say. "It might not start again."

Graham pulls his hand away from the ignition. "Good idea."

When I left the bonfire, I asked a few people for a ride home, but everyone was heading to other parties. Then I noticed Graham Wilde about to jumpstart his car. I helped him hook up the cables and then he offered me a lift.

When I open the passenger door to get out, Graham says, "Say hi to Emma for me."

I lean my arms against his lowered window. "Can I ask you something? When the two of you were going out, did you ever really like her?"

His headlights dim slightly, so he taps the accelerator and they brighten again. "You're her good friend, right?"

"Yes," I say. "I am."

"I did like her," he says. "But neither of us wanted any-thing serious. It was just fun, you know?"

I look away for a second. I can still see him groping Emma in the dugout.

"Emma's awesome," Graham says. "If I did want some-thing long-term, she'd be hard to top."

The headlights weaken again, and I step back from the car. Graham puts it into reverse and backs away, waving out his window.

When I open my front door, Mom and Dad are read-ing magazines, pretending they haven't been waiting up.

"That didn't sound like Sydney's car," Dad says.

"It wasn't," I say, walking up to my room.

* * *

I TURN MY RADIO to a low volume and then sit on the floor, my back against the bed. Next to me are the eight charcoal sketches from earlier.

Downstairs, there's a knock at the door. I can hear Dad answer it, followed by they voice of . . . *Tyson*? Seconds later, two pairs of feet come charging up the stairs.

"Get up!" Tyson says, flinging open my bedroom door.

Kellan stands beside him, wearing my black sweatshirt. "You heard the man!"

I put my hand on the mattress and push myself up. "What are you doing here?"

"We're here to make sure you and—" Kellan stops talking when she notices the sketches. "Did you draw those?"

"Focus!" Tyson says to Kellan. "Besides, I can't even tell what they are. Go back to drawing Tweety Bird, Picasso. Okay, so here's the deal. We're kidnapping you."

"You *and* Emma," Kellan says.

"Obviously, neither one of you were having fun tonight," Tyson says.

"Not just tonight," Kellan says, looking at Tyson. "They've been like this all week!"

"Guys!" I say. "What's going on?"

Tyson steps forward. "What we're saying is, the night's not over."

"And this time, it's going to be all four of us." Kellan puts her hands on her hips. "*Just* the four of us. We talked to your parents, and they've extended your curfew until one o'clock."

I can't believe it. "Seriously?"

Tyson nods toward Kellan. "The girl's got charm."

"Now we need to get Emma," Kellan says.

When Graham brought me home, I noticed Emma's car in her driveway. I looked up to her bedroom window, but the light was out.

"She went to sleep early," I say.

Kellan raises her hands in mock frustration. "I don't care! She doesn't have a choice."

"How are you going to get hold of her? You can't call her this late."

Tyson pulls a flashlight from his back pocket. "The four of us go way back," he says. "I know how you and Emma used to communicate."

Kellan picks up my sketchpad, then she pulls a marker from my desk, and starts writing a note.

Tyson walks to the bathroom, slides open the window, and shouts, "Emma! Wake the hell up and look outside!"

Kellan laughs as she tears the note out of the sketchpad. "Oh, there's no way her mom heard that."

I shake my head and follow my friends into the bathroom.

64://Emma

SOMEONE SHOUTED outside my window, pulling me out of my sleep.

The last thing I remember is my mom peeking into my room around eleven. I didn't say anything as she kissed my cheek and then closed my door.

I stretch across to my nightstand and press the top of my alarm clock, lighting up the red numbers. It's only 11:20 PM.

The voice isn't as loud this time. "Hold it steady."

Is that Tyson?

I push off my covers and walk to the window. When I look out, I cover my mouth so I don't laugh. Tyson has his forehead pressed against the screen of Josh's bathroom window. He's holding a sheet of paper against the glass. Someone else in the bathroom is shining a light on the note. Thankfully, my pink binoculars are still in the top drawer of my desk.

> *Get your butt*
> *downstairs*
> *in 3 minutes*
> *cuz we're*
> *kidnapping you!!!*

When I lower the binoculars, Tyson waves and removes the note from the window.

"And I'm serious!" he shouts.

Kellan appears at the window with the flashlight shining beneath her chin. "We're both serious!"

When Kellan and Tyson leave, Josh walks up to the window. He doesn't say anything, but he smiles and shrugs his shoulders. Kellan pushes him out of the way, holds her wrist to the window, and points at her watch.

I give her a thumbs-up, wriggle into some clothes, and tiptoe downstairs.

* * *

TYSON'S TRUCK IS PARKED at the curb with him in the driver's seat. Kellan is squeezed next to him, and Josh is standing outside holding the door open for me.

He smiles shyly as I hop in.

"It's going to be a tight squeeze," Tyson says.

Josh climbs in after me, but the door won't close all the way.

"You'll need to get squishy," Kellan says.

I press as close to Kellan as I can. Josh slides over until our bodies touch from our shoulders down to our knees. When he slams the door shut, Tyson shifts into gear and the truck jolts forward. Josh lengthens the seatbelt before handing it to me. I stretch it across both our laps and buckle us in.

"Where are we headed?" Josh asks.

He had nothing to do with this? I glance over at Kellan, but she continues looking at the road with a smile.

"There's only one thing we all need right now," Tyson says.

He and Kellan throw their fists in the air and shout, "GoodTimez!"

*   *   *

I'VE NEVER BEEN to GoodTimez Pizza after hours, and it's eerily quiet. Tyson entered the security code at the door and flipped on a few lights. Thankfully, he didn't turn on the disco music.

Within minutes, Tyson and Kellan are having a heated competition over a game of Pac-Man. Kellan is gripping the joystick, shouting, "Suck it, ghosties!" every time she eats a power pellet. She's wearing Josh's sweatshirt, but I'm not going to ask if she found anything in the pocket. I'll consider it a good sign that she still has it on.

I wander away from the arcade and sit in one of the dining booths. After a little bit, Josh slides in across from me. "We've got some weird friends."

"True," I say. "But the boy is weirder."

"I'll give you that," he says. "And yet, I have a feeling the kidnapping was Kellan's idea."

"Did you have to sneak out, too?"

Josh shakes his head. "They talked my parents into letting me stay out until one."

"No way!"

We don't say anything for a minute, but it's not awkward. It's good to be with Josh again. Even if he's with Sydney, we can still be friends.

Josh glances toward the arcade. It's Tyson's turn at the joystick now, with Kellan jumping around, shouting, "Get him, ghosties! Get him!"

"There's something I need to tell you," Josh says, running his finger over a nick in the tabletop.

"What is it?"

He breathes in deep and then slowly exhales.

"If you want, I can go first," I say. "Because I need to tell you something, too."

He smiles. "I would love it if you went first."

"It's gone," I say. I glance over at Kellan and Tyson, still absorbed in their game of Pac-Man. "We can't get onto Facebook anymore."

Josh leans into the table. "Really? How'd that happen?"

"Tonight, fifteen years from now, I cancel my account," I say. "Originally, I was just going to change my password, but then the whole thing disappeared like it was never there."

Josh leans back, obviously shocked by the news.

"Now it's your turn," I say.

He places both hands on the . His face is flushing from his cheeks to his ears.

"Just say it, Josh."

"I don't know what's going to happen in the future," he says. "And I guess neither of us will now. But I've decided not to be with Sydney."

I don't know how to respond.

"It never felt right," he continues, and then he looks at me. "She wasn't the one."

A blue plastic ball smacks the side of Josh's head. We both look over at the ball pit. Kellan's already in there, and Tyson is pushing himself through the entrance in the netting.

After he dives in, Tyson shouts, "Come on! Less talking, more ball-pitting!"

Kellan tosses a bunch of the rainbow-colored balls into the air.

Josh looks at me and we both smile. We head over and look through the mesh. Kellan and Tyson are stretched out, hogging the area beneath the slides. I go in first, sinking down to my knees, and Josh tumbles in after me. The balls rise and shift around us, covering us up to our chests.

Kellan tosses me a yellow ball and I catch it.

"When did we take that picture of the four of us in here?" she asks.

I think about my copy of that photo, currently ripped in pieces in my journal. One day I'll tape it back together.

"Last year," Tyson says. "I've still got mine in my locker."

"Me too," Josh says. He chucks an orange ball at Tyson's chest.

Kellan tosses another yellow ball at me. I catch it and throw it to Tyson, then lower my arm back into the pit. As I do, my pinky finger touches the side of Josh's hand. I'm about to pull it away, but instead I leave my hand where it is.

A moment later, Josh lifts his pinky over mine.

65://Josh

ALL WEEK, I've known bits and pieces of my future, and I've wondered how my current actions affect me in fifteen years. But when Emma's finger touched mine, I was only thinking about now.

If I moved my hand away, I knew Emma would play it off as an accident. But I didn't want that to happen. So I slid my finger over hers. When she didn't pull away, I went one step further. Now I'm covering her hand completely.

"Want to see something?" Kellan reaches for Tyson's palm, and then drags her index finger down to his wrist. "This is your career line."

"My career line?" Tyson says. "Where's my *love* line? Show me something sexy, woman!"

Kellan lets go of his hand. "You're hopeless."

Emma laughs. As she does, she turns her hand over,

lacing her fingers into mine. For as many nerve endings as I thought I had in my hand, I now realize there are a hundred times more.

"You guys are being quiet," Kellan says. She looks carefully between me and Emma. "Are you plotting your revenge for being kidnapped?"

Hardly.

"Hold on!" Tyson says. He lifts both of his arms out of the ball pit. "*Shhh* . . . Listen. If any of you can read stomachs, tell me what this means."

We all wait patiently until his stomach growls.

"Never mind," he says. "That was easy. I'm *starving!*"

Kellan grasps the netting around the ball pit and hoists herself up. "There's an entire kitchen back there that we can raid."

Emma slides her body lower until the plastic balls touch her chin.

Kellan staggers across the pit and pushes her way outside. Tyson follows after her.

"You guys want to come?" he asks.

Emma squeezes my hand.

"I'm not hungry," I say.

"I'm good," Emma says.

"We won't be long," Kellan says. "We'll probably just heat up some garlic knots."

"Take your time," Emma says.

When I hear the door to the kitchen swing shut, I finally

look directly at Emma. She smiles at me. I push aside a few of the plastic balls so I can see her entire face.

"Much better," I say.

Emma leans her head back and her smile fades. "Josh, I need to tell you something else. And this is probably the worst time to say it."

I groan. "This doesn't sound promising."

She shifts onto her side and looks up at me, still holding my hand. "School will be out in a few weeks, and I have a feeling this could be the most incredible summer," she says. "But my dad asked me to spend the summer in Florida. I really want to see him and Cynthia, and I especially want to get to know Rachel."

Even though I'm holding Emma's hand for the first time, I already miss her. It would be amazing to spend this summer together. A big part of me wishes she wouldn't leave. And yet, I'm happy for her.

"I know how much that means to you," I say.

"I know you do."

"Of course, I'd be stupid not to try talking you out of leaving for the *whole* summer."

"I'm not leaving for the whole summer," she says. "Probably just six weeks."

"Or maybe four?"

Emma grins. "Five."

"Four and a half and I'll throw you a welcome back party."

She laughs. "You don't throw a party for someone who's only been gone four-and-a-half weeks."

"Then how about a really nice date?" I reach across and find her other hand resting on her stomach. My balance shifts and I slide a little lower into the ball pit.

"In a way, I'm glad Facebook's gone," Emma says. "I hated obsessing about what I didn't want in my future."

"It's better to focus on what you *do* want," I say.

Her lips part slightly. "I'm starting to figure that out."

"But I'd love to know," I say, leaning closer, "what this will change."

I feel her breath on my lips as we both whisper, "Hopefully everything."

With immense gratitude, the authors wish to send Friend Requests to the following:

JoanMarie Asher

Jocelyn Davies

Ryan Hipp

Magda Lendzion

Penguin Young Readers

Jodi Reamer

Laura Rennert

Jonas Rideout

Society of Children's Book Writers and Illustrators

Ben Schrank

Mark Zuckerberg